I LOVED HER ENOUGH

CHANCE, TRAGEDY, LOVE, AND FRESH AIR

DIANE LANE

Diane Lane
Lewes, DE 19958

First Edition, 2019

ISBN 978-0-578-48727-4

Front Cover Image: Copyright Eilleen Jandreau Spence
(Eilleen & Sarah, Slaughter Beach, DE)

Back Cover Image: Aleksandra Boguslawska, via Unsplash.com
Cover Design & Interior layout: Crystal Heidel (Byzantium Sky Press)

INTRODUCTION

My Mother never laughed more than with her best friend Eilleen. Together, those two were outrageous; entertaining anyone within earshot, even captivating strangers who'd end up laughing with them most of the time. Their sense of humor was infectious and part of their magic. They were young children when Eilleen and my Mom became best friends; the very summer Eilleen arrived by train with the Fresh Air Program. That's all I ever knew.

In 1967, my Mom died. Later I married and moved to Milford at the same time Eilleen's daughter, Debbie, moved there too. We reconnected, instantly became best friends and had a blast raising our children together. Debbie happily shared her mom with me. She dearly loved my children and became "Ba-Ba," the grandmother they were missing.

But it wasn't until the children were older, I asked Eilleen to tell me the whole story of *how* she came to Milford. What was her early life like in New York? What happened to her parents?

The story that surfaced blew me away. How we shared so many years without us knowing a peep of this was astonishing. Getting her to talk at first was difficult, but soon, she became passionate about reliving those days and sharing every detail she remembered so we could record this history for her kids and future generations. If not, they'd never know "exactly how they got here." It's like they say, true stories are always the best ones because you just can't make up stuff like this.

It took me years to check the local archives, researching the original places they went back then and the events that happened, and simply, just to stick with it. It's been a big project for me since I am not a writer. But maybe that's best because I wrote this story the way it was shared with me. Eilleen's story begins in 1933 and covers one year in the life of a five-year-old and all the adults around her. The facts of chance, tragedy, love and the unusual circumstances are all true, I merely connected them. It's a story that is so powerful I knew it had to be written. I loved her enough to give it my best shot.

Milford, Delaware
1997

"Now hold on a minute.... You'd like to do *what*?" Eilleen popped her eyes as large as she could, screwed up her face and started laughing. Remaining in that dramatic state of being shocked and in total disbelief, she reached for her sweaty glass of iced tea and downed a big swig as if she wished it were a shot—only thing is, this lady didn't drink.

"Sugar tit, honey, I don't know. I'm not sure if I can do that, Diane. I made a decision a long time ago, back when I was just six years old, never to mention those days, not to anyone," Eilleen stated firmly as she looked across the room, pausing a bit to think before she continued. I could see her wheels were turning.

"I will tell you this though, it certainly would have been a whole lot better if I'd had enough sense to tell the kids when they were little, but I didn't want to hurt my Mother and Dad. I couldn't have loved those two anymore than I did. Besides, life was going great for us, so I always figured it was best to keep moving forward. Heck, why should we go back and dig up old dirt?

"I had nothing but the best of intentions for staying quiet, but boy, that backfired the day Debbie found out. I'll never forget it. She bust through the back door one day after school, bawling her eyes out, upset as if she'd just watched a squirrel get run over by a car, or witnessed a murder or something; the way she was crying and screaming for me. 'Mom... *where are you?*' she yelled, as tears streaked down her face, she was crying so hard as she blurted out, 'Mom, a girl in school told me… I'm NOT Nana's and Big Byo's real granddaughter... because YOU… *you aren't even their daughter!* You're *ADOPTED?*' She struggled to get her words out between gasps. 'THEN, she told me that... *you're just* some POOR *kid...* they took in... *off the streets of New York?* And that…you came here on a *train?* Why would she say that to me, Mom? She was so mean! I told her she was crazy and to get out of my face! Then she said to me, *Your mother's not who she says she is and if you don't believe me… just go home as ask her yourself!*'

"Those tears couldn't stop pouring from Debbie's eyes that were now such a vibrant blue, I swear they looked like they could glow in the dark, surrounded by such a red face. It pierced right through me, watching my daughter sob, that upset and distraught, oh, it was awful," Eilleen said dropping her chin and rocking her head as she was vividly remembering. "I never wanted my kids to be upset or affected by what happened to me when I was little. That chapter of my life was over and done with and it had been filed away years ago.

"But you need to understand, it wasn't like I was harboring some deep, dark secret. I never hid a thing. Doc knew soon after we started dating, long before we were married and so did your Mom and all my friends. Heck, I always figured, why would anyone else care or give a hoot?

"Later on, that same afternoon, as soon as Tommy and Byo got home from school, I sat all three of my kids down to set the record straight. I remember it like it was yesterday. I told them, 'Kids, the first thing you need to know is I AM Nana's and Big Byo's daughter as sure as I'm your mother who's standing right here in front of you. Don't you ever doubt that for a minute, you hear me? But, that girl in school today is right. I was a poor kid from New York. You three don't know this, but I don't have a single memory of ever laying eyes on my real father; and my mother died when I was only five years old. That was the very same summer I came to Delaware on a train as a part of the Fresh Air program. They arranged for poor children like me to have a chance to get out of the city for a couple of weeks to get a break and have an opportunity to sample rural life.

"You know how much my Mother and Dad love me. Well, I love both of them too, with all my heart. The thing is, well… we were just blessed to become a family in a little bit more unusual way is all, and that's the end of it. Now that you know the details, you need to remember this too—it doesn't change a cotton-picking, single thing, understand? We're still the same family and I love ALL of you! And, I believe you love me too, right? So, you see? Not a darn thing's different.'

"Both the boys just sat there, frozen in place with blank faces. They were so stunned they were speechless and for Tommy that was just about impossible, probably the first time in his life, but Jesus, Mary and Joseph, you might have thought the world was ending for Debbie. To be fair, I can see how her core foundation was abruptly shifted by this kind of news, but I never dreamed she'd be so upset. Mostly, I think it was the shock. Debbie stomped upstairs to her room, slammed her bedroom door and bawled for hours in there like someone had died. You best believe after that, I've never opened my mouth to say a peep about my childhood or anything else about those days in New York."

"But from what you've told me Eilleen, the odds of you even

being on the train that day were what? One in a million? Good Lord! Can you imagine *if* you weren't? Everything we know would be different." I remained still for a moment, thinking that over and trying to conger up a completely different version of our lives.

"There wouldn't be any of those zany, best friend 'Wharton and Murph' stories Mom always told me. Not to mention, Eilleen, you've become the only grandmother my kids have ever known and to think... we could have missed all of this on one single chance day, that long ago? It's hard for me to wrap my head around the slight thread of circumstances that pulled together to create an outcome that got you here in the first place. Good grief, it's like the movie *It's A Wonderful Life*, pieces and parts of everything we know would be incredibly different for all of us if you weren't here. Wow. The 'what-ifs?' are staggering. I wouldn't even have my dearest friend Debbie. Whoa, this is almost too much to even consider.

"We've got to write your story Eilleen. I want to know every detail you can remember. Come on, what do you say? Let's do this. Let me officially interview you and write it all down. Pretend I'm Diane Sawyer or something," I suggested, hoping to make it seem fun and more official, I was that serious.

"I don't know honey. I've never spoken about any of this. They were hard times, and boy-o-boy, the last time I tried it sure didn't go so well," Eilleen said, teasing and making another crazy face, but I could tell the whole time she was giving the idea serious thought.

"I understand, but that was years ago. Besides, we're not 'kids' anymore, heck we're all grown up with our own children. Now's the perfect time Eilleen, and you're the only one with the details. If we don't record your story for future generations, it could end up lost forever and besides, think how much fun we'll have. You'll be doing this for your grandkids and their future kids, too. I think it would be some amazing history for your family to have."

She smiled and agreed. It was decided. We made a plan, and in a few days, we got right to work.

Over the next several months we drank numerous glasses of fresh brewed iced tea and found ourselves laughing one minute, only to be bawling the next, shedding plenty of those sweet, sudden, unexpected tears that uncovering a precious memory can provoke. During this time, I witnessed many changes in Eilleen's expressions and her tone as she shared and described details and events that sprung up as old memories were finally released and allowed to run free. Those bittersweet days played out sharp and clear in her mind, triggering plenty of complex feelings that stirred her soul. Our time together was powerful and insightful. I tried to imagine being a little girl like she was back then and living through such hard times, experiencing so many unexpected twists and turns and finding such surprising love, all while being five years old.

During one conversation several months into our work, Eilleen mentioned with teacher-like seriousness, "Diane, do you realize you're the only person on this earth I've ever told my entire story to?" Then she snorted, crinkled her nose three quick twitches, snorted and added, "Guess that's 'cause you're the only one who's ever bothered asking!" Laughing in her contagious way, she suddenly switched back to dead serious, as quick as changing a channel with a remote, and in a thoughtful, soft voice added, "Truth is, I'm really surprised how much is coming back to me now that I'm allowing myself to go back there for the first time in my adult life and really think about all of this. Do you realize that I've been able to recall every story Dad used to share about how much he loved having me come into his life? He used to tell me stories all the time while I was growing up, and right now, I swear, I can hear his voice and his every word just as clear as if it were yesterday. He adored me you know. Mother loved me too, but with Dad, I don't know, we shared some kind of a special bond.

"It's funny, but I feel free to talk about it now that Mother and Dad are gone. There's no one who could misunderstand or get hurt from me speaking the truth and you know what? I really do believe this project is going to be therapeutic for me. Revisiting these old days now at my age, I've got to say, it's surprising to me how it all seems far less tragic to me now. It really is a beautiful love story, isn't it?" She marveled at how surprised she was to realize that for the first time; and for a few moments she sat as still as a lake at dawn, lost in her new thoughts about her old life. Her face beamed; she looked positively radiant and glowing. "When we're done, those kids and grandkids of mine are going to learn exactly how they got here. Aren't they in for a big surprise!"

Laughing again, she took another sip of tea and we went back to work; she, prying open an unvisited vault of memories that immersed her back into life as it once was; while I feverishly took notes, capturing every word as the story surfaced and came into focus. Truth is, she was one hundred percent on board now and excited to delve in and relive those days to uncover every detail. Soon after we began, I realized there was far more to this story than anyone ever knew.

"The first thing you need to know Diane, is back then, things were hardly copacetic. It was a desperately bleak period in America during this time. In 1933, our country was about four years into the grips of the Great Depression.

"I was born Eilleen Gladys, one of the three little Jandreau sisters, living in the slums of Queens, New York. We were born in America to French and German immigrants who came to the United States with their parents who had a dream in their hearts to give their children a chance for a better life in a free country, like so many others did back then. The entire section of New York where we lived was full of different nationalities, French, Irish, Polish, Italians, Germans and even others. With hard work they were convinced they could achieve the American Dream. But, could they really during such tough times? I'm here to tell you, it wasn't easy.

"At that time, immigrants were arriving in massive numbers; most had limited educations if they had any, and all of them faced language barriers or struggled to learn the English they needed. None of them understood one another's ethnic background, let alone all their various customs. Jobs were more than scarce. No one had any money, heck, all the banks were failing, so it was only natural for nationalities to stick together like glue, giving any jobs they had to family members or close friends; they had to for survival. But even those who were working soon found their pay cut back due to the hard times and soon, even a well-earned paycheck was not enough to live on.

"Every week the soup lines grew longer. With little money and such poor diets, illness was on the rise. Tuberculosis had reached a point of being a full-blown epidemic. People with need were everywhere you looked, folks in every direction around us were either desperate, sick or hungry. This was a very sad time in America, the poverty was staggering...." There was a long pause as a veil of sadness fell over Eilleen's face. "... and our family was right in the middle of it."

George Luke Jandreau

"My father, George Luke Jandreau, was French. He was a bright, hard-working man with a kind heart and a big, beaming smile, from what Grandmother Anna, my mother's mother, told me. His hazel eyes would practically dance when he'd tell one of his stories. Seems he loved to spin a good tale and used to throw in all sorts of exaggerated details every chance he had to achieve the fullest effects he could possibly muster up. That talent, mixed with his happy, energetic spirit, attracted him many friends, like spilled honey draws a swarm of flies.

"Grandmother Anna told me I have his spirit, and that I reminded her a whole lot of him. She said it was a good thing, and that's where my energy and spunk came from.

"But I don't remember my father. Grandmother said he was a taxi driver by trade and was hardly ever home, but when he was, he would get upset when Mother complained, and I understand that's pretty much all she ever did. Often, he came home after he'd been drinking, as if it was the only way he could cope with the disappointment of our pathetic life.

"Seems he really did try from what Grandmother said, because all he ever did was work. He'd drive his taxi all day, going nowhere and back again, and when that didn't earn enough money, he took on all sorts of extra odd jobs, working from sun up till sun down. Grandmother Anna said he never got a single thank you at home for all that hard work and she hated how Mother constantly told him he was responsible for our bleak life and all its misery. Grandmother said Mother's harsh words wounded him deeply and hurt him far worse than any man's fists to his face ever could. Seems he couldn't look at Mother without seeing the reflection of our suffering and poverty in her eyes when she glared at him.

"To say his soul became weary was an understatement. I guess the disappointment of our life and his inability to make it better was far too great a burden for a naturally carefree man like George Luke. One day, he simply left for work and never returned. I was just a baby."

Caroline Mawlback Jandreau

"My mother, Caroline, was miserable from the day I was born from what Grandmother Anna told me, She was always thinking things couldn't get any worse, but she was wrong, because they sure did after, my father, George Luke left. His departure left my mother bitter and wondering where was that God in heaven Grandmother Anna always talked about? Life was so unfair! How much more was she supposed to take?

"Despair blanketed over Mother like thick storm clouds that never cleared; leaving her living in a place so far down and dark not a single ray of light could reach her. Nope. So, without any light at the end of her tunnel to help her find her way, she simply expected to stumble and fall into every hole and pitfall she already knew was out there waiting for her. There were no answers to fix her life from what she could tell. And even if there was a God in Heaven, she wasn't about to go looking for Him, after all, shouldn't that be his job, to come find and save her? And when he didn't, she just got mad at God, too.

"So, like everyone who folds in upon themselves from the weight of depression, she found no other choice but to do nothing. While choosing nothing, sure seems like a choice to me, it wasn't one she felt responsible for, oh no, not in the least, because every miserable day of her life, without question, was still *all George Luke's fault!*

"Mother cried so long all her tears dried up and finally she grew so tired, fatigue stole her desire to ever cry again. Seems that's when she turned to drinking, seeking its numbing effect as an easier way to treat her misery and pain. She'd leave the house and when she came back she didn't, or maybe couldn't, care about anything—even her own children.

"It's hard to know when she became sick for real, but I can remember when she stopped eating. Grandmother consistently tried to get her to eat, but Mother would say mean things like, 'Well, maybe now there will be some extra scraps for the girls.' But what did she know? She never even looked at us anymore. She had abandoned us, right there in the next room, every bit the same as if she'd packed up and moved away too.

"I can remember her lying there in her rumpled bed, so ghostly pale and unkempt with her long-tangled hair scattered across the pillow, hacking and coughing something awful when she wasn't asleep, sick to death with the worst deep, horrid, rattling chest cough I'd ever heard. Her body grew wafer thin in time. Finally, she didn't even try to get up anymore... but, why would she, when she hated everything?

Anna Mawlback

"My Grandmother Anna moved in with us as soon as I was

born, to help out with the new baby and she never left. Thank goodness for Grandmother Anna. Without her, we'd have been thrown out and into the streets and left to fend for ourselves, there's not a doubt about it.

"Anna Mawlback was raised and grew up in Germany. While she had lived through her share of tough times, even the worst of days she could remember paled in comparison to what she witnessed going on with us, for the way we were living was beyond tragic.

"My Grandmother Anna never suffered heartbreak during her marriage. No, she had married a good man, God rest his soul. During their marriage, they shared trials and tribulations, said grace every meal, no matter how little they had to put on the table and every night before bed, they gave thanks for their blessings. And there were many times she used to tell me, they had to look pretty hard just to find one, but it's like she taught us: blessings are always there, you have to take the time to look. But looking is a choice and there certainly are times when life beats you up so much, even wanting to look for a few blessings sure does take work.

"In their difficult times, Grandmother Anna told us she and my grandfather spoke to each other with kindness because they believed tenderness and compassion was a big part of what makes a marriage. If those things don't come from the one you love, well, just where in the world were they supposed to come from? Certainly not from alcohol or lashing out with harsh words. Kindness was the unspoken golden rule they lived by all their married years. It became their standard, and it sure made living through life's tough times more bearable.

"Together, she and my grandfather brought my mother to

America when she was a little girl. Grandmother Anna always knew her life was full of countless blessings, but she realized it far more after she began living with us. She used to recall how her husband's steady, reassuring voice would tell her, 'things will be just fine,' as he'd brush away loose hairs back from around her face with his callused hand. And he was right too, because ultimately, somehow, they always would be. My, oh my.

"Well, he was gone. And our poor Grandmother Anna found herself stuck with us; cast smack dab into a life she hardly expected to be living during her final years on earth. She never imagined having to watch her daughter grow so desperately ill right before her eyes without proper medical care or to have to witness her granddaughters doing without—going to bed most nights hungry. Her children had never gone hungry! But the fact was, our situation was a real mess and there sure weren't a lot of options.

"Our biggest blessing was that Grandmother Anna truly loved us. We were the only family she had and by God, she was bound and determined to be devoted to us until her dying breath. She had decided, what she lacked in physical strength, she'd compensate for by using wisdom, love and plenty of faith, too. She always read to us from the Bible, but we learned far more by watching her example. We certainly needed and put those skills to use.

"But the love she gave us wasn't an easy or pampering kind. Heck no, our situation required her to dish out plenty of tough orders, stand firm and make some demanding requests of us even though we were only scrawny little girls. But little or not, Grandmother Anna was out to teach us, one way or another, how to make do, rise up and survive, so we'd be able to when the day came that she wouldn't be there to guide us.

"That was the big question, how long could she hold up at her age? The hour glass of time was not on her side, especially for raising me. It was a constant concern that provoked a powerful fear in Grandmother Anna, one she squelched the only way she knew how, with lots of prayer.

"Oh, I remember, she sure did pray a lot. When things grew worse than the ordinary awful, when our food ran out, and there was no money to buy bread or to pay the landlord, or when mother's health kept on declining right before our eyes, or we were getting too cold inside, for it was almost always all of those things at once, she'd gather us girls up on top of our bed and tell us we were going to bundle up all our worries into a tight little package, stuffing in every detail that bothered us, then send our whole pile of concerns and worries straight up to heaven... and place them into God's hands. She'd say, 'Girls, you need to know, He always knows just what to do even when we don't.' And you know what? I believed her because over the years, she had witnessed plenty of good results that only served to strengthen her faith. We relied on her promise that things were going to improve… somehow… even when we didn't have the foggiest idea how they possibly could.

"But, here's the best part, answers would arrive. Oh yes, they did. And most of the time it was in surprising and unexpected ways. Now, not always on an ideal time schedule, mind you, but they'd come, just in the nick of time too. So, we'd huddle together real close, like a nest full of baby chicks and send all our worries off in a big old prayer bundle to turn our whole mess over to God. After that we were able to sleep better for another night since results just might be coming in the morning.

"Grandmother Anna decided years ago to give up second guessing the future—it never seemed to do a bit of good, anyway. She taught us that trust was a word for the living... but Faith, now that was far more important, because that was trusting in God. But fear? Well that meant you weren't using a lick of faith.

"Around this time, faith was about all we had going for us, things had gotten pretty bad, our apartment was almost as cold as being outdoors; Mother's wheezing and cough were worse and there wasn't a day I can recall when we weren't hungry. Thinking back, I wonder in Grandmother Anna's weakest moments, did she ever think the day would come when faith wouldn't be enough? I guess I'll never know, but I do know this, she fought hard to prevent fear from taking over her mind. She used to say, 'When your faith gets shaky, it leaves the door unlatched for fear to come busting in and take over and if it does, it'll crawl right through you, settle right into your bones and scare you half to death,' and she wasn't about to stand around and wait for that to happen.

Sisters Jene and Marie

"That last winter I was in New York, Marie was twelve, Jene was ten, and I'd just turned five that September. My sisters were kind and they always looked out for me. Marie was such a mother hen, bless her heart.

"We shared a tiny bedroom. I remember we had this big 'ol cast-iron radiator that would hiss away, trying its best to warm things up, but that poor thing didn't stand a chance competing with the frigid draft that would blow in around our tall, rickety window. There was this one harsh winter storm I remember when our window panes rattled so hard, I thought the glass would fall right out. Water trickled inside and froze in fat trails that looked like icicles. We could see clouds from our breath it was so cold.

"I used to whine about being cold. I remember Marie teaching me: 'What you focus on is what you're going to notice.' She'd say, 'Instead of the cold, try to focus on how warm you'll be once we are under the covers.'

"When it was time to get ready for bed on the coldest of nights, Jene would prompt us to race, to speed things up, but do you have any idea how hard it is to rush and unbutton with cold little fingers? Oh, when the shoes came off and our little feet hit that icy floor, Lord have mercy, we'd get to jumping and hopping around like three little Mexican jumping beans! We'd be laughing, jump into bed and jerk up those heavy quilts over our faces only to discover our sheets were freezing too! Then we'd squeal and laugh even harder. But it wouldn't take long, snuggled together like we were, before our trapped breath would warm us up just like Marie promised. That little shabby room was barely bigger than the twin bed we shared. We lined our pillows down the long side of the mattress and slept crosswise, just to fit. I was always in the middle.

"The night of that big blizzard, I remember listening to the storm howl as it ripped through the streets below, while sleet hit our window so hard it sounded like the ice pellets might crack the glass. Powerful wind gusts shook our room like a tremor. Temperatures had to be in single digits because thick ice covered everything for as far as you could see outside. We three little girls laid there all night knowing that in the morning, we'd get up, get ready and walk to market. No matter what... ice, snow, wind, rain or slop. It didn't matter, off we'd go. We didn't have a choice. It was that or go hungry. Can you even imagine?

"It was a long time ago when we were those three little girls, but I clearly remember the night of the ice blizzard. Jene got us to race while getting ready for bed. We rushed, changing as fast as we could and jumped into bed between freezing cold sheets but it didn't take long before..."

Chapter 1
New York City 1933

The shivering stopped, and the giggles subsided soon after the girls snuggled and squirmed close together. In a matter of minutes, they warmed and relaxed under the heavy pile of covers and quilts while the winds whipped, and the fierce storm raged outside.

"I won!" Eilleen announced, "I'm first!"

"Oh no you don't!" protested Jene, "I was first! I *let* you get in the middle so really, I won!"

"Let's not argue girls," Marie said, "just be happy we got here so fast, so settle down. Tomorrow's market and we have a busy day ahead." Marie rolled over with a deliberate thump, closing her eyes, snuggling into her pillow.

Marie, being the oldest, knew how important her role in the family was. Without a single spoken word, she stepped up, followed every instruction and carried out every request from Grandmother Anna without so much as a soft sigh about it. Just one look at her tired, old grandmother, with those dark circles under her baggy eyes and listening to her mother's sick coughing coming from the next room, said it all. The family needed and depended on her.

Marie was scrawny, and overall, very small for her age. She wore her dark auburn hair tightly braided and always seemed so serious for one with such a sweet face; but she was a very busy girl. On the occasions when Marie did engage in laughter, it was sweetly infectious, her hazel eyes would crinkle and for that moment, everything seemed right in the world. She did own the most wonderful, almost musical laugh. It was magical.

"Marie?" Eilleen asked while little fingers tapped her chin thoughtfully. "I heard some good news today, several times really, so it must be true. Is this a happy new year? Mrs. Gillespie told everyone in the hallway. Do tell, is it true?"

Marie smiled, rolling over to look at Eilleen and sighed before speaking, "Oh, you dear little girl, 'Happy New Year' is a greeting, not news. The same as when someone says 'Happy Birthday.' Tomorrow happens to be January first, and 1933 begins, so people greet one another saying, 'Happy New Year' wishing them to have a grand year," Marie explained.

Eilleen's eyes widened and she popped up in bed as if she were a puppet connected to rubber bands instead of strings, "I know. Let's wish for ours right now! I want a happy new year, don't you? I want you to have one too. Should we wish on a star? Oh, let's!"

Then her voice fell as she turned and looked out the window, "Oh no. Do you think we can find a star out there in this storm? Should we wait until tomorrow when the stars come back? Or, will that be too late? Where do the stars go when there's a storm anyway? Do they blow away?" she asked all at once in her overzealous fashion her sisters were used to, there wasn't time to get a word in edgewise.

Marie searched for the right words while the cover's warmth was trying its best to melt her into sleep. "The storm clouds that rolled in are floating between the stars and the earth, so they're just blocking us from seeing them for now, but they're still up there, shining... right along the edge of heaven. Tomorrow night we'll see them again and we'll make your wish, only now, you need to go to sleep... OK?" Marie pleaded in a soft voice, more than ready to drift off.

"I know! How 'bout we just squeeze our eyes shut and *pretend* to see the stars and make a wish tonight! Then, tomorrow night ... we can wish again on real stars? Two wishes couldn't hurt do you think?" Eilleen insisted, her eyes wide and glowing as if it was just the best idea she'd ever thought of.

So, the older sisters gave in to the little one's persistence and joy for such a simple thing. Who would want to dampen that kind of hopeful thinking?

Together, the three of them squeezed their eyes shut and in unison, sincerely wished for a happy new year. And, they knew without a doubt, they'd be wishing on a bright star out their window tomorrow night as well.

A happy new year. What a splendid idea.

CHAPTER 2
MARKET DAY

"Time to get up girls," Marie said, poking Jene's arm in the still dark room. "Are you awake yet Jene? Looks like the storm's passed, but everything outside is frozen solid. It looks like an ice world out there, so wrap up extra well. I'll go start breakfast."

A sleepy "um-hum" was the only sound Jene made as she rolled away, hoping to steal a few more minutes of sleep. She couldn't help but notice how the air around her face was so much cooler than the warm temperature caressing her curled up, relaxed little body cocooned underneath the covers. Oh, it would be so easy to drift off again. Ice world? Oh no, brrr.

Marie called out again, "JENE! Get up for heaven's sake! What on earth would you have us do for food? Take a bite from your pillow? Try that a time or two and I bet you'd get serious about going to market on time. Come on now, let's go!" Marie finished dressing and marched out of the room to boil water for oatmeal and stir up a pitcher of the powdered milk they drank so often.

"Hold your horses, Sis. *Good Morning to you, too,*" Jene replied in a mocking singsong fashion. "*Fine sunny day*, you say? Did I hear you mention... *food?*" She continued with an edge of sarcasm as she sat up rubbing her eyes, "Perhaps sausage and biscuits? With fresh butter, strawberry jam and hot, spiced ginger tea? That's what I'm having everyday once I grow up. Well, I'm awake now and I'm hungry."

"Rouse Eilleen and help her dress, will you?" Marie called

from the kitchen. "Lots of layers and two pairs of socks if you can still pull on her boots."

"Rise and shine Eilleen, you little snookum's," Jene said as she gently rocked her little sister's shoulder. "Got a good song in your heart for market today? We need to dress you warm, so get over here and let me help."

"Morning Jene," Eilleen said in a soft, sleepy little voice. "I'm up. Is breakfast ready?" Lingering hunger was tugging and pinching inside her belly too.

"We've got to bundle you up," Jene said opening the sock drawer. None of the socks matched, but the trick was to match the thickness, never mind the colors. Good old Miss Maggie.

Miss Maggie was Grandmother Anna's closest friend with six grown children of her own, an Irish immigrant who took in washing and mending. She'd save a good sock when the mate was beyond repair, tossing it into a basket stashed under her sewing table.

"A single sock's perfectly good and a thousand percent better than no sock a-tall. Why, can't be put on more than one foot at a time. Ah, never mind, feet don't have eyes for noticing the matchin'... only feelin' for the warmth. So I say, if it's warmth you be after, these odd, one-of-a-kinds can do it in grand style!" Maggie would boast, "Call it a trick of the trade, or waste not want not, but I'm here to say not one of my six ever had cold tootsies! And I'll see to it for you girls, too. You can bet your lace britches on that! Ya sure can."

During the summer, Jene turned ten. She was stronger and stockier than Marie with more pink to her fair skin, and she sported freckles sprinkled across her cheeks. Her hazel-blue eyes changed color in different lighting and possibly at times to reflect her mood as they sure seemed intensely vivid whenever she was mad or grew stubborn. Her reddish-brown hair had a natural luster and would shine after she brushed it, so she brushed it often, and tied a cloth strip about her head to keep it back off her face.

Whenever the days were excessively wet or freezing, Jene wished they could leave their little sister home. Eilleen seemed far too little to have the job of family fund raiser but, she was the one blessed with the extraordinary talent for singing. It was a skill the girls used to their full advantage, earning the money they needed and depended on. Working together, they made a good team.

Eilleen had the brightest, most clear blue eyes you've ever seen, topped with perfectly shaped, dramatic, movie star looking eyebrows that gave her childish face a sophistication that everyone couldn't help but notice. She was a beautiful child. Her light blue eyes appeared even brighter in contrast to her olive complexion. Her thick, brown hair had reddish highlights and it curled easily. Why, with just a few rags tied in her hair overnight, she'd have ringlets that resembled a doll baby sitting in a downtown store window, that would last for days.

Eilleen was curious, inquisitive and quick to learn. No one knew how she managed to sing like she did or where on earth she ever learned the lyrics. You'd hear her singing songs she'd make up while she worked making a bed, sweeping or cleaning up after dinner. Music and melody flowed from her little soul as natural as the air she breathed entered and exited her lungs, simply without thinking a thing about it. The final blessing was that she wasn't the least bit shy. She never greeted a stranger without looking them straight in the eye, so it seemed natural when she became their little star entertainer.

Being the youngest, she'd also escaped knowing the weight of grownup responsibilities her older sisters carried; but this protection allowed her to remain far more innocent and carefree. Staying a child also allowed her to provide an important contribution back to her sisters, a bit of balance. It was Eilleen who could bring them back into the world of being the children they still were, with her fun, silly songs and her endless requests for telling stories and make believe.

At bedtime, Eilleen always asked for stories, or begged if necessary, until her sisters finally gave in. At first, they'd recite classic lines as if doing their duty in a "let's get this over with" tone. Only a funny thing would happen, within minutes as Jene and Marie took turns, they would venture a little deeper into the story, get caught up and begin adding interesting details, supplying drama and building excitement and that's when changes would begin to take place. Pretty soon the storytellers would get swept away as they allowed their minds to travel down paths that lead them to create fresh and unfamiliar plots from ideas that lived along the limits of their imagination. They could still pretend up a storm, when given half a chance. Eilleen loved it when her sisters played with her like this.

Princesses and fairies often showed up in the tales, having grand adventures, meeting pirates, or stumbling into encounters with dragons and wizards. Stories became so vivid, with runaway horses, sword fights over piles of gold and treasures, or situations with wild animals lurking and spying nearby about to pounce, there were times you just had to yank the covers up over your face. Intermissions must be held sometimes, just for time to calm down or go get a drink of water, but always in a rush, being so intensely captivated and consumed with curiosity to discover what in the world was about to happen next. As the stories wound down, they always ended surprisingly well, Marie would see to that. A sweet peaceful sleep easily followed every happily-ever-after conclusion.

But in the next room, things were not going as well. Their mother's lingering chest cough had grown worse. The deep coughing now had the added sounds of consumptive bronchial rattles and gasping sounds that were desperate and frightening. The hankie she held over her face became stained red.

This morning, the "what-if's" seemed unthinkable. It was far too bitter and icy outside for the girls to walk to market. Even inside it was too cold for humans to live without a real risk of getting sick. Grandmother Anna stood in the kitchen wrapped in a blanket, Indian style, feeling helpless and overwhelmed. Caroline was desperately sick yet, there was no medicine, no money and right now, not even enough food to eat this very evening. *If the girls aren't able to...NO! Oh no you don't woman!* She stopped her thoughts and the sting of impending tears at the last minute by remembering that sometimes, help arrives in surprising and unexpected ways. She sighed.

"Dear Lord, please, you must look out for us today. Something needs to change.... somehow, and fast. But I will leave it up to you," Grandmother Anna whispered to herself so as not to alarm the girls.

She took a deep breath and proceeded like normal to dip up the oatmeal while pretending that all young girls bundle up, walk blocks across a frozen city, behave nicely as they sing and beg for scraps, staying cheerful and grateful, saying thank you to return home with enough food to feed everyone. All of this was to be accomplished by three, skinny little girls with pocket change, since that's all she had to give them today. If the girls had the slightest hint of how afraid for them she was this morning, they'd become scared and that would never do. Nope, the best she could do was try to keep them warm and send them off with an attitude of hope...and keep praying until they returned.

Marie reached for some mismatched glasses from the cupboard for milk. Tattered napkins and worn silver-plated spoons were set on the pine table while the bowls of oatmeal steamed away as if they were sitting outside when placed on the breakfast table.

After grace, Grandmother Anna delivered her pep talk, "Girls, you know, the Bible says that God cares enough to feed even the smallest sparrow. So, don't you think he will see that we're fed too? Of course He will! We must never doubt it for a second." Then she reached in her apron pocket and revealed a small red tin full of cinnamon and sugar, to sprinkle over their bowls of tasteless cereal. The girls were delighted. Truth be known, this was her way of making sure they walked across town today with full stomachs.

Anna knew there would be fewer vendors gathered at the Market in this weather. Plus, most of the shop owners found it necessary to shoo away beggars without even looking at their faces, for there were far too many of them these days. If a merchant was seen giving out anything, they ran the risk of being swarmed by droves of needy kids, all with their hands out. The vendors creed was if you can't give to all of them, then don't give anything to any of them. It was a rule they stuck to.

But, the Jandreau girls didn't beg. No, they attended market with a plan. First, they'd sing and entertain the shoppers while collecting donations, then they'd shop buying seconds, damaged goods or the less than perfect items that a few of the merchants saved aside for them. The girls appreciated any kindness in the way of dramatically reduced prices, or at least, a few extras to be thrown in since they made it a part of their job to smile, be grateful and always to sincerely thank every booth owner and merchant. It certainly helped.

"Hey Eilleen, come over here," Marie said. From inside the hall closet, Marie pulled out a pair of hand-me-down green wool gloves that Miss Maggie had sent over. "These are a bit big, but they'll be warmer than bare skin tucked in cold pockets."

Marie kneeled to button-up Eilleen's coat and reminded her, "Be sure to say 'thank you' today, no matter what's offered to us, understand? We must smile and be grateful. I promise you tonight, Grandmother's going to cook us up a pot of the most delicious, hot tasty soup you've ever had! It will be wonderful and we're going to sleep like babies after that with full tummies."

Grandmother handed Marie her small change purse with a little money she knew wasn't nearly enough. "Just do your best today girls. That's all I ask... and I know that you will. Stay together, be careful and don't slip." She kissed each one of them on the cheek.

So, out the door they went, on their mission. Little did they know, whether they would get to eat tonight or not, would depend on the success of the next few hours.

CHAPTER 3
OFF TO MARKET

A harder than normal shove was required to open their building's tall front door pushing against the storm's remaining strong gusts. As the girls exited, they were instantly struck by a blast of bitter cold, swirling air that tugged at their scarves and stung their cheeks making them glad they'd taken the extra time to bundle up. But the sun was strong and there wasn't a cloud to be seen in the clear, bright sky. Light was reflecting off of thick ice that seemed to be covering everything. Walking between tall buildings blocked some of the wind, but they had a long, blustery, slick trek ahead of them.

Making the final turn, the girls could see a few booths and displays being setup. They continued to their favorite spot right beside Sophia and Antonio, the kind, older couple who sold steaming cups of fresh brewed Brazilian coffee, rich, imported cocoa and hot spiced cider. A cold day like this would mean big business for them, conditions were perfect.

Rich, comforting aromas of roasted coffee beans and imported spices filled the air. Upscale customers stopped and lingered here while sipping their piping hot drinks. If shoppers could afford this luxury, they had some extra money, and folks with time and money, well, that was the girl's meal ticket too.

"Psst.... *psst*," Sophia hissed, nodding in the direction of a customer, their signal to get busy. It was Mrs. Anderson, ordering a hot chocolate. She was a regular and a good customer for them, if they could act fast.

"Start with *Amazing Grace*, Eilleen. Mrs. Anderson loves that one," Jene suggested in a whisper.

Eilleen took a step forward as if to position herself on a grand stage and tugged up her drooping gloves. She knew her job and loved it. Taking a deep breath, she lifted her head, stood tall, remained silent for a moment, then began. "*Amazing grace.... how sweet the sound.... that saved a wretch like me... .I once was lost....but now I'm found.....was blind....but now I see.*" The words were as rich and as sweet to the ear as the hot cocoa was to the taste buds. Other shoppers also enjoying their beverages listened and held their steaming cups suspended mid-air and were suddenly mesmerized. What a precious child. What a talent. Her perfect pitch couldn't go unnoticed.

Eilleen continued with winning songs that earned the best tips—current hits to Broadway show tunes—but she always ended with *America the Beautiful.* Kind patrons dug in their pockets searching for spare coins. Everyone could see need stamped on the clothing and faces of these sad looking little girls even though they wore bright smiles.

Folks who passed by would nod, making comments the girls would overhear: "Such a darling face," ... "that voice, what a gift" ... "poor dears, look at them practically in rags"... Or even worse ones, spoken in tones of disgust: "Where do you suppose their mother is?" or, "What kind of parents train their children to be street beggars?" or, "They should be ashamed of themselves, sending little children out on a cold day like this!"

But the girls had gotten used to hearing harsh things and over time had become somewhat calloused after hearing such comments for the umpteenth time. Yes, they were poor. But they were also smart and entertaining, and for that, they were proud. Grandmother Anna told them to hold their heads up high and enjoy their unique talents. They were out in the world, learning important life skills and learning how to work with people of all types, and that alone was a valuable education no one could ever take from them.

Maybe it was the sun shining after so many stormy days, or a bit of left-over Christmas spirit, but the girls were having a profitable day. Eilleen's singing seemed to improve at each market. Regulars made it a point to shop this end of the street when the Jandreau sisters would be there to entertain them; it was a treat to enjoy a happy song or two during these hard times.

A new face was out in the crowd today, a fancy lady with pale hair the color of yellow gold, wearing a thick, glossy, full length fur coat and lipstick that outlined her smile in a red so bright it made her teeth look as white as her pearls. She walked over to Eilleen, knelt to her level and looked her over from top to bottom before saying, "Why you darling, sweet child! Do you have any idea of the marvelous talent you possess? I sing on stage, uptown in the theater and you, my darling, have impressed the socks right off of me this morning! I declare, your voice is simply a joy to behold." Then taking both Eilleen's shoulders, she got close to her face and looked her right in the eyes. "You must promise me that you'll never stop singing. Here, I have something for you." Reaching for Eilleen's hand, she removed one of the droopy green gloves and placed two silver dollars into her warm little palm.

Eilleen saw the silver coins and gasped, "Thank you! Oh... my goodness! You're too kind!" Beaming with a smile that lit up her face, she instantly flung her entire body into the fur coat giving the lady such a sudden, forceful hug, she almost toppled backwards. Excited to show Marie, Eilleen turned so quickly she dropped her glove. Bending over to grab it before it blew away, she slipped on a patch of ice and fell... dropping the money. Both coins took off rolling in the same general direction at first, then rolled apart. One bumped the wheel of Antonio's cart and stopped while the other traveled straight for the street, jumped the curb and plopped straight down the storm drain.

"OH NO!" Eilleen screamed, "Jene! HELP!" Eilleen wailed and tears streamed down her face at the instant loss of a gift, the likes of which she had never seen before.

"Don't cry Eilleen. It's OK. We'll get your money...please, don't cry. Oh dear..., stop screaming... good grief. Please, honey... breathe! No! No... come on now, BREATH! EILLEEN!" Jene hollered, becoming more concerned by the second. Eilleen began turning blue! No more sounds were coming out. She was completely out of air and just at the moment everyone feared the child was going to pass straight out on the pavement... she breathed. Her face turned bright red making her eyes look the color of Caribbean water, strikingly bright and glassy with tears.

Such a vivid display of anguish sent several volunteers rushing over offering their assistance and positive assurance they would see to the coin's recovery, pronto. The grate was lifted off the drain by a couple of young men after they cracked away some of the thick ice. It wasn't far down to the bottom, but the street opening was narrow.

Eilleen peered over the edge of the hole and was quick to notice that she'd fit. Besides, no one wanted to get their hands on that coin more than she did.

There it was, shining with sunlight reflecting off the silver. "Come on, lower me down boys. I can get it!" Eilleen said with enthusiasm.

"Are you sure little girl? There might be some spiders or slimy things down there. My boy is about your size," one of the men offered, "He can get it for you."

"Gosh darn it, I'm not a scaredy cat! I can do it sir, if you'll just help me," Eilleen said with solid determination.

"OK. You seem pretty sure," he said as he held her under the arms and lowered her inside until her feet touched bottom, then he let go of her. The top of her head was only about fifteen inches below street level.

A moment later the crowd heard her cry of victory, "I GOT IT!"

Shoppers across the street heard her call out since the acoustics inside the pipe echoed her voice with an enhanced volume that surprised everyone.

"Golly. Did you hear that? My voice sure has some super power down here. YOOU-HOOOO!" Eilleen called as she tested the sound she could make inside the pipe. "Isn't this just the best?" she said thrilled as she looked up at her sisters and then, doing the most natural thing she could think of, started singing!

"*Oh, we ain't got a barrel of money... maybe we're ragged and funny... but we'll travel along... singing a song... side by side. Through all kinds of weather... what if the sky should fall... just as long as we're together... it doesn't really matter at all. When they've all had their quarrels and parted... we'll be the same as we started... traveling the road, sharing our load... SIDE-BY-SIDE! Haaaah!*" she ended so jazzed up she even threw in outstretched arms at the finish.

The group that gathered to help soon grew into a small crowd of curious onlookers. The music was clear, up-beat and amplified as if by magic. Folks joined in and started singing along. The quality of the sound was so unique it held them all spellbound. Everyone began offering donations that had Jene and Marie running around in all directions accepting coins from outstretched hands, thanking everyone while stuffing their pockets. "Hey kiddo... whatever you do... don't stop now!" Jene hollered down to Eilleen, "You sound terrific!"

Thirty minutes later, both sisters laid on their stomachs, reached down and pulled their little sister out from under the street, giddy from the success of what accidentally just happened.

"Are you thinking what I'm thinking, Jene?" asked Marie who was practically breathless from excitement.

"Are you kidding? Almost losing that silver dollar was the best thing that's ever happened to us! I'm telling you. We must have collected, oh I don't know... so much money Grandmother's gonna think we robbed a vender!" Jene stated through her giggles.

Eilleen emerged beaming with a grin stretched from ear to ear as she brushed off her coat. She lifted her head, looked toward the sky and said, "I think I am a star! Did you hear how wonderful that sounded? Everybody thought so! Did you hear them clapping for me? My voice was really big down there. That was the best fun singing I've ever done in my whole entire life! It was just like my own *ample theater!*" She was standing tall, beaming with pride.

"It's amphitheater, silly" Marie corrected, "but you're right. We've discovered the future singing stage for our very own little star. Everyone here certainly loved it."

"Oh my..." Eilleen suddenly froze standing as still as a statue, inhaled deeply while her eyes grew wide before she continued in a bold, airy whisper, "HOLD ON! Guess what? I think it was *our wish* last night ... don't you? We wished for a happy new year and look, it's already started! It's coming true. Isn't this fun?" She squealed and began bouncing up and down in the street.

"One thing's for sure, it has been the most peculiar morning," Marie agreed. "Now, let's get the items on the list and see what money's left over. We must come up with a surprise for Mother, definitely some tea and honey. Oh, Grandmother will be so proud of us. Not to mention, a tad bit surprised, don't you think?" The girls laughed.

On their way to shop, Marie suddenly stopped in her tracks, barricading her sisters with outstretched arms as if grave danger lay straight ahead. "Wait a minute, girls," she said, turning to them, "we need to collect ourselves. If we seem overzealous today the venders might think something is up. We can't seem this happy, act rich or show off at all right now. This extra money we have today must be saved for times when things are not so good for us. We better hold back our celebrating for when we get home and are behind closed doors." The girls nodded in agreement. They knew she was right.

So, with more serious faces they shopped for a sack of flour, an un-plucked chicken, some pasta, a loaf of brown bread and an assortment of vegetables. After a vote, they added raisins, a bottle of olive oil, a bag of loose tea and a jar of honey for Mother. There was still money to take home along with both silver dollars.

The sisters hardly noticed the long walk home that afternoon, toting their reward of brimming full baskets, even with freezing toes and wind-burned, rosy cheeks. Before they knew it, they spotted their building up ahead, a dreary, run-down apartment house, sandwiched between two equally neglected high rises that matched the rows of forsaken soot covered structures that lined their street.

Building after building, the entire city was stone and concrete, block, brick and pavement. The only sky the Jandreau sisters could see was limited to a small view of blue straight overhead or narrow patches peeking from in between buildings. There were few grassy areas, not many trees, and certainly no wide-open spaces to view an entire sky. Not where they lived.

Up ahead, the ice wagon was making its rounds and the old, sway-backed dapple gray was clomping along the memorized route at a weary pace. Eilleen's short legs were tired. She slowed and began walking in time to the old horse's rhythm. At their front stoop Eilleen took a deep breath and with an exhausted sigh questioned out loud, "Why do we live up so many flights of stairs? You know what? When I grow up, I plan to live behind the first door that's inside the building. Yes sir-ree-bob, that's my plan."

Back at home, up on the sixth floor, the sisters opened the door to a small, two-bedroom apartment that revealed nothing but cramped living conditions for their family of five, complete with peeling wall paper, chipped paint and linoleum so old, tired and worn out it exposed large bare spots. The living room's secondhand furniture was as dingy and gloomy as the rest of the old building. Neighboring structures hovered so close they cast never-ending, long shadows. Any small path of sunlight that did manage to reach their windows fell upon glass so dirty it had to filter through years of grimy haze before shining in, diminishing the light and permanently preventing the room from ever experiencing a truly sunny day. The faded flower-printed curtains looked as sad as the lives of this struggling family who lived in this place they called home.

This was their life in the New York slums and it was harder than most of us could imagine or ever understand.

CHAPTER 4
WINTER IN MILFORD, DELAWARE

About two hundred miles due south of New York City, it was January 1933 in a place so different from the bustling city it was completely like another world.

Sarah Wharton and her husband Bayard enjoyed a fine life of proper living in their small town of Milford, Delaware. Sarah was a woman of quiet strength. She was refined and actually seemed to be showing some signs of turning prematurely grey well before her time since she was only forty-three. She was a tall, slender woman, about 5'9" and she had soft hazel eyes that sparkled and spoke far more at times than her words ever did. If you really wanted to know what was going on with Sarah all you had to do was look at her face, for she could not hide her thoughts; it was fair to say she would never be good at poker. Active in Avenue United Methodist Church and the ladies Circle, Sarah had earned her place in the local society. The women in town knew whenever there was a job to be done or if a special need arose in the community, they could always count on Sarah.

This year, she'd become curious about a new project the church was supporting called The Fresh Air Fund. Tonight, a representative from the Fund was coming all the way from New York and would be speaking, right after the Woman's Circle Supper. Sarah was very curious, so she was eager to learn more.

The ladies discovered long ago that hosting a home-cooked church supper was a marvelous idea if you wished to spike attendance. Why, just the mention of a Circle Dinner and *voila*, it worked like magic to pack the house. Tonight's menu was chicken and slippery dumplings with all the trimmings: mashed potatoes, sweet peas, cranberries and applesauce, hot buttered yeast rolls, topped off with an assortment of baked goods for dessert. Yes, the ladies knew a meal like this would get the husbands to attend, and you best believe they did too; one hundred percent unless one was stricken with an illness.

Pulling up in the church parking lot right on time, Bayard finished his cigarette while he pictured his wife, Sarah, inside running around. She had been bustling in there for hours by now since he knew she arrived mid-afternoon with her niece, Dorothy, to help set everything up for the big shindig.

Bayard never lost his boyish grin or that devilish gleam in his eyes. He had an abundance of energy and was in great physical shape for being forty. Here was a man who liked to be in the out-of-doors and most of all, this was a man who truly loved his wife. Removing his favorite wool beret, he rolled it up and stuffed it in his jacket pocket before entering the church hall.

Dinner was served family style. When the supper dishes got whisked off the tables by the older children in the church, the rattling of silverware, plates and glasses traveled off behind the double swinging doors to the kitchen, only to have them swing back open by the ladies serving chocolate cake and fresh apple and pumpkin pies with steaming pots of hot coffee and tea that produced an aromatic trail that soon filled the room with its soothing scent.

As soon as dessert was served, Mrs. Edwards took to the stage in a hurried pace, "Good evening ladies and gentlemen and welcome to tonight's special program. Let's start off with a big round of applause for that fine supper. Wasn't it simply delicious?" she prompted the crowd.

As the clapping subsided, she continued, "I am pleased so many of you have turned out. I know you want to learn more, so without further delay, let me introduce, all the way from New York City, we are delighted to have with us.... Miss Milly Pennypacker, from the Fresh Air Foundation!"

Miss Pennypacker walked on stage. She was beautiful, a tall and slender young woman with an air of sophistication. From her tailored tweed suit, with its nipped waistline, to her stylish hair-do done with deep set waves, every detail distinguished her instantly as a lady from the city where cutting edge fashion was readily available. There was not a woman in the room who wasn't craning her neck to observe everything about her, right down to her perfectly applied makeup, her nail color and that strikingly rich shade of scarlet lipstick. They knew she was displaying the future fashion that would soon be arriving from New York, for these styles had not yet been seen even at the most fashionable of shops as far north as Wilmington.

"Good evening and thank you all for coming," Miss Pennypacker began. "I'm honored and very happy to be here. The Fresh Air Fund was established in 1877 by Reverend Willard Parsons, the minister of a small rural parish in Sherman, Pennsylvania. Originally, he asked several members of his congregation to help provide a few country vacations by becoming volunteer host families for some of New York City's neediest children. Turns out it was a surprisingly big success.

"Since then, the program has grown and continues to be a great success for both the children who are selected to attend and for our hosting families. With great support in helping us getting the word out from such fine publications as The New York Tribune along with many positive stories coming from our supporting families, just like all of you, we continue to grow every year. The simplicity of our program is its strength. Even as we expand to serve far more children each year, our basics remain exactly the same: we arrange for city children to have a chance to visit the countryside for a few weeks in the summer."

A vivid picture of how tough city life could be for these children was portrayed as Miss Pennypacker continued, "Many of our inner-city children live from childhood until old age never having the chance to leave the city to discover the pleasures you enjoy down here. Ordinary things like your backyard gardens, livestock grazing out in the fields, walking along a wooded trail, or seeing wide open skies with distant horizons would be a sight to behold for these children. Why, just the simple things all of you see here every day in Sussex County would be extraordinary and would never be able to be imagined by our group of city born and raised children.

"If your family would like to join in and play a part in our program, all you'd have to do is simply sign up, become a host family and share your home and your way of life with a child for two weeks this summer, nothing more. In June, when your child arrives, just bring them home, do what you do, go where you go and eat what you eat. In doing so, you'll absolutely delight and astound these children," Miss Pennypacker said as she scanned the room smiling, confident in her belief that what she said she absolutely knew was true.

"Do you realize that most of these children have never tasted vegetables picked straight from a garden, let alone they have never seen them while they're still growing on the plants.

They've never seen corn growing, up tall on the stalks, like all of you have. You won't have to entertain these children while they visit, just your everyday life will do that.

"Our children are scheduled to arrive by train at the Harrington Station in June and shall return by train at the visit's end. We make all the arrangements and provide the transportation.

"Let me stress, each child is hand-selected by need, but it's important for you to know, that each one of them is thoroughly screened to be certain every hosting family will receive a good child, one with the necessary manners you'd expect, and proper values. After all, no one would want to house a naughty child and the program simply could not stand to have that kind of reputation. No, let me assure you, there are far too many sweet, good children out there for us to choose from to allow that to happen." Miss Pennypacker wanted the crowd to trust that fact.

"In conclusion, let me say this, sometimes in life, just when we think we are doing a kindness for others, life has a way of surprising us. Most of the time, by the end of these visits, our host families tell me they believe they got far more from the two-week visit than the very child they brought home. I call that part of the program, God's reward.

"Please walk over to the back table and speak with me. I will be happy to answer all your questions. Together, let's look forward to making many little New York City children very happy this summer. Thank you all so much for coming tonight." Miss Pennypacker smiled and exited to the sound of excited applause.

By the end of the session, Sarah was one hundred percent on board and eagerly accepted taking on the position of being the

Coordinator for Sussex County. "Think of the lives we'll touch, Bayard," she said, "I can just imagine all those delighted little faces. Oh, isn't this program such a wonderful idea!"

Sarah loved children, but she and her husband were never blessed with any during their marriage. In fact, it took forever before she even agreed to marry him in the first place. Bayard courted her for almost nine years before she finally said 'yes'. At first, she worried about being three years his senior, but more importantly, she was extremely proper and... well, to be frank, he wasn't. Not always anyway, but his heart was in the right place and he was very fun and charming, but he could be devilish, not to mention... relentlessly persistent. He finally worked up the nerve one year, to move right next door to the Banning home, where Sarah was still living with her parents. After that, she felt like she saw him every time she stuck her head out the door. Teasingly, she used to say she married him just to get rid of him and put an end to his blasted and constant pestering. They had been married for six years now, had a strong bond and shared a loving and compatible marriage, but as for children... well, they just didn't talk about it anymore.

The idea of this program had thoroughly energized Sarah. "Oh, Bayard, just think of a little city child getting the chance to see our sandy beaches along Delaware Bay, not to mention how exciting a trip to Rehoboth Beach would be for them, strolling along the boardwalk and their first sight of the Atlantic Ocean, watching the big waves roll in. Or, how about the first time they'd see a chicken sitting on her nest of eggs. Or looking at orchards with apples still growing right on the trees!" Sarah excitedly said thinking out loud, her mind racing with possibilities.

"Why, Sarah my love, do you want to know what I think?" Bayard asked. "I think we need to get on that list. Look at us, why we have our little cottage sitting right on Slaughter Beach with more than enough room plus the guest room is all made up and just going to waste if you ask me. I think it's ripe and just waiting for a little bit of company. What the heck, why not? What could be a better use of our summer? Go on. Get on over there and sign us up." Bayard said as he nudged Sarah off balance, bumping his elbow across her back.

If the truth were known, anything that brought this blush of excitement to Sarah's cheeks was just fine with Bayard. He loved to watch his wife's eyes sparkle when she was enthused for something important like this. He held the secret belief that if his wife had been born a man, she'd have made one hell of a businessman. She just had the head for it.

The Wharton's did live a happy and fulfilled life. They adored and respected each other about as much as any married couple could. Sarah was a good wife, kept an immaculate home and was a wonderful cook. She was smart, well read, kept active with her many interests, and could hold her own in any conversation in mixed company.

Bayard was a successful businessman and the founder, co-owner and operator of the automobile parts store, Wharton & Barnard. He participated in the town's legislation as well as being involved in various church activities. Together, they had many dear and loyal friends. Yes, their small-town life was pretty darn good.

That very night, the Wharton's easily agreed and without any further discussion, signed up to host a child and support this fine program. Heck, it was only for two weeks. Oh yes, they might be a little bit set in their ways, but they could manage to change it up a bit for just a couple of weeks.

How exciting! Yes-siree-Bob, this was shaping up to become a very interesting summer.

CHAPTER 5
THE COTTAGE

The warmer days by the end of May was the signal it was time for the Wharton's to close their large home on South Washington Street in Milford for the season. They would pack some necessary belongings and move down to their cottage in Slaughter Beach to escape the hottest months of summer. A short, eight-mile drive East ended at the coastline along the Delaware Bay. Bayard looked forward to the move every year as if he were twelve and about to go off to a much-anticipated summer camp.

Slaughter Beach, with its smattering of cottages, was located south of the mouth of the Mispillion River that twisted west to the center of downtown Milford. From the shore, you could watch steam vessels travel down river, enter the bay then make their slow turn north toward Philadelphia. The *City of Milford* completed the trip in three days, and yes, while it may be faster to travel by train, at least you didn't arrive soot covered when you sailed with Captain Murphy.

Summertime at the beach still had its own share of stifling hot days and plenty with sticky, high humidity, but cooling bay breezes almost always blew in across the open water. Somehow, down here you felt as though you were hundreds of miles away from home. Slaughter Beach was a quiet haven, a retreat from the usual pace, and it provided the Wharton's their favorite time of year.

At night, small waves lapping over little stones and sea shells along the water's edge created a rhythmic sound that was so soothing it was almost hypnotic. The combination of that sound with a whisper of the evenings cool bay breeze was heavenly as it floated through Sarah and Bayard's open bedroom windows and lulled them into a sleep unlike any they'd ever known, almost an unconscious sleep that arrived so fast, they couldn't remember its beginning, recall ever dreaming, or even notice if their bodies even moved a muscle during the night. They woke completely rested, so different from back at home, and that alone was a big part of the magic they enjoyed at the beach.

Mornings began as the light of dawn filled their room in a soft orange glow as the first peaks of sun appeared rising over the bay. Early sunlight reflected off the white sand and flashes bounced off small waves, causing them to sparkle. Cries of sea gulls announced another new day had started, and Bayard would stand in the open window every morning, drinking it all in.

"I declare Sarah, there can't be a better way to wake, nor a more beautiful sight to behold than all of this." He would stay in place, scanning the horizon, observing every detail of the pure and natural beauty.

The Wharton's cottage was smaller than their home in Milford. It was a simple but lovely, well-built, square structure, sided in cedar shake shingles with large windows. Raised up on a tall foundation, the cottage was built to be ready for any unusual high tide or storm surge. The boardwalk was right off the front porch, the favorite part of their cottage. This large, wraparound porch was situated just feet from the water's edge. Time spent there in a rocking chair proved ideal for resting up, and perfect for gazing or daydreaming. On many occasions, it was the simple porch that became the most important spot to do some serious business thinking, too.

Wicker rockers and several sofas—all with comfy pillows in their seats—filled the porch space; poised, ready and waiting for guests. Each seat had a lamp nearby for evening reading. The wooden porch swing—hung by chains looped over hefty hooks mounted in wide ceiling beams—made the most wonderful creaking sound when going back and forth. It added another layer to the mix of pacifying sounds: waves rolling in out front and frogs and crickets croaking and chirping from the back marsh. Those critters could sing up a storm after dark, but when mixed with the beach sounds, it created a rhythm and hum so relaxing; it cast a spell over you that made it hard sometimes just to get up out of the rocker to go to bed.

Inside, rooms were simple and spacious. The living room had a staircase along one wall and was furnished with a davenport, a few stuffed chairs and a rocker with a walnut bookcase near the fireplace. Further back was the drop-leaf table and chairs set, and a glass front cabinet that held dishes. The table was used for every meal and was also the ideal spot for numerous games of cards or checkers and was perfect for spreading out a five-hundred-piece jig-saw puzzle, especially if it rained for a few days. Oil lamps scattered here and there, were ready in case the power went out.

Across the back was the simple kitchen, neat and clean as a pin, with freshly painted white cabinets. The deep enameled sink and icebox were on the front wall, leaving the entire back wall with a long working counter beneath windows that overlooked the vast wetlands, a perfect spot for doing meal prep work, canning or making jelly. There was more shade across this back section of the house and it often caught a good cross breeze that helped to cool down this busy room. Quite a bit of sweat got worked up over that gas stove from all the delicious cooking that Sarah did. She enjoyed preparing nice meals for her husband about as much as he enjoyed eating them, and never once did he ever fail to praise a meal and her tasty cooking. He was a smart man. However, Sarah wasn't fooled, she knew what he was up to with all those compliments, but she enjoyed hearing them, anyway.

With limited indoor plumbing, their out-house was down a short, sandy path, and stood right behind the sagging, weathered garage. While that garage sure wasn't much to look at, it kept the car out of the scorching sun and housed some critically important summer items one needed while living at the beach; like the vital clamming rake, a seining net, some very necessary string-tied crab lines, along with a bushel basket for the catch. Most importantly, the dip net and a few salt water fishing poles—all wearing shiny, well-oiled Penn reels— hung on nails, ready and waiting to go. Bayard never turned down an offer for a fishing trip from his friends, Heimie and Bud, who owned boats. He always brought the lunch and squid or live minnow for bait and often wondered, did he get invited for his good company or for Sarah's delicious box lunches?

Upstairs there were four bedrooms. The front bedroom was painted a tranquil green. Since it faced the morning sun, there was no need for any additional brightness. The double bed was centered to take in the panoramic views of the bay and wore a crisp white chenille bedspread. A rack at the foot of the bed held a couple cotton quilts for cool nights when an extra cover to snuggle under felt delightful and allowed them to keep the windows open longer. Only roll-up, straw blinds were hung at the windows. A set of pink floral lamps sat on top of the night stands. Smooth, wood plank floors were scrubbed squeaky clean with rag rugs to prevent sand from getting in the sheets.

The back bedroom was a soft buttercup yellow and its double bed was painted in a high gloss white enamel that looked as shiny as cake frosting. The bed was topped with a patchwork quilt and an eyelet dust ruffle. A swing arm lamp that hung over the night stand with an oval rag rug beside the bed. The room was as sweet as could be, complete with purple blooms of an African violet sitting on one of Sarah's mother's embroidered doilies, soaking up soft, filtered light from the back window.

The far bedroom was done-up in fresh cornflower blue and fresh white and was the room reserved for niece Dorothy whenever she was down. Being a twenty-five-year-old school teacher, she enjoyed her summer off and made sure she found lots of time to spend with Aunt Sarah and Uncle Bayard while they were at the beach.

The cottage was everything Sarah and Bayard needed and nothing more. Simplicity at its finest. What mattered here was relaxing and resting from the regular year-round, fast-paced schedule while retreating from some of that stifling summer heat. Plans included sleeping well, long, leisurely walks and beach combing, occasional boat rides, catching and steaming jumbo blue-claw crabs or frying up freshly caught trout and serving whatever the catch-of-the-day may be with garden vegetables picked that very afternoon. A refreshing swim a few times a day was a must—at high tide of course. Or just sitting out-front in a high-backed canvas chair by the water's edge under the shade of the beach umbrella to catch up on overdue reading was indeed a treat.

Evenings brought out the neighbors for a stroll along the boardwalk and provided ample time to chat and keep tabs on who'd nabbed the largest fish so far. Conversations that started on the boardwalk often led to a card game in someone's porch, and many times it was the Wharton's, with plenty of stories and lots of joking and laughing while they sipped iced glasses of squeezed lemonade or fresh-brewed Red Rose.

Everyone ate well at the beach. As far as a menu goes, you could count on plenty of oyster fritters, clam chowder, lump crab cakes, trout, flounder and even fried fish roe; served with garden tomatoes, squash, steamed corn on the cob, shucked pole limas or fresh cucumbers, onions and vinegar; or as Bayard put it, "the best damn eatin' of the whole entire year!"

Cantaloupe and watermelon slices accompanied every breakfast plate and the buttermilk biscuits— with a drip of local honey or a smear of homemade jelly or preserves made from local peaches or strawberries—was served, breakfast, lunch and dinner.

Truth is, this mix of breezy, salt air and sunshine, sparkling bay water, great food, dear friends, plenty of laughter and the best sleeping in the whole wide-world made Slaughter Beach pretty much the perfect place.

The Wharton's felt lucky to have their beach cottage and always believed that life couldn't possibly be better anywhere else. Especially these days when everything seemed to be dramatically changing in the country and right about now, none of those changes were for the good.

CHAPTER 6
SPRING IN NEW YORK

As temperatures grew mild and warmer breezes began to whisper the promise of spring, times were growing dismal at the Jandreau home in New York. Caroline Jandreau was dying. She was in the final stages of TB—tuberculosis, a dire condition she had far longer than anyone knew.

Grandmother Anna began to fear for the health of the girls, heaven knows they didn't eat the best. TB was deemed an epidemic, sweeping the city, with thousands dying all around them. The threat was certain; they would be next if Caroline remained coughing in the next room and it scared Anna to her core.

Anna began to feel as if her prayers weren't being answered. So, was that it? Did God wish them all to die? Well, maybe he did. Maybe that was some part of the big plan she didn't understand. She was overwhelmed and with so many concerns, she had become deeply bone tired, but even so, something deep down inside kept nagging her, telling her to fight and keep going for those beautiful little girls, they were... Knock, knock, knock. Bang. BANG! Loud pounding on the door interrupted her thoughts. "Oh my. Hold on, I'm coming!" Anna said, as she opened the door to the hallway.

"Good gosh, Mr. Geneille, forgive me, for pity's sake. Do come in," Anna said as she discovered it was her landlord. "I'm sure you're here for the rent money. Mercy me, how the days have slipped by," Anna said, rattled as her face instantly flushed with color.

She scurried off to the kitchen to collect the money so fast Mr. Geneille couldn't even say "Hello." That's when the coughing began from the next room. A deep, horrid, choking type of coughing that was followed by the sound of someone struggling and gasping so desperately to inhale it seemed as if it could be their last breath. That was followed by strong consumptive wheezing and bronchial rattles.

Mr. Geneille's face turned pale. "Why Anna," he said as he reached for her hand, "I had no idea Caroline was this bad." He continued in a voice so low it was almost a whisper, "Why on earth didn't you call for me?" He asked with genuine concern showing across his face.

"Oh... I... don't know..." Anna's throat closed, and she choked on her words before breaking down with tears that instantly turned uncontrollable. Overdue sobs surfaced so suddenly they poured out with a force from a place so deep and soulful that it overtook her ability to do a thing about it. Her cries sounded as raw and sorrowful as the pain she had been carrying. In between crying breaths, she tried to utter, "My poor little girls," but no more words could follow in the state she was in. She was terribly afraid and had been for weeks. Fear got into her bones and it had taken over.

But right now, Mr. Geneille was here. His comforting hug instantly told her he cared and understood. Anna leaned toward him and fell limp, letting go, leaning in to his firm shoulder. She was desperate for someone to care and relieve her. She proceeded to wilt into a good bawling cry, the kind that left her exhausted with jerking breaths, snot running everywhere and puffy, red, swollen eyes. It was a pent-up cry that had been stifled far too long.

After allowing a few minutes to get the tears out, Mr. Geneille began formulating his thoughts, while the whole time, patting Anna on the back. "OK Anna," he said in a strong voice, "Here's what we are going to do. I want you to have Jene stay here with her mother. And you Jene, get over there and close that dang bedroom door, and for Heaven's sake, keep it closed from now on, do you understand?

"Anna, you are going to come with me. I think I know a place we can move Caroline to. We need to get her away from everyone. Come on now. We've got to act right away, before the rest of you get sick. Lord knows, TB could devour half of us in the building if we don't do something and I'm not going to stand around here and let that happen. No, we're going to put this plan of mine into action right now.

"Anna, you listen to me, this is most important, you're not to worry about this anymore, understand? We need you to be strong for the girls. Let's go and speak with Mrs. G. She'll work on rounding up some other folks who are going to help us. It's going to be alright." Mr. Geneille concluded with his plan developed clearly and firmly in his mind. And that's just what they did.

Neighbors gathered quickly and working together, a section of the basement began to get prepared for Caroline. Everyone knew, without any money, plus with Caroline's TB being as advanced as it was, there would be no assistance coming from a hospital for them. Besides, at this stage, there was nothing to be done but to keep her hydrated, as comfortable as possible, and isolated.

Stacked boxes and wooden crates were moved out of the

storage room. The brick walls were scrubbed with stiff brushes dipped in buckets of hot sudsy pine oil disinfectant and as soon as the walls dried, every inch was white washed. The room was prepared and ready by the end of the second day.

Back on the sixth floor, the time had come to move Caroline to her new quarters. Four strong men arrived with boards to slide under her mattress for them to create a make shift stretcher.

"Please, do come in boys. Oh, how can I ever thank you?" Anna said, as she hugged and greeted each of the young men she knew since they were little. They were pleased to be of service and help her out for a change.

"Miss Anna, times around here are plenty hard enough," one of the men said, "you don't need to be thanking us. Why, look at the countless times you've helped us out or made a pot of soup for our families when we've had an illness or a new baby. We're just sorry we can't do more to make this easier for you and the girls," he nodded respectfully.

Anna turned toward the girls who were huddled together on the opposite side of the kitchen, wide-eyed with worry and all too quiet. "Girls come on over, but no farther than right beside me and say your good-byes to your mother. Just blow a kiss to her from here and she'll know you love her."

Jene was the first one over beside her Grandmother. She quietly whispered, "I love you mother and I will pray every day you get better." Then she looked away as her chin dropped and her eyes filled with tears.

Marie and Eilleen walked over together. Marie squeezed her hands together, intertwining her fingers, but words caught in her throat that suddenly was too tight and restricted for any sounds to slip past. Her chin quivered. She blew mother a kiss and stepped back.

Then Eilleen piped up, "Oh Mommy, you must get better, really fast! I want you to hear me sing at the special place we found at market. As soon as it gets warmer, we'll take you there. When your cough is all gone. I'm sure it will be soon." She blew her kiss never taking her eyes off her mother.

"OK girls, move back now, let's get your mother to her special room so we can get her settled and make her comfortable," Anna said as she put her arm around Marie.

The men easily lifted the frail woman lying on the mattress and were soon walking down the hall, balancing and guiding their load, easing it slowly down the staircase, one step at a time.

Mr. and Mrs. Geneille had been busy putting the word out about Caroline's situation. Many in the building owed a debt of kindness to Anna, now it was their turn to help. Most feared without their help to sit an around-the-clock vigil, Anna would be the one to drop over dead long before Caroline; she looked that tired and spent. A schedule was posted near the mailboxes and right away, every shift was covered; but the worst days were still ahead.

Anna could think of nothing more to do, but at least for right now she had something to be thankful for. Yes, she was mighty thankful for having such wonderful friends in her life.

Nine long days later, Caroline Jandreau passed away. The children never saw their mother alive after the day she was moved to the room in the basement. But, it was finally over.

The three sisters bunched close together along the top railing of the first-floor landing the afternoon Caroline was removed from the building. Her body was completely covered, draped with a white sheet. All that was recognizable was their mother's long flowing hair that trailed down one side of the stretcher from under the cloth as they rolled her body out the front door.

Grief stirred the children, but even that emotion wasn't as strong as the fear they felt as they looked over at their tired Grandmother Anna. They couldn't help but think, "What will we do if something happens to her?" That topic was never discussed between the girls. They didn't know what would become of them now that they were orphans, but Grandmother Anna had taken care of them so far, so maybe, somehow, she always would.

CHAPTER 7
CHECKING THE LIST

By the middle of April, the Fresh Air Fund in New York was beginning to launch their plans for summer and the office was bustling with activity. Coordination efforts at all the various locations had sprung into action. References had to be researched and screened one by one, for only children with enough manners not to be offensive, could be selected. While some lack in the social graces was predicted and certainly understood, outright rudeness or blatant bad manners would not be tolerated. Approved children could never have been known to ever lie or steal, regardless of their poor living conditions or their tough family circumstances. Such behavior displayed in a sponsor's home could be the ruination of the whole endeavor. Those who worked the program were strictly trained on the importance of that rule and there would be no exceptions.

The volunteers felt like Santa, researching the names on the list and checking them twice. It was terribly hard to cross off a child's name. One couldn't help but wonder what a difference a trip like this might make in the life of a child, but in the end, the program had to think of the greater good as numerous children and family backgrounds were scrutinized. Many names must be scratched off before summer, for there were never enough homes for all these dear, deserving children.

Miss Pennypacker was in charge of the Queens region and scheduled to conduct interviews at Trinity United Methodist Church on Wednesday. When Mrs. Geneille, who was a member there, learned about The Fresh Air Fund and the summer trips for children, she decided it would be such a lovely idea to add the names of Caroline's daughters for consideration for this year's trip. Such a good idea in fact, she finagled a dear friend of hers into arranging time for a private moment for her to speak directly to Miss Pennypacker herself.

"Thank you so very much for seeing me Miss Pennypacker," Mrs. Geneille said smiling with both the pride of her marvelous idea and its potential impact. "Let me assure you, these three little girls are very good, and they've suffered so much, first by having no father, and then having to watch their mother waste away like she did before her death. Oh, it was months and months before the TB finally took her." Mrs. G teared up, her voice becoming thin and weary, recalling what she had witnessed firsthand. "Why, the entire household has lived through one tragic thing right after another. The idea of your program, well it would simply be wonderful—for all of them. They're being raised now by their elderly grandmother and it would be such a blessing for her too, a chance for her to get some much-needed rest. The girls are twelve, ten and five and I tell you, their manners are fine, I can vouch for that myself. The little one, Eilleen, has been losing weight. Did I tell you, she's the one that sings at market for coins? It's how those dear girls manage to make ends meet," she told Miss Pennypacker with so much genuine love, she had to fight back impending tears.

"I am so very sorry Mrs. Geneille," Miss Pennypacker said as tenderly as she could, "they sound really lovely, they do, and I'm sure they are, but it's much too late for me to possibly even consider them for this year. You see, we stopped gathering names last fall. There are hundreds of good children already under consideration right now, and to be honest, there are never enough homes to go around." Miss Pennypacker spoke with sincere sadness in her voice. This was the part of her job she hated the most. As she continued speaking, she used the rehearsed, unemotional, strictly business voice she had trained herself to revert to for moments like this. "Perhaps you'd like to put their names on my list for consideration for next summer's program?" How she desperately wished there were more homes, one for each and every one of these deserving children.

"Oh please, could you just consider little Eilleen and maybe give that dear child a chance? She's absolutely darling and..." at this point emotions took over, stealing her ability to utter another peep. She realized she couldn't continue without completely breaking down and it was not her intent to make a spectacle of herself, so she stopped. Looking away, she reached into her purse and retrieved the cotton floral hankie tucked inside and quietly dabbed her eyes.

She watched Miss Pennypacker slowly shake her head, adding, "I am very sorry, but you do understand my position."

"Yes. Of course, I do." Mrs. Geneille was too much of a lady to insist anymore. She blotted her eyes one more time, took a deep breath, put her hankie back and snapped the purse shut. She collected herself and forced herself to sit up straight and inhaled deeply before saying, "Thank you for listening. I know you do all you can. I guess only God can make a difference for these girls now. I really do understand there are not enough homes, so I shall be praying for your program tonight, and for many nights to come, but please, would you say a prayer for these girls, too? Especially little Eilleen? I believe God still works miracles sometimes. Don't you?" With her heartfelt question asked, her voice cracked, so she made a quick turn of her head, followed her lifted chin and slipped quietly right out the door.

Mrs. G. was certainly glad she'd not breathed a word of her wonderful idea to Anna and the girls. What a huge disappointment this turned out to be. Imagine if she had given them false hopes by painting images of a summer vacation spent in the country. Heaven forbid. Well, she certainly wasn't going to speak of it now, not to anyone.

At least she had tried her best. And, it truly was a splendid idea.

Mid-June arrived with temperatures rising a bit more each day, but the early morning hours were still refreshingly cool. Mrs. Geneille decided it best to do her baking bright and early, while it was still comfortable enough to run the oven. Sliding in the second tray of oatmeal cookies to bake, she heard a terrible commotion, like someone running wild down the hallway. Before she could see what all the ruckus was about, beating and banging began on her door along with someone hollering. "Mrs. G! Mrs. G!"

"Heaven's sake, Tommy, what in the world's going on?" Mrs. G. asked in the open doorway wiping her hands on her apron. "Is something wrong? Why, it's not even 7:00 a.m."

"Nothin's wrong Mrs. G!" Tommy boasted, wildly excited, bent over and panting, trying to catch his breath. "I got this here note for you. Seems you got a real important message! It come in, just now, on the telephone line, over at the church. Reverend Samuels told me to run straight here, fast as I can and don't stop for nothing till I put this note in your hand. He called it, Rrrr-gent!"

"Let me see this." Mrs. G. said as she took the paper note from Tommy's sweaty hand. She started reading and her face softened."Well... I'll be." As she kept reading her face lit up. "Oh Tommy! Thank you, son, thank you. Here, have a cookie!" She handed him one still warm from the oven. "No, here you go, have some more." Then she yelled, "Yippee!" as loud as she could, something she'd never done her entire life. Tommy discovered to his amazement, whatever "Rrrr-gent" meant, it must be a pretty-darn, swell thing, that's for sure.

Breathless, Mrs. G. ran to the stove, turned off the oven, pulled out the half-baked trays, then practically pushed Tommy, with his hands full of warm cookies, backwards out the door as she fled for the stairs almost running. Yelling began again before she hit the top step on the sixth floor, "Girls! GIRLS! JENE! MARIE! GO FIND ANNA! Boy-oh-boy, have I got some big news for you! Open this door. And for heaven's sake, get Eilleen!" She was almost screaming, but in an excited, good way.

When the door to the apartment flung open, three frozen faces looked at Mrs. G. with puzzled expressions, not knowing what on earth to think. They remained standing like statues, still in their night clothes. "Whatever's going on Mrs. Geneille? What in heaven's name is all this fuss about?" Anna asked, wondering if she should be concerned but detecting a strange sort of happiness about something going on.

"Do you girls know where your mother's old suitcase is? Oh, if not, you can use mine. Girls, your sister is going to get out of this city. She's going to get to go to Delaware for two weeks! I just got the news. Eilleen's been chosen as a fill-in for the Fresh Air Program!" Mrs. G. was crying and laughing as she spoke.

"I can hardly believe it. Some poor kid got sick today, seems they had an asthma attack, bless their little heart. But a spot opened-up, early this very morning. I just got the word, just now! It seems Miss Pennypacker remembered me and called the Minister on the church telephone line with the news. God sure does work in mysterious ways. SO, if we can get her ready in time, she gets to be the one to go. Good grief, we've got to get busy, Miss Pennypacker will be here herself to put Eilleen on the train in a few hours. Marie, go find that suitcase. Jene, go run some warm bath water, honey. Hurry girls, I need your help. Isn't this thrilling?" Mrs. Geneille said with so much excitement it was instantly contagious.

"Where is that dear child anyway?" Mrs. Geneille asked as she spun a complete circle searching the room for the missing little girl.

"Marie, go out in the hall and see if you can find her out there." Grandmother said.

Sure enough, Eilleen was in her nightgown at the far end of the hall on her tip toes with her head inside the laundry chute.

"For pity's sake, what are you doing?" Marie asked, "Did you drop something down there?"

"Oh Marie... look!" Eilleen said holding out her hand full of copper pennies. "I'm singing inside the laundry shoot and folks are dropping down pennies to me from the top floors. My voice sounds really good inside here, too. It's working almost like the storm drain." Eilleen said. "Come over and listen for yourself."

"Good grief. Get your head out of there. You need to come with me, right now. Something big is going on." Marie said in a way that Eilleen knew something important was up.

The energy in that old apartment had never been as bright or as alive as it was in the next few hours. Glowing smiles literally lit up the room as excitement bounced off everyone. Anna kept shaking her head saying "Oh, my gosh... can this really be happening?" Everyone kept giving Eilleen big hugs. Anna looked straight up as if the ceiling were as transparent as glass and she could see the heavens, saying, "Thank you God!"

Jene was twirling circles. Eilleen was clapping, jumping and whirling all over the place. She didn't have a clear idea of what was happening, only that she was going on a wonderful vacation.

"I'm going... *where?*" she asked in a voice that giggled. She never stopped dancing, while they explained the trip, she jumped the entire time they were packing and even as they brushed her hair, she wiggled, danced and bounced. Excited energy like this wasn't to be contained inside that child's body, not without some of it flying out her limbs in different directions. Nobody minded, not today.

Grandmother Anna packed a nightgown, her tooth brush and the rest of her clothes, folding them tightly, trying to remove the wrinkles, then added a sweater in case it got chilly. There wasn't much time. Jene came running to donate her precious hair brush to be packed, for she couldn't imagine going so far away and not being able to brush your hair.

Mrs. G. wished they'd had more time to scrounge up some better clothes than these, but they would just have to do. Eilleen was soon scrubbed, buffed and dressed in the best she had, which wasn't much. They choose a faded green and rose floral print dress with a tie sash and Peter Pan collar that had been handed down several times even before Marie wore it then dug in the sock drawer to come up with a pair that almost matched.

Suddenly, Mrs. G. got an idea and took off running back downstairs only to return carrying a happy, carnation pink silk ribbon they tied in her hair. Admiring the results, who would notice anything but the smile on that child's face topped with that wonderful pink bow! They had done it. It was time to go down stairs and wait.

At precisely 9:10 a.m. a black Chrysler sedan pulled up in front of the apartment building and stopped. They couldn't miss it. After all, they'd been looking out the front window in the downstairs hallway every two seconds all morning.

Grandmother Anna kneeled down and faced Eilleen, "Now, be sure to be a good girl and use your best manners. I want you to bring us back all the stories filled with every little detail, so we can hear about all the fun you're going to have. You be gracious and happy, no matter what, understand, *gracious and happy*. You remember that, OK? We love you, child!"

Miss Milly Pennypacker practically jumped out of the car wearing a smile so big it matched everyone waiting curbside, and gave everybody a handshake, "Good morning ladies! I'm sure you all have been very busy scurrying around like crazy this morning. You must be Grandmother Anna, it's lovely to meet you. And you must be Eilleen, I am so glad you get to come today. You know, it's moments like this that make all my hard work so worthwhile. As soon as I got the word we had an open spot, I thought of Eilleen straightaway."

Miss Pennypacker was the most beautiful woman Eilleen had ever seen up close. Every bit as beautiful as any princess she ever imagined in bedtime stories. She was young, had polished finger nails and was wearing a lovely, navy blue suit and real nylon stockings. Miss Pennypacker seemed as excited about this bazaar twist of fate as everyone else.

"I'm so glad you took the time to come and speak with me Mrs. Geneille. Seems someone's misfortune turned out to give us all this great surprise. You know, the cancellation came to me so last minute, but right away I remembered your words. So, I thought to myself, if you would be willing to pull this off in a flash, we just might be able to make it work out, and look, we did! I do believe you're right Mrs. Geneille, sometimes God does work in strange ways. I think this trip was meant for Eilleen.

Grandmother Anna, I left some paperwork for you at the church. Please go pick it up when you can, it's got all our trip information inside the envelope. Ok everyone, I guess we're off! We will see you all back here in two weeks. I'll personally drive Eilleen back here myself. Thank you everyone. Good-by."

Even at her tender age, Eilleen could read faces and understood body language but in all her short life, never had she witnessed everyone this happy at once, so in her mind, any worry she may have thought of was eclipsed. There couldn't be a doubt about it, wherever she was going had to be the best place in the world. She didn't fret a single second or shed a tear. She met Miss Pennypacker as though she had known her all her life and promptly bounced into the back seat of the sedan to be driven to the train looking as confident and grown up as if she always traveled the world. With a big wave out the back window of the automobile, she was off.

They arrived at the train station well before the other children and Mrs. Pennypacker proceeded to set up tables alphabetically, so each child could pick up their packet and a tag. Name tags were to be pinned on each child's shirt or dress. Tickets were collected as the children were accounted for and were presented by the bundle to the Red Caps for boarding in groups. Since accommodations were limited, they were crammed for space, so children had to bunch up. The foundation received a nice price break on their group tickets, that came with no frills included.

Eilleen was tagged and as she boarded, the Red Cap couldn't help but notice her, maybe it was the pink bow. "Good afternoon little Miss. Welcome aboard my train. Aren't you a little cutie-pie!" said this kind, dark man with a huge grin. "You know, things be a mighty bit crowded in this 'ol train compartment of mine today. You just stick by me 'til I get everyone settled in, then I'm goin' to find a good spot for you." he said in his smooth, deep, southern voice.

Why, he looked happy too, so Eilleen waited and he kept a watchful eye out for her while he squeezed in the other kids. Soon the rush was over. The whistle sounded several times and the train started moving. They were on their way, traveling Southbound.

"Okey-dokey, little lady. I'm puttin' you up in a special place for safe keepin'," the Red Cap said as he flashed her another powerful big smile. And with that, he swooped her up. "You can settle in right here." The Red Cap had folded a blanket and placed it across an upper luggage rack for her. He knew it would be a long ride, first to Philadelphia, then on to Wilmington before going south and reaching their final destination, Harrington, Delaware. "Now, I'll be back by to check in on you, so, stay put, ya hear?"

The rack provided small, but comfortable quarters and he'd even added a little pillow, so she laid down and started humming along to the sound of the train as it began clunking, rocking and moving down the tracks. She peeked out a few times, but soon settled into the clacking and swaying rhythm of the wheels that were rolling beneath her as the train picked up speed and really got underway. When the Red Cap returned, he discovered she was fast asleep.

Before the sun would go down this very afternoon, she was going to step off that train in a totally new place. A place so different from her home, it would look and feel almost like another world.

CHAPTER 8
SUMMER BEGINS AT SLAUGHTER BEACH

Toting a warm bucket full of sudsy Spic 'n Span, that was smelling every bit as good as they said it would on her favorite radio program, Sarah climbed the stairs to the guest room. She raised open the back window and proceeded to scrub the little yellow room from top to bottom. Fresh off the clothes line, crisp, clean sheets got tucked on the mattress, feather pillows were plumped and for the final touch, a fuzzy teddy bear was placed on top, waiting to welcome their visiting child.

Together, Bayard and Sarah made several shopping trips. They visited the pharmacy for zinc oxide, to prevent their child from getting sunburned along with a cobalt blue jar of Noxzema, in case she did. At the hardware store, Sarah had to have the darling brown little teddy bear, (it could end up being very necessary you know, to help with sleeping). They picked up a jar of bubbles with a wand inside, a tin sand pail with a red shovel, a nice coloring book of farm animals and a forty-eight-count box of Crayolas. After all, what on earth did they have hanging around the place that might keep a child entertained?

With a few basics ready and that great big sandy beach out front, they felt off to a good start. Once the child arrived, it might be fun to take them shopping, maybe break the ice those first days and help things to go a little smoother, should there be an adjustment period. And, besides, toys were expensive, better to have the child in on the decision than to waste money.

Bayard watched the extra spending that Sarah had been

enjoying these last few weeks. Not too much mind you, but none the less, it had never crossed his mind what a child could cost if you had one around all the time. Seems they required quite a list of things.

In fact, Bayard hadn't really thought about children over the years much at all. Oh, he was fond of children, of course, but he hadn't missed having a baby when other couples their age did. He'd never really saw what all the fuss was about, and besides, he'd been far too focused on growing his business. But right about now, their friend's babies had grown up a bit and were turning into some pretty interesting and entertaining little people. As a matter of fact, having one of these children around might not be too bad. He liked sitting on the porch, watching as they rode their bicycles by weaving back and forth, serpentine style, and he'd always smile when he heard them laughing as they romped and played tag out front on the beach.

By gosh, it dawned on him, he was getting excited about the arrival of this little visitor. Maybe as much as... now hold on a minute... come to think of it, might he even be a tad more excited than Sarah? Well, what do you know. Bayard stopped rocking to ponder that thought and decided he'd just keep that notion to himself. But it did surprise him.

The next few weeks passed quickly. Finally, the big day arrived, and it was just about time to leave for the train station, but Sarah, as it turns out, was not feeling well.

The last few days had really taken its toll. Why, just yesterday, she thought she was going to faint dead away when she got the news that two of their host families backed out... *yesterday* mind you! Seems one family got an outbreak of chicken pox and the second one had an unexpected death in the family. Ladies from the church circle came to the rescue, scrambling to find quick replacements. Seems there were a few families who wished they'd registered but hadn't, so their names got put on a waiting list. Now, this wasn't a list Sarah ever thought to create, mind you, but one of the ladies had, so at least that was one big problem that had been averted. Thank Heavens it worked out, but not before causing Sarah to realize how quickly a big problem could pop up.

That got her to thinking. For the moment things were fine, but what might happen next? Sarah couldn't help but conger up thoughts of all kinds of potential problems and possible chaos and once she started down that road, her thoughts ran wild. All those children and families converging in a few hours and it's going to be my job to keep them safe and sound and get every child distributed to a strange family, most of whom, I've never laid eyes on. Good Grief. A train full of other people's precious children. She couldn't stand it as the details of imagined problems climaxed in her head giving her nothing but worries and doubts.

Children would be scattered all over Sussex County. What if a child got lost? Or sick? What if one was missing when the train arrived? Oh, dear Lord, could one of them have possibly gotten off along the route before reaching Delaware? Who knew at this point. One thing was clear, any problem that arrived with that train was going to end up right in her lap. What had she been thinking? Anxious thoughts like this worked her into a dither. This wasn't fun anymore. No, this was a monumental responsibility, one she didn't take lightly and honestly, it was just entirely too much.

Then... if all of that wasn't enough, there was the added looming mystery about the strange child they would be bringing home. While that thought seemed to be like an idea straight from a fairy tale back in January, this was June and let's face the facts here, this child was some unknown kid from the streets of New York. A total stranger. What if the child wouldn't talk to them... or wouldn't listen? Or worse, screamed things like, "You can't tell me what to do!" What if they cried... for days, "I want to go home. Where's my Mother?" Oh heavens! Where in the world had her mind been? She'd lost touch with her good senses, she was sure of it!

"Gosh darn it, I've tried my best and worked hard, for months now, and I've damn well earned this pounding headache," she decided. So, Sarah—blinding, sick headache and all—marched out on the porch where Bayard was reading the morning paper, stood tall and summoned all her self-control so as not to breakdown.

"Bayard," she said in a strong tone, "When you pick up Dorothy today, tell her I'm sorry, but you must also tell her she needs to take over for me at the train station. I fear I've developed a debilitating headache and I'm simply not able make it."

Niece, Dorothy, was her sister Mimi's child, a young school teacher who lived close by them in Milford, one block over on Walnut. "Dorothy has worked hand in hand with me ever since the launch of our program and she knows all the rules; and besides, she works with young children every day, so she's used to them. If you don't mind, see if you can help her out too, would you? I'll give you the envelope with all my written instructions. She'll know exactly how to tend to it all. I think our visiting child should arrive to the cottage and find the lady of the house calm and not a headache-sick, total nervous wreck. Don't you? After all, the program is designed to be a pleasant experience. I am sure you understand, Bayard, but I must confess, I'm at my wits end."

Bayard calmly stood, put the paper down, and kissed his wife on the cheek while noticing the dark circles under her eyes and her pale coloring. "Yes darling, Dorothy and I will handle it just fine. Why, I feel sure she's equipped to do this, she's practically memorized every child's name on the list. You just go inside and lie down a while. Try a cool cloth on your forehead and don't worry your pretty-little head about this anymore. We'll be back shortly."

"Yes, that is exactly what I'm going to do." And with that she turned and went upstairs.

So, it looked like he and Dorothy were on call for greeting and distribution duty at the station. Another first. Bayard checked his watch and decided he better get rolling. He folded the paper, put on his beret, lit a cigarette and walked out to fire up his 1931 Ford Sedan Tudor.

Now, this man loved any excuse for a nice long drive in his new car and while technically, it wasn't quite "new" any longer, but it sure felt like it after driving that old Model T. He enjoyed the feel of the improved quality every time he took to the road. They used to say, "Henry's made a lady out of the Lizzy" when these Model A's came out with their 40 hp, 4-cylinder, flathead engine. She certainly had some pep and the new three-speed shift with "glide" was as smooth to operate as they advertised.

A ton of Model A's were sold when they first came out in 1930, why they couldn't even keep up with production there for a time, but by 1931 with the economy falling off the way it did, sales really dropped off. He had gotten a sweet deal on this honey by waiting. And another thing Bayard always loved was making a good deal.

"Look, I see the train!" "It's here!" "Finally made it!" Folks called out from the crowd gathered at the Harrington station. Hearing a blast from the whistle, the gatekeeper walked from the station onto the middle of the tracks and held up a large, round, black and white enameled sign that read STOP, indicating it was no longer safe for cars to drive across the tracks. Chugging southbound with black smoke surging from the engine, the cargo of anticipated children arrived. With a screech of metal brakes pressing against the steel wheels, the train slowed down until it crawled to a stop to the delight of everyone eagerly waiting. Red Caps suddenly appeared in the open doorways and got busy placing steps below the doors to the passenger cars. In a few minutes, children began exiting and looking around at new surroundings, searching for a friendly face. Dorothy along with several volunteers with clipboards, began meeting and matching the names on the tags to the waiting families.

Bayard lit another cigarette and nervously held on to the name of the little girl that was to be theirs, Grace Anne Wilson. As the children emerged, he scanned various tags, searching for "Grace Anne", but nothing yet. When the stream of exiting children ended, Bayard located a Red Cap and asked, "Excuse me sir, could you please do me a favor and make a quick check through inside, just to be sure there still isn't one of our children left on board. We want to be certain we get all of them off."

"Oh Lordy! I sure am glad you brung that to my attention, sir. Why, I put a real little one up top for safe keep'n. She's no bigger than a minute. Let me go check and make sure we done got that that sweet child off this train before we pull out." The warmhearted Red Cap chuckled and wearing a beaming smile, reentered the train compartment.

A few moments later, the Red Cap returned carrying a little girl in his arms who had been asleep since Philadelphia, and announced, "Could this be the little one you is looking for?" He placed her and a small suitcase down right in front of Bayard. She rubbed her eyes and looked straight up at Bayard. Instantly and without a thought about it, he dropped his cigarette, crushed it with his foot and extended both hands toward this little girl and she jumped up, right into his arms. This must be Grace Anne. What a darling little girl. His heart raced as he checked her tag... but no... it read "Eilleen Jandreau." This wasn't his child.

Immediately Bayard scanned the crowd, searching for Dorothy. As soon as he spotted her he called out, "Hey, Dorothy, you need to get over here, and be quick!"

"Oh, would you look at our little girl! Isn't she simply precious! And what a darling bow in her hair. Aunt Sarah is going to be so excited." Dorothy said in her sweet teacher voice.

"No, Dorothy, this is not our little girl, but I'm telling you, she's going to be if I have anything to do about it. And you're going to help me." Then Bayard lowered his voice, "Look, this is the child I want, Dorothy and by gosh, you need to know, this is the one we're taking home, so here's what we are going to do. We're going to switch these name tags you see, right now, then we'll be off and on our way before anyone catches on. Come on now, hurry, we don't have much time."

"What? Oh, Uncle Bayard! I can't do that." Dorothy replied in a surprised tone. "You have another child's name. I don't know how I could ever make a switch like that, and with all these folks standing around? Oh no, I just can't!"

Bayard knew these next few moments were precious, "No one ever has to know exactly how a couple of tags got mixed up. Now, come on, I'm telling you once and for all, go find Grace Anne and bring me her tag. I'll do the switching if I must, but make no mistake, this is the child I'm taking home. Now, no one is going to think a thing about it. Pshaw, who's even going to notice? Now, are you going to help me or not?"

Dorothy had known Uncle Bayard her entire life, and this was not a tone she was accustomed to hearing from him. Right then, Dorothy decided, if ever there was a special advantage to having your wife be in charge of this whole mess for all these months, well this just might be it. She'd do it... but only because it was him asking, and she'd just have to think up an excuse for the mix-up later, when her head was clear. She felt her face flush and her pulse raced just thinking about what she was about to do.

Uncle Bayard was right, there wasn't a moment to lose before the confusion would die down and others might catch on they were up to something. Over near the table stood a remaining group of about six children. Yep, there was Grace Anne. Uncle Bayard already had un-pinned Eilleen's name tag and slipped it into her hand. More families were arriving by car now that the crossing guard was waving at them that it was safe to cross the tracks again. Possibly one of them would be Eilleen Jandreau's claimer. *Oh boy. Hurry up Dorothy, just don't look as guilty as you feel.*

In a flash, the deed was done. With a quick clip of a safety pin, Eilleen's name tag was pinned on Grace Anne, swapped right while Dorothy appeared to only be carefully reading names. Cautiously, she casually glanced over her shoulder to see if anyone was paying attention, watching her commit the crime, because that's sure how it felt. Nope. No one even looked her way.

Dorothy thought, *At least Grace Anne's old enough to tell everyone her correct name later.* Why... she's just as cute as a button too, thank goodness. Oh, good heavens, what a terrible thought, that's not what matters. *No one is really going to mind, right? Oh, let's hope not. I think Aunt Sarah would kill me on the spot if she had any idea of what I just did.* Dorothy's thoughts flashed nervously across her mind as she felt a hot, guilty blush burn her cheeks.

"OK Uncle Bayard, the real Grace Anne is labeled Eilleen. So, take our 'real Eilleen' and get the heck out of here before I change my mind, or before someone catches me and has my head on a plate. And be sure to do something with the tag that says 'Grace Anne' before you get home and Aunt Sarah sees it." Dorothy said as she slapped the Grace Anne tag in his hand. Bayard slipped it into his pocket as quick as a world class magician pulls off a disappearing trick.

Dorothy breathed a sigh of relief as she watched what she thought must be about the happiest man in the world, heading off to his car with his prize catch. Uncle Bayard was beaming from ear to ear. He'd orchestrated a swap more exciting than any business deal or stock trade he had ever worked on. Dorothy knew she should feel bad, but somehow, she felt down-right pleased with herself. Just looking at those two, they seemed right together. She'd certainly made Uncle Bayard's day, and she didn't plan on letting him forget it either. No, he was going to owe her for this one.

In a matter of minutes, the families began to scatter and drive off, each with a happy child in the car driving away about the same time the train pulled out of the station. Dorothy plopped down on a bench and watched until the last of the cars and the train disappeared. In only a few short minutes, the station became as empty and quiet as if all that commotion had never happened.

Dorothy felt relieved and satisfied. It went well. None of the children were scared, no one cried and every one of them was accounted for and happy, even with a switch-a-roo in the mix. She took a deep breath and relaxed.

If today was any indication, who knew what in the world might happen next? There was something different about Uncle Bayard today. Now, the question remained, *should* they or *would they* ever tell Aunt Sarah? Boy-o-boy, she decided she was going to leave that totally up to Uncle Bayard to figure out.

CHAPTER 9
DELAWARE'S FRESH AIR

From the moment Bayard crushed out his cigarette and scooped up Eilleen from the train platform, he never put her down. Heading toward the car, he had so much spring in his step, she was practically bouncing in his arms.

"Welcome to Delaware, Eilleen! I happen to love your name, by the way. Why, I do believe it might just be my favorite name of all times," Bayard said as he looked over his shoulder to see if the coast was clear for a clean get-a-way as he waved Dorothy to come over to the car.

Dorothy had not taken her eyes off of them and responded with a quick nod. *So far, so good* she thought, but at that moment, if anyone questioned her, she knew she would pass out cold, right on the spot! Thank goodness everyone was occupied, busy with the excitement of children and their host families meeting for the first time.

Bayard plopped Eilleen down on the passenger side of the car, pushed her bag behind the front seat, then slid in behind the wheel. As Dorothy approached, he asked, "Dottie, would you mind terribly much checking with Fred and Mildred on the chance you might be able to catch a ride back to Milford with them. Just tell them I'm too excited to wait around here. I sort of feel like a bandit that needs to get the hell out of Dodge before the Sheriff discovers the safe's been robbed. I'll wait here while you ask. I won't leave you stranded." And he flashed her a wink.

"Lands sake, yes!" Dorothy said, "I know I'll feel better when the two of you get out of here, too," and she hustled off to inquire about the ride. As soon as she had the OK, she cupped her hands around her mouth and called out, pretty loud, "It's fine Uncle Bayard! See you back at the beach! You hurry-on now, I'm sure Aunt Sarah can hardly wait!"

What a good touch to throw in, Dorothy thought, giving everyone within earshot a reason for Uncle Bayard's hurried exit. Well, it was mostly true. *What a devilish thing we did*, she thought, but part of her had to admit, it was also the most exciting thing she'd done in a long time, her cheeks had to still be blushing, she could feel them burn. She needed a moment to sit, so she plopped down on a wooden bench facing the tracks, still clutching her clipboard, glad this task was over.

"I am very glad you're here, Eilleen. My wife and I have been looking forward to your visit. So, tell me, how was the train ride?" Bayard asked his little passenger who, up until now, had remained quiet. *Good grief*, it dawned on him, she had to know what they were up to surely wasn't standard protocol. He hoped their actions hadn't frightened her.

"I'm glad to be here too. The train ride was swell, and it was very long too, because it's far away from where I live to get here. I took a big nap," Eilleen said while looking around out her window, intensely panning the surroundings and taking in the scope of things, the way an excited golden retriever might.

"Yes indeed, you certainly have come a long way. Are you hungry? Did they feed you any lunch on the train?" Bayard looked over and caught another glimpse of those vivid blue eyes noting there wasn't a scared expression or a worried bone in her body. *What do you know.*

"Yes sir, I'm *really* hungry! They passed out apples on the train, but mine is *gone.* My sisters say that I'm always hungry, but I promise you, it's true, I *really am!*" The answer was delivered with enough emphasis to convince him even if he did have some doubt.

Forget "proper" or "manners," by gosh, here was a direct, point-blank answer stated with nothing but pure, unfiltered honesty, one of many to come, that was going to put a smile on Bayard's face. That's what he liked by-golly. Just tell it like it is for Pete's sake. How darn refreshing.

"Hmm, maybe we should forget about spoiling dinner, after all, we do have a bit of a ride before we get down to Slaughter Beach." Bayard said. "What are your thoughts about you and me heading over for some ice cream, just to tide us over. What do you say?"

"Ice Cream? That sounds like a *very fine* idea to me, if you are asking what I think about it!" Eilleen bubbled back then lowered her voice, adding, "I've had enough spoiled dinners to last me. Blah. I've had ice cream twice. Un-huh. It was during special times at my church. I was there with my sisters. Vanilla and chocolate are the flavors I tasted; in a little cardboard cup with a tiny wooden spoon wrapped in paper and glued to the lid. They were wonderful!" She announced as if she were auditioning for a part in the school play.

Bayard could swear her eyes grew twice their size each time she emphasized a word. He couldn't get the smile off his face, thinking, *well, she sure doesn't sound homesick.* He turned the car toward downtown Harrington and crossed the railroad tracks where they could see the train preparing to depart off to their right.

On the left they drove past Reese's Theater where the marquee read: *Warner Bros. Presents....* 42nd Street. And, *Coming Soon... Little Women featuring Katharine Hepburn.* "Look over here Eilleen, this is one of our nice theaters. Do you like to go to the movies?"

"I've never been to the movies. Have you?"

"Oh, sure I have. And I'll make you a promise, before you leave, my wife and I will take you to see one. Would you like that?" he asked her, expecting those big eyes again.

"You really mean it? Golly gee! Just wait till I go back and tell everyone about this! They want to hear everything I get to do you know, but I never thought there would be so much to talk about already. Heck, I just got here!" Eilleen giggled with a relaxed, genuine smile.

Her sincerity and thrill from such simple things and those darned enlarging blue eyes brought unexpected tears to Bayard's. Bless her heart. Never been to a movie. He didn't know of a single local child who hadn't been at least a few times; why during holidays around here they offered free matinees for all the kids. Wasn't there anyone back home to take her to things like that?

Downtown was bustling this afternoon, but a produce delivery truck was preparing to pull away from the curb, so Bayard waited for the spot. They parked in front of Wilbert Jacob's Dry Goods and Grocery and walked over to Cupid's Ice Cream Shop, a favorite spot to stop by after shopping, and especially after catching a movie. Bayard lifted Eilleen and placed her on a tall stool at the counter. The shop was small, very long and narrow with two paddle fans slowly swirling overhead. Compared to being outside in the bright afternoon sun, it was dim and nice and cool inside the screen door. Behind the counter, hung a large decorative mirror with fancy designs cut into the beveled glass.

"Oh look!" Eilleen pointed out, "Bring your head over here. See, if you look in certain spots you can find rainbows inside all the little curlicues! See them? Aren't they simply beautiful?"

Bayard was speechless. And to think they worried about finding enough to keep a child busy for a couple of weeks. That certainly wasn't going to be a problem.

"OK Eilleen, what flavor would you like, you can have whatever your little heart desires, only let's get it in a dish so I don't bring you home to Sarah all sticky."

Little did Bayard know that comment would prompt a long discussion when Eilleen asked the soda jerk to precisely describe just what each of the seven flavors listed on the board tasted like. She first decided to try a scoop of chocolate and peppermint stick. Then changed her mind to chocolate and cherry vanilla… no wait, chocolate and orange ice sounded really good too. It was hard to choose.

The soda jerk leaned one elbow on the counter and said, "I have the perfect idea for you sweetheart. How 'bout I make you a cup we call the Cupid Rainbow Dish. I'll scoop little dips of chocolate, peppermint, cherry vanilla and orange ice in a dish and put a cherry on top. How's that sound?" He had to do something, or he would never be able to finish washing dishes and stocking up cones for the crowd after tonight's movie show.

"That's perfect! This way I'll taste them all! Can we come back next time, so I can try more flavors? Maybe after we go to see our movie?" She practically squealed she was so excited.

Bayard smiled, nodding yes.

"Will you remember me when I come back? And remember how to make the Cupid Rainbow Dish?" Eilleen asked the young man who was dipping the final flavor.

"Oh, don't you worry about that doll face, I'll remember you!" The soda jerk spoke with a smile over his sarcasm. Bayard was sure he would too as the two men connected glances and couldn't help but share a laugh. Eilleen was much too busy conducting her ice cream taste test to even notice they were laughing at her. Bayard ordered two dips of orange ice on a cake cone. As he took a lick, he couldn't help thinking.... when was the last time he actually thought about how good an old homemade ice cream cone really is? This one sure was, right down to licking the last drip off his fingers.

The wonders never ceased during the drive home. It didn't take long to realize this little girl's world had been extremely limited. Why, she marveled at large birds that turned out to be a few old sea gulls, but she viewed them as if they were a flock of majestic eagles. She was thrilled to discover such a big sky "going on forever" over every open field they passed. As they circled Haven Lake, sprinkled with a few floating ducks and geese, it was as exciting to her as if they were driving past the Barnum and Bailey Circus. She couldn't get over the woods as they drove by saying, "Look at those trees! Why, there're more trees living all together right here than I could ever count!" Of course, she would say these things having lived in a concrete world.

Approaching the first working farm, Bayard felt it best to pull over and get off the road in fear she might jump right out of the car when she spotted black and white cows standing out in the open field. He parked the car, they got out and walked to the fence where she stared across the farmland and inspected every detail.

"Why, they're so big, but they seem awfully calm. So, are they related to horses or dragons?" she asked with her eyebrows knitted as serious as any adult.

"Dragons? No, of course not, they're cows. They give us the milk you drink. You see, when you pour milk from your bottle back home, this is where that milk comes from. I guess all this time you thought it came from the milk man," Bayard explained as he laughed at his joke while he watched the cows grazing.

"Not my milk. Ours isn't in a bottle and we don't have a milkman either. We make ours from dry powder in a box. You add water and stir it up, it's OK, but truthfully, I don't like it all that much," Eilleen said as she wrinkled her nose and squinted looking straight up at him.

Could it be? Has this child never tasted fresh milk? This wasn't cute anymore for Bayard. For God's sake, just what were the conditions this little girl had no choice but to live in? At that moment, stooping down near her, next to the fence around the cows, a feeling poured into Bayard's heart he had never experienced before. She had not asked for a thing, yet he strongly felt a need and pressing desire to protect this little girl... and... make a difference in her world.

The late afternoon sun caused trees to cast long shadows while its beautiful orange glow continued to kiss the fields and shine through Eilleen's reddish brown hair while she was still admiring the cows. Bayard felt sure she would have stood there for an hour or maybe more if he allowed her to, taking it all in like a tourist who had traveled to visit the Grand Canyon or Niagara Falls might do.

Never had he seen such a beautiful child. It was obvious the moment he laid eyes on her but, in just this short time, he discovered she possessed additional beauty inside. She was pure and sweet and unspoiled and upbeat even though her life seemed to him, sadly deprived. He wanted to make it up to her. Why, it seemed to be her nature to be happy and wouldn't it be the most fun thing in the world to show her everything she's missed and to spoil her rotten?

Back in the car Bayard said, "Now Eilleen, no matter what comes our way, or what we may see next, we're not stopping another second. You see, if I don't get you to Slaughter Beach in the next thirty minutes, Sarah's going to call out a search party for us! One thing about me, I am always prompt and I never dawdle. But, today, I must admit, I have not behaved quite like normal… and guess what, I think we had some darn good fun! Don't you, kid-o?"

"Oh, yes sir! I've had the most fun ever!" Eilleen agreed sitting up straight with a big smile.

Fishing boats, tied to the docks, lined the banks of the Mispillion River that afternoon as they crossed the low draw bridge at the entrance of Slaughter Beach. Another mile or so and they would be home. Cottages sat scattered all along the shoreline just off the road facing the water.

"Eilleen, we're now at the coast of the Delaware Bay, and it's where we have our cottage. The beach runs about twelve miles south from here to Lewes Beach and that's where the mighty Atlantic Ocean meets the Delaware Bay, right at a spot they call Cape Henlopen. Our bay waters are calmer than the ocean, so you'll have more fun bathing along the water's edge here. Mmm, we're probably going to need to get you a swim suit. I want you to see the Atlantic Ocean, too. We'll take a trip to Rehoboth Beach and walk the boardwalk," he said while he was thinking to himself, *We're almost here. In just a few minutes you are going to get to meet...* and he paused. *Sarah? No, that would never do. Mrs. Wharton? No, too formal... Aunt Sarah? Naah.*

"You know what Eilleen, while you are here in Delaware, my wife and I are going to be your Delaware mother and father. Of course, we aren't your real mother and father, but we will be your *Delaware mother and father.* So, if you want to, you could call us Mother and Dad. How's that sound?"

Eilleen looked straight at him and gave this some serious thought as she rolled up her eyes seemingly to look for an answer in the top of her head. Her eyebrows scrunched, and her mouth twisted, then her lips tightened. She had never known her father and always wanted to have a Dad, and she certainly liked this man. As for her mother, well she was gone too, so, she really didn't have anyone to call Mother. No one at home would be upset with her she was sure. So... if she wouldn't hurt anyone's feelings AND she could have someone to call Mother and Dad while she was visiting the best place in the whole entire world, there seemed to be no doubt in her mind. She straightened her face and beamed as she said, "Yes! I would be gracious and happy to call you that!" She recalled being told to be "gracious and happy," those were the exact words she was sure of it. Look at how Dad was smiling!

Sarah had been watching for the car to return for hours by now. She'd brushed and rolled her long, prematurely greying hair into its regular bun at the nape of her neck, only to release it free, brush it again and complete the perfect bun for a second time. *Why did I do that when it was perfectly fine the first time? Surely must have something to do with a bad case of the nerves. What on earth could be taking him this long? Is something wrong? Was there a mix up at the train station? Did the car break down? What on earth is he thinking... leaving me to worry like this? It isn't like Bayard not to be prompt.*

As the car turned off the road, there was a different sound when the wheels rolled over crushed clam shells that ran up the driveway to the back of the small cottage. Overhead, seagulls were crying out and flying over the reeds in the vast open back marsh region. The air was muggy and warm with a slight breeze, fragrant from the back marsh, smelling clean but salty and yet so fresh all at once. Eilleen noticed it the second she got out of the car. She couldn't help but stop and stand very still to take it in, looking and listening to every detail that was so different from the city noises and scents of her world. She had to be very far from home now, but everything seemed so nice.

"Come on, let's go inside and meet Mother!" Dad said.

When Sarah heard the car pull up she looked out the upstairs window and there seated on the passenger side was a little girl. She forgot all about being the least bit worried and flew down the stairs to meet them at the kitchen steps.

"*Mother*, I would love for you to meet someone very special, this is Eilleen. Eilleen, this is Mother, your Delaware mother." Bayard formally introduced them as he flashed Sarah a huge grin accompanied with a wink. Sarah could see he adored her already!

"Why, hello, Eilleen," Sarah said as she extended her hand only to clasp it and pull her in for a tight hug. "Oh, you are simply beautiful my dear. We're so excited you're here to spend some time with us. How was your trip? Are you tired? I bet you're hungry and ready for some supper. I've got it all ready," Sarah said.

"It's nice to meet you. Thank you, but I'm not hungry. My sisters would never believe I just said that!" she said giggling. "They think I am always hungry. The trip was long, but it was fun. I'm too excited to be tired and I know I'm too full of ice cream to be hungry right now. Dad said we would spoil our dinner with ice cream, so I mustn't eat, throwing up spoiled food would be a terrible thing to do since I just got here, don't you think?" Eilleen said as fresh and precious as ever.

"Oh... So, Dad took you for ice cream... I see. That might explain why I had plenty of extra time to pace upstairs looking out the windows every few minutes," Sarah said smiling as she folded her arms across her chest and cut her eyes over to Bayard, giving him a look. She was teasing now since she was far too happy to be scolding. Why, if she'd been in his shoes, she would have taken this dear child for ice cream too.

"I have a big pot of clam chowder on the stove and strawberries are sliced and sugared down and the shortcake's cooling, so we can wait until later for when you are good and hungry to eat our supper. How's that sound? Why don't we get *Dad* here, to bring your bag upstairs and I'll show you your room."

Calling Bayard "Dad" felt odd, since she had never called anyone that besides her own father, but it felt fun too. Eilleen seemed as though "Dad" was the perfect thing to say, so Sarah shook her head and smiled. This was going much easier than she imagined. What on earth had she been so worried and worked up about?

"Here's your room, all ready for you Eilleen," Sarah said as she opened the back-bedroom door.

All Eilleen could say was, "Oh my, it's so beautiful," as she walked around looking at everything as if it should belong to a princess in one of the fairy tales the girls told. She knew the walls must be made of gold since the whole room was glowing a soft yellow. Pretty, soft colors were everywhere. The rag rug had lots of odds and ends of colors that were bright and fresh and without any stains and the bedspread was made of patches of many prints with hundreds of soft colors, but not all dull and faded like the quilts they had at home. Eilleen ran her hand over the cloth as she examined every detail, right down to the eyelet lace dust ruffle. "I wish I had a dress that looked like this." Everything was clean and shining and smelled fresh and sweet. The bed looked huge and the pillows so soft, then she spotted the cute little teddy bear sitting right between the pillows. She had to hop up just to see if it felt as good as it looked. Sitting on top, she knew it did. "This has to be the best bed in the whole world!" she said, then she slowly scooped up the little bear. "Oh look, isn't he cute, what's his name?" She asked.

"You know what, he's been waiting right there for you to arrive so that you could give him a name," Dad said.

Without hesitation, Eilleen inspected the little bear, rolling him around and studying him hard before announcing, "I'm naming him Tony. After Mr. Antonio. He's the very nice man who owns the coffee and cocoa cart at market. Why, little Tony here is just the color of the cocoa and coffee with cream."

Both Delaware parents beamed, they were pleased, but

more than that, they were amazed to see how everything made this dear child so very happy. Even this simple little bedroom delighted her.

"Why don't you take some time with Tony, look around your room and settle in. Then come on down whenever you want," Dad said.

Back downstairs, Bayard asked, "Isn't she just something special Sarah? I tell you, I knew she was the one as soon as I laid eyes on her. I just scooped her up as soon as they got her off the train. After that, I knew, I just had to change the name tag with the kid we were supposed to get, so I got Dorothy to help me."

"You got Dorothy to do... *what?*" Sarah gasped, placing her hand over her heart.

"Now Mother, if you want me to take her back and exchange her for the other child, I'm sure it won't take us too long." Bayard teased.

"No. I guess it's done now." Sarah went on still in disbelief he would think up such thing, "Did anyone see you do this... switching caper? How on earth did you ever talk Dorothy into doing such a thing? I can't imagine her going along with such a crazy idea. But... as much as I hate to admit it, at this moment, after meeting her... I suppose I'm glad you did. She is a wonderful child, you can tell right away." They both started laughing then she playfully punched him in his upper arm. "Bayard Wharton, you are such a devil!"

"You know Sarah, we make choices all the time in life. Why, I chose to marry you didn't I? Of course, as you well know, I wasn't hasty about that. Oh no, I had to give that marriage idea some careful consideration... mmm, yes, it took me a long time... many years in fact!" he teased since it was almost nine years before she gave in and said yes to his numerous proposals.

"You know, I think I've done alright for myself. I've built a successful business by taking my time and making careful, well thought out, deliberate decisions. But today, I don't know how else to say it, but I acted on pure impulse. One minute I was looking for a child with a name that I held in my hand and then, in a flash, I had this other child in my arms and I don't know why, but I knew... she was the one. For the life of me, Sarah, I don't think I would ever be able to explain to another living soul exactly why I did it. Something came over me and ... it was the right thing to do. Just as clear as when I knew it was right to marry you. I think some things must be bigger than us and maybe they get planned by fate."

"I understand Bayard," Sarah answered. "She is precious, I already can see that. We might learn a thing or two before these next two weeks are over, but I've always known one thing... you... are a rascal... even before this craziness got into you!" she added being playful. They ended up laughing like two little kids.

"I think you might be right... *Mother!*" Bayard teased back.

CHAPTER 10
ON THE BEACH

After the last plate was submerged in the deep kitchen sink for soaking, Dad said, "That sure was a delicious dinner, Mother. You know, I've got a great idea, let's go for a stroll along the boardwalk, right now, so Eilleen can see what's down here and we can show her off to the neighbors. And I'll tell you what, I'll even wash up the dishes when we return," he added as a bribe for being so spontaneous.

Residents would often go for a walk, visit and chat after dinner while daylight lingered a few extra hours before the sun would sink, seemingly in slow motion over the back marsh, taking with it the hottest hours of the day. That mixed with the evening's soft bay breeze, created conditions that beckoned them to stay outside as long as possible enjoying those glorious cooler hours. There wasn't a bay-side cottage, no matter how small or rustic, that didn't have a little screened front porch for keeping out the no-see-ums, marsh bugs and greenhead flies, while providing a wonderful place to gather and comfortably linger out of doors.

Every neighbor up and down the beach knew weeks ago the Wharton's were hosting a child from the Fresh Air Program this summer. They made a point to come over to greet her and offer friendly hellos.

Walking back toward their cottage, Bayard reached for Eilleen's hand and said, "Come on with me little city girl, it's high time you get a first-hand look at the beach!" They took off their shoes, went down a few steps and crossed the soft, still warm on top, sand and strode right up to the water's edge to do some exploring.

Mary Liz, Frances and Audrey, some of Sarah's close friends and all mothers, began to inquire, "So, tell us, how are things going? She seems like such a lovely child and it looks like she is settling in really well."

"Oh girls, we're having so much fun, Eilleen is simply darling… and she's sharp as a tack too. She must get lots of attention from her family. But I have to say, they must be poor as church mice. Why, when I opened her little suitcase to put away her things… well…" she paused, shaking her head, "you can't imagine what I saw. Now, her things were clean and neatly folded mind you, but the clothes this child brought are either faded, stained or old as dirt. None of it is fit to wear and should be tossed straight in the rubbish. We are talking about hand-me-downs that I swear have had more lives than nine of a cat… and an alley cat at that." Sarah said, not to complain but just to share what conditions back home must be.

"Tomorrow we plan to go back up to Milford and pick up a few things. Heaven knows she needs them." Sarah looked out and spotted Eilleen down on the beach. "Bless her little heart."

Audrey piped up, "For starters, I know I have a swim suit she can have. My sister gives me the ones her daughters outgrow, so I stash them away in the linen closet. You know every kid who visits wants to go for a swim, so they come in handy. I'll bring a couple down for her to try on. Did you know, next week, the Red Cross swimming lessons start, right in front of the Fire Hall? Elaine is signed up, and I bet Eilleen would like to learn to swim too. Oh, we do have to introduce the girls, they'll have a big time playing on the beach."

"Thank you, Audrey, that will be nice!" Sarah said as she felt her heart swell with a feeling of pleasure that was completely new to her.

Bayard and Eilleen enjoyed walking in the sand and noticed how the colors of the sunset blended peach, coral and purple across the horizon, creating a decorated sky that kept changing while they were talking. Eilleen was asking questions non-stop and Dad was doing his best to answer.

"Hey, what are these big brown things? They look like they are wearing armor. Look, I can see their eyes! Do they bite? Can they hurt you with these long, pointed tails?" Eilleen asked, backing up a few steps, just in case.

"No, those guys are pretty harmless. They are horseshoe crabs, but the locals call them King Crabs."

"I bet that's why their tails look like swords! Where are their crowns?"

"No crowns sweetie, but guess what? Inside of them, they have blue liquid instead of red blood. Royals, like Kings and Queens, are often referred to as blue bloods, hence that's where the King Crab nickname comes from."

"What's this?" she asked picking up a large, curled white shell.

"That's a conch shell, only look, this one's without the conch inside. They're kind of like large, saltwater snails that live inside these shells. Hold it up to your ear and listen, you will hear the ocean inside," Dad said.

"Yes! I hear it! Can I keep it? Could I bring it home with me? Will it work back in New York?"

"Of course, you can. Yes, it will work, so no matter where you are, so long as you have it, you'll always be able to hear the ocean."

The twilight of evening began to slowly slip into darkness on the beach. Golden lights began blinking on inside the small cottages sprinkled along the shore. Further down the beach, a group of folks had started a roaring bonfire that sparked, shooting off orange cinders that circled, swirling upward and twinkled as they caught the rising draft. Fishing boats had been dragged up to the dune line to prevent the incoming high tide from washing them away overnight. Near the boardwalk, the fishing nets, draped and hung to dry, looked like giant cobwebs while they waited for tomorrow's catch. Eilleen turned her attention away from the treasures in the sand along the water's edge and began to notice the sky that was slowly becoming filled with stars.

"I've never seen so many stars in all of my life." she said in a soft, fascinated voice. "I think this must be the biggest sky in the whole wide world. My sisters and I wish on stars sometimes. We wished for this happy new year. Do you ever wish on the stars? And, what on earth is that?" Eilleen asked as she stood up, pointing straight up in the sky to an almost full moon that seemed extra bright and pearly white against tonight's dark night sky.

"That's just the moon," Dad answered. There was nothing extraordinary about that.

"The moon?"

"Surely you've seen the moon?" Then Bayard noticed how much brighter the glow appeared to be tonight, and it held his attention.

"No. I don't think I really have. I've heard of it... the cow jumped over it and all, but I've never seen it before. We can only see a small spot of sky from our bedroom window. There are tall buildings all around us," she said as she held up her two index fingers like the number eleven in front of her face to show what a small sky she was able to see back in New York. "And it's never this dark at home. It's so dark here. The moon looks like it's shining from the inside. Look! You can see its reflection way out there, lighting up a long path out across the water! It almost looks like we could walk on it. Isn't it beautiful?"

Yes, it was. Bayard froze in place and his face relaxed as he observed the sheer beauty of the pure white moon and its rippling reflection and the hundreds of stars that quietly sparkled against the deepening night sky. Then he plopped down on the sand like a dead weight, thoroughly astonished. What has he been doing his whole life? How out of touch has he been? For right now, this very moment, he realized he saw, no, really saw, the moon, too. Stunned he took time to focus on each star, noticing just how many there were, sprinkled across the vast darkness going on for as far as you could see. It was dazzling! Looking down around where he was sitting, he could see the little stones and sea shells, hundreds of them in their various whole or fractured shapes and noticed how the colors were deeper on the wet ones than the dry, sun bleached ones further up on the dry sand. Underwater pebbles and small shells were being tumbled, sucked in and out by the current, looking like pieces of glitter. He heard the sounds the small waves made rolling in, curling over and kissing the shells. It sounded like a lullaby he had never heard before, but one he had longed to hear his whole life. He filled his lungs with night air and noticed the smell of the beach—and how he could pick up hints of seaweed and marsh, freshness and salt; mixed with the hint of distant burnt campfire wood as it was blending into the singular, soft nighttime fragrance—that was a familiar smell of the beach, yet tonight, distinguishable with separate notes he could uniquely identify. He felt so alive at this moment. Did this mean he hasn't been?

A few minutes ago, he was excited for this little city-raised child to see the beach for the first time, and turns out, he needed her before he could see it for himself? For he knew, he never really had... not until this moment. How shocking. Bayard Wharton was sitting on the damp sand, dumbfounded, in front of his own cottage with Eilleen, while they both observed all the marvelous beauty the world had to quietly offer them on this ordinary summer evening along the shoreline of the Delaware Bay.

Her views had been limited by living in a big city, but… what was his excuse? First it was the taste of the ice cream, then that odd peacefulness that came over him while he watched some plain old cows... and now this? Whatever was happening, it sure was about time. Might he have missed ever noticing the simple beauty of the entire world around him if left to his own devices?

Tonight, he was a middle-aged man going on twelve, discovering with fresh eyes what had been right under his nose all these years, how astonishing. What an extraordinary day!

Chapter 11
Making Memories

First thing, after breakfast on Monday morning, Bayard drove the girls back to Milford to do some very necessary shopping without Eilleen realizing that it was, since they made sure to keep their comments to each other discrete. Certainly, no need for her to be aware how they felt about her pitiful clothing, after all the remedy was easy, just like Bayard said, "Here's one problem that can be instantly fixed with just a little bit of shopping."

Parking on Walnut Street right as the "open" signs were being hung in store windows, they began to go through the checklist. The first stop was to J.C. Penney, the town's newest department store that opened in 1929, giving J.C. Penney a store location in all forty-eight states.

They found a darling cotton nightie made of a perky pink and yellow daisy print, picked up six pairs of white cotton undies (with elastic that worked mind you) and three pairs of anklets, added a plaid romper, a peach sun-suit and the cutest little light blue seersucker dress Sarah had ever laid eyes on, that would be perfect for summer. Now they'd have a few choices on hand when some of her things were in the wash.

They walked down to H. P. Van Kirk & Co. for a new pair of shoes. After looking over the oxfords and the ties, Sarah choose a sweet pair of Buster Brown's in dark cherry red leather with cut-outs over the toes and twin straps that buckled on the side. Eilleen was instructed to put on a pair of her new socks first, to be sure the shoes would fit properly. She practically pranced as she walked back and forth, looking in the low angled mirror while Sarah watched making sure they didn't slip on her heel. She stepped up on the new-fangled Fluoroscope housed in a walnut cabinet they had in the store where you slid your feet—shoes and all—inside the box-like part, pushed a button and you could see the bones inside your shoes; making sure you had a good fit. You could even watch your bones move when you wiggled your toes, it was just like having X-ray vision. The shoes were perfect. Eilleen loved the round sticker inside with Buster winking next to his dog, Tige. Delighted, she wore them right out of the store absolutely knowing she could run faster and jump higher than ever before. Old shoes were left behind and with a wink and nod from Bayard, the clerk knew exactly what to do and put them straight in the trash can. They were making progress.

Walking back, Sarah stopped in front of the Deputy Dry Goods, Notions & Etc., with *Calicos, Cottons & Chenille's... Plain & Fancy Trimmings & Notions* painted on their window and in they went. Eilleen ran her hand across the arrays of fabrics, speechless as she studied the beautiful, colors and textures of the various bolts of cloth.

"Go ahead and pick out two bolts of fabric that you like Eilleen. I'll select a pattern and let's have a couple of dresses made for you," Sarah suggested. Eilleen choose a pink with navy polka dots and a green calico with small flowers in fresh colors. Sarah measured her and got the clerk to pull the correct size McCall's pattern from the wooden drawer in the long cabinet behind the flat cutting table. She selected a basic, sweet little dress that all the little girls were wearing. They placed the bolts on the counter and watched as the clerk rolled out the fabric and cut the yardage. They added in some trim, ribbons, buttons and matching spools of cotton thread. On their way out of town, they'd be sure to stop by Mable Murphy's and in no time, she'd have the new frocks sewn up.

Bayard felt these dresses may be a little bit more for Sarah than Eilleen at this point. But the truth was, he couldn't quite decide which one of them was happier, the way they both were beaming. He loved it.

Baskets of fresh produce were on display out front of The American Store. They bagged some sweet corn, filled a sack with snap beans, selected a cantaloupe and a few summer squash. The tomatoes looked good, but they already had plenty. A cucumber, onion and a bottle of vinegar finished the list along with a dozen brown eggs and a quart of milk. At the check-out counter, Bayard reached around Sarah to slide in a bag of Campfire Marshmallows and said, "Come on, you know we must roast marshmallows on the beach Mother, don't you think? I believe our roasting sticks are in the garage. Hmmm, what about some hot dogs? Let's get some wieners and rolls!"

"Can you pick up a loaf of bread for us too?" Sarah asked.

Bayard saw a sign hung above the bread that read: *Penny wise & Health foolish... cheap bread vs Huber's... buy Huber's Bread.*

He got a loaf of Huber's then found the wieners.

Sarah laughed, remembering how long it had been since they'd built a fire on the beach. What was happening to her husband? Never mind, this was fun. Bayard returned with Oscar Mayers, the loaf of bread, plus... a box of Cracker Jack?

And so, it began. They made many campfires on the beach, enjoying the summer's offering of cooler breezes after a hot day. They roasted hot dogs on sticks; that smelled so good while they sizzled and swelled up and sweated while turning crispy brown. Using green sticks Bayard had whittled down to create pointy ends, they roasted marshmallows until they plumped, and their edges became toasty and golden brown. Eilleen learned the trick was to see how long you could roast them without them igniting into sudden balls of fire that charred them into black blobs of soot. The winner could roast his marshmallow golden brown outside with a soft gooey melt all the way through without burning or falling off. It wasn't easy, but it could be done. With an entire bag of marshmallows to practice with, you got to start over any time you lost one to the flames, or it melted and dripped off the stick, always practically perfect before falling in the sand. And many good ones were ruined too, for you can't brush sand off a sticky, cooked marshmallow Eilleen learned first-hand after trying to save a few. There was a lot of laughing, "do-overs" and yes, plenty of sticky fingers.

Never had Eilleen eaten so well, or tasted so many delicious new things, and guess what, she loved all of it. Clam fritters: she watched as clams were shucked from the shells; corn on the cob: she helped husk and remove the delicate silks; and fresh fried trout required "cleaning the fish". That meant scraping off their scales, slicing them open from the belly up and scraping out their inner guts before beheading them with one swift slice of the knife then cutting off their tails too. Yet even witnessing all that did not stop her from taking a single bite.

After every fish cleaning session, the heads and tails were dropped into a small pail and walked over to Heinie's, so he could use them to bait crab pots. To try to explain eating those bright orange steamed Delaware blue claw crabs, well, there are no words to describe how messy that was. Crab eating was sloppy and down-right disgusting to look at but turns out one of the favorites of all the seafood Eilleen tried. She never knew what they would be eating next, things pulled from the garden or harvested from the bay. One afternoon she even asked Dad, "Do we ever catch and roast the sea gulls?"

After a few days, Bayard returned to work, leaving Sarah and Eilleen to set about meeting some of the other little girls who would be spending summers at the beach. Eilleen was registered for Red Cross swimming lessons that began at 9:00 a.m. and that's where she met a tall girl named Gertrude, Elaine Townsend and Francis Pettyjohn for the first time. The girls hit it off right away. They all loved romping on the beach, splashing in the waves and giggling over just about anything.

When the whistle blew signaling the end of the first morning's lesson, the girls doggy paddled to shore and ran up to dry off with their warm cotton towels that had baked turning saltwater-crunchy while spread out to dry from previous use. The giggles didn't stop as they wrapped up and clutched terry towels around their wet little bodies with shriveled fingers. They made plans to meet back on the beach right after going back to their cottages for a quick Skippy sandwich and a glass of milk. Eilleen loved playing with her new friends even more than eating; now that was a first. She'd never had friends her own age before, let alone any designated time to just "go play."

Sarah loved to recline on her canvas lounge chair out front

under their stripped beach umbrella with a book and a glass of iced tea, but found it was impossible to get absorbed in a novel's plot when these girls were so much fun to watch. Sometimes Audrey would join her, and the two of them would sit, watching them for hours. It was wonderful fun and so rewarding. Sarah couldn't understand why really, since all they did was watch.

One evening, Bayard surprised the gang by bringing home some old, patched up inner tubes he thought they could use to float on. The girls eagerly gathered near the garage and watched as Bayard used the hand pump to inflate the tubes for them. You might have thought they were the best toys in the world. They spent hours splashing, floating and drifting in the sun. Sometimes they remained lazy, relaxing and bobbing along on their wet shiny black tubes and from the beach, it appeared like they were riding dolphins. Other times they'd race, swimming off-shore a bit before they'd line up, holler "GO" and see who could paddle to shore, run out of the bay to be the first one to stand flat footed across the finish line they'd drawn in the sand. Oh, the games these girls could make up, what one couldn't think of, the other one would.

Every day Eilleen added a few more shells to her collection. She'd take them up to her room and place them around the blooming violet next to her back window. She could be heard singing while she arranged and organized them. The white conch shell with soft pink inside had a place of honor under the table where no one would step on it.

During this first week, Eilleen had already gained a little weight, her eyes seemed brighter, her hair showed sun-kissed streaks and her skin had some color and a healthy glow replacing the inner city, pasty pale complexion she arrived with. Why, she was radiant, and to sum it up, she didn't even look like the same child. The new clothes helped, but when you looked at Eilleen, all you ever really noticed was her smile, her bright blue eyes and those darned unlimited expressions of hers!

Sunday morning, Eilleen wore her new seersucker dress and Buster Browns to Avenue Church in Milford. Most of the families hosting Fresh Air children were there, sharing news of the week, and eager to connect with the other children. The program was turning out to be terrific and a grand success. Sunday marked the beginning of the final week of the children's stay. The days were flying by.

After church, they stopped by Mabel's to pick up the two new dresses. She'd sewn them right away knowing the child's time here was short. Mabel even fashioned matching hair ties out of left over fabric to surprise her. Eilleen was distracted at first; bent over a small cardboard box, petting new kittens and was surprised when she looked up to see the dresses, "My stars! These are so beautiful. Why, I feel just like a rich kid," she boasted with pride as she tried them on and of course, twirled, danced a little and giggled a lot! Both frocks fit perfectly.

It was still early afternoon when they left Mable's. Dad said, "Since it's Sunday, I think it's fitting we should take a little drive. Let's go out for dinner and take Eilleen down to get a look at the ocean."

While driving south to Rehoboth Beach to stroll the boardwalk and see the Atlantic, Dad decided to give Eilleen some information and bring her up to speed on some splendid attributes of this ocean they were about to see.

"Did you know, they say the waters from the Atlantic Ocean can cure what ails you? Why, it seems, a good soak can even restore your youth and vitality... not that you're in any need of that my dear child. They say, if you get the jiggers while hunting for blueberries, you can just stand in ocean water covering the infected areas for an hour and you'll be rid of them. Bet you didn't know that. Yes, the articles I've read promote that bathing in Atlantic Ocean waters is known to be good to develop firm muscle, courage, strength and force of character. Why, it's no wonder so many fine people flock to our seashore. And just wait until you see the tempting treats they offer all along the boardwalk. Oh-boy-o-boy, you'll see!"

Surprised by the size of waves that would rise, curl and crash down on the sand, creating sheets of white foam that washed ashore in frothy piles, Eilleen said, "I sure wouldn't want to be in my inner tube out there in that water. Waves that big would toss me right over. I might even wash away out to sea. My favorite beach is still Slaughter Beach, but the ocean is beautiful."

They settled on the Hotel Rehoboth for dinner as it would be Eilleen's first experience inside a fine dining restaurant. They arrived at 4:45 p.m. to beat the rush. Eilleen couldn't believe the choices on the menu and that all of these people could afford to come to a fancy place like this to eat dinner for the sheer fun of it. Platters were fifty cents and Dinners, seventy-five cents. The orchestra music played from 5:00-7:30 p.m. during dining hours. Their meal was served soon after the music began so, not only was everything exciting and delicious, but the whole experience was down-right swanky!

After dining, they strolled over to Playland that housed amusements and some rides. Bayard got tickets for them to ride the beautiful Carousel sitting in the center of it all on a packed dirt floor. Eilleen selected her horse carefully, inspecting each one, going from horse to painted horse, finally choosing an all white one with sapphire eyes and bright floral decorations painted in its mane. "This is the one! He looks just like a horse a princess would ride!" she said delighted with her choice. The pipe organ music began, and they were off. Circling around, first overlooking the boardwalk then catching a glimpse of the ocean then zooming around to see it all again. Seated high up on her beautiful horse, Eilleen took it all in while the peppy, carousel music filled her head and the spinning thrilled her insides making the whole experience something she'd never forget.

Later, they stopped to watch folks making saltwater taffy as it stretched and spun, and even got to taste a sample but decided on a box of Dolle's sticky caramel popcorn they enjoyed from a boardwalk bench that enabled them watch both the waves and the people as they strolled by. By evening, the unspoken rule of Rehoboth Beach dictated you best be dressed if you planned to stroll the boardwalk after 4:00 p.m. You'd be sure to see lovely outfits and all the latest in fashions that showed off both quality and taste being worn by the ladies. The gentlemen sported light pants with navy jackets or navy pants with light jackets which seemed to be the current rage, all worn with light colored shoes of course and most of the gentlemen sported straw hats. It was great fun to observe so many dapper folks walking by. Promenading and displaying the latest in fashion was a very important part of summer in 1933 on the boardwalk.

Eilleen smoothed her dress and looked down at her bright white socks peeking out of her new, red Buster Browns and for the first time in her life, felt like she belonged to be right here with all of them. She felt important, groomed to perfection right down to her freshly filed fingernails. It was an important moment, feeling worthy and beautiful like this for the first time in her life.

While they snacked and watched the sights, Sarah spotted Harry Holden approaching. Harry was an older gentleman, about seventy years of age or so, who was a regular on the boardwalk selling roasted peanuts. He stood tall and erect and wore shiny black shoes with gray spats, gray well pressed dress trousers topped with a morning coat. He carried with him a silver topped walking stick along with his basket of peanuts he sold for ten cents a bag. Harry was a lifetime local. When he'd sell out of nuts, he'd stash his basket under a nearby bench and continue to stroll the boardwalk enjoying the sights for the rest of the evening. Just by looking, one would think him to be a man of great wealth, but this was the Depression and the sad story was that Harry was no longer a wealthy man. He was known for saying, "Ain't no need of being poor and acting poor all the time too." Personally, he'd decided he was entirely too proud to be poor, so he just decided never to act like he was. Bayard bought a bag of Harry's peanuts to take home.

Driving back, Eilleen fell asleep to the hum of the Ford's purring engine, long before they reached the cottage. "Mother, let's not wake her. If you will, just close the door after us, I'll carry her up." Bayard opened the car door for Sarah, then propped open the kitchen door and returned to scoop up this precious sleeping child to carry her inside. Halfway up the staircase, Eilleen opened her eyes and said in a sleepy voice, "You don't have to carry me, I can walk."

Dad replied, "I know you can sweetheart, but I've never had my own baby to carry upstairs to put to bed so, you just put your head on my shoulder and let me enjoy carrying you, cause, right now, you are my baby." Eilleen smiled, closed her eyes as he climbed the stairs and tucked her into bed. That was the beginning of a long tradition the two of them shared.

Now that Eilleen was tucked in, Sarah remembered a letter they were given at church she slipped into her purse that was from the Fresh Air Foundation. She retrieved it and sat down on the sofa. Bayard sat down next to her, "Wonder what they have to say?"

Sarah read the letter. "They want us to be at the station in Harrington on Saturday by 10:45 a.m. We need to pack a lunch to eat at the station while we wait for the train and they suggest we pack a snack for Eilleen to take with her for the ride back."

"Pack a snack? Well, how jolly good of us!" Bayard said, jumping up from the sofa, perturbed. "Yes, let's do that. Let's just take her to the train, give her lunch and a snack and send her back to God knows what. A place where she doesn't even get to drink real milk? Oh Sarah, I don't know about this." Pacing, he began rubbing his forehead, rolling his head while looking at the floor.

"I know Bayard, but you know that's the program. Think of all the fun she's had here. We'll sign up right away and have her return next summer. Why, she can come back every year." Sarah suggested trying to help change his mood.

Bayard took the letter and walked out to the porch where he stood staring out over the bay, lost in his thoughts… powerful thoughts. *There's no need for me to share any of this with Sarah, not yet, but I've got to do something.* He pinched the bridge of his nose and thought until he finalized a plan. *In the morning, I'll just reach out and contact Miss Pennypacker directly, why, the telephone number's right here on the letterhead. I'll offer to extend Eilleen's visit to have her stay with us for the rest of the summer. Then, well, I'll simply drive her back home to New York myself, before school begins. This way the child can have a proper vacation and that would give us enough time to enjoy the balance of the summer, together. Yes, and maybe her visits can be every summer for all of June, July and August. Of course! I'll drive to New York and pick her up early next year. Why, that might work out just fine, but this train ride out of here on Saturday? No, that's not an option I can live with.*

Hmmm, it was that same overpowering feeling griping and driving him; he simply knew he needed to do whatever it took to keep her, for a little bit longer. There was no doubt, it was clearly the right thing.

The secretary at Wharton and Barnard had to place several telephone calls to the Fresh Air Foundation in New York before connecting with Miss Pennypacker, then she immediately put Bayard on the line. He cleared his throat as he prepared to share his thoughts with her.

At first Miss Pennypacker responded, "You know Mr. Wharton, folks often get caught up in the moment and have grand ideas, but our program is restricted to the limit of two weeks. It's a big program and we can't make separate arrangements for each child. We are responsible to get them there and back again on time."

But it wasn't long into their conversation before she felt and understood the sincerity in his voice. Plus, the situation at Grandmother Anna's household was different, Eilleen didn't have any parents waiting for her at home unlike the rest of the children; she finally gave in and agreed. They decided to arrange a telephone call for Anna and Bayard to discuss his idea directly on Wednesday morning at 11:30 on the church phone, close by where Anna lived. She gave Bayard the church's telephone number and pledged to have Anna there in time to receive his call.

"You must realize, Mr. Wharton, it will be up to Anna to make a decision like this." Miss Pennypacker stated. "So, don't get your hopes up. If this is not a plan that Anna agrees with, then I must insist you place Eilleen on the train Saturday. You do understand?" Miss Pennypacker asked, using her most stern tone.

"Yes, of course I do. I only want to help make things better for everyone. I know Anna loves the child. Eilleen speaks so fondly of her. The girls are fortunate to have such a wonderful grandmother trying to care for them, but it's got to be hard. I don't believe either of us can imagine just how hard either. Whatever the outcome, you need to know, I'll be fine with it. I've not spoken a word of this to Sarah or Eilleen. I'll make the call on Wednesday. After that, I promise to agree to whatever the plan needs to be. I'm a man of my word. Thank you again Miss Pennypacker."

Wednesday's call came quickly. "Good morning Anna. You'll be happy to learn, Eilleen's well and has not been the least bit homesick. Why, she's eating all the local seafood down here, has learned how to do the doggie paddle in her swim class, and she has three little girlfriends and let me tell you, they do nothing but play and giggle all the time. She is simply having a grand old time, and that's the reason for my call. I feel that with all she has been through, and you as well, it hasn't been nearly enough time for her, or for you, to rest up. It would delight us if you would allow her to continue her visit with us for the balance of the summer. If you would agree to it, my wife and I will personally drive her home to you ourselves in September. She'll be back in time to start school."

Anna heard the generous offer, but more importantly, she heard something else, there was "something" about the way he spoke, a tone she remembered, sincere yes, but even more. There was a protective tone. Why, Bayard reminded her of the way her departed husband spoke of his children.

New York was stifling hot and miserable, too hot to sleep most nights. They were struggling to have enough food and things they did have spoiled so fast in this heat. Nothing at all had changed for the better. Yet, here's Eilleen with a chance to sleep near bay breezes and wake to spend her days with girlfriends... splashing in the cool waters of the bay.... What was there to think about?

Anna decided quickly, "Yes, my goodness. Thank you so much, it's very generous of you and your wife. I think it sounds wonderful. As long as you're sure you don't mind driving her home in September? She is such a lucky little girl! Thank you again, Mr. Wharton."

"Oh Anna, please call me Bayard, and thank you! I want you to know, Eilleen speaks so well of you. You are a wonderful grandmother. I promise you, we will take good care of her. I'll place a call as we get closer to September. I can't wait to tell Eilleen we've spoken and made this plan. Good-bye, Anna."

"Hump! Saturday... on the train with a snack. Well, I don't think so." Bayard declared after he hung up the phone. "Hot Damn!" Triumphantly he pounded the desk with his fist, what a victory. "Looks like our summer visit isn't over yet!"

He couldn't wait to tell the girls.

CHAPTER 12
SUMMER CONTINUES

How often does good news arrive to completely disrupt your thoughts? So extraordinary, it disturbs you to your core, to the point you can't even conduct your normal affairs? Not often. Possibly never before that Bayard could remember. Sitting here, he couldn't concentrate on a darn thing except this feeling of joy that had traded places with a fear that must have been in his every fiber, prior to that call.

Gratitude and relief swept through him as stress vanished from his muscles, leaving him almost weak. Having Eilleen stay the remainder of the summer must have been desperately more important than he ever realized because at this moment, emotional tears were rolling down his cheeks leaving him, a big boss, sitting at his desk, dripping in a stream of unstoppable, happy tears.

Wait until Eilleen hears this news! Bayard thought. *She's going to light up like a firecracker she'll be so happy. Won't she? Oh, of course, she will. But, if not? Well, that would change everything, cause, if this idea isn't okay with her, then we'll do what she wishes. But staying the summer? Could that upset her? Naaaah. She's going to be thrilled!*

"I can't sit put around here any longer, Delores. I recon' I need to get out of here and go on home. I'm utterly worthless. My head can't think about anything that resembles work today," He announced to Delores, who was busy typing at the front desk. He stacked up a few papers and walked out of the office, formulating another good idea on his way to the car.

After swinging by Geyer's Dairy for a pint of heavy cream, he stopped by the Milford Ice Plant for a sack of cracked ice. He knew they had plenty of rock salt at home. *What a perfect occasion to churn up a freezer of ice cream*, Bayard thought, *Elaine, Francis and Gertrude can come on down after supper for a dish too, then I'll break the news to the whole gang! Won't it be swell to sit back and watch the girls celebrate! (that's what all the kids are saying today, isn't it? Hmm... more of that middle-aged going on twelve stuff. I like it!)*

Then he had one more swell idea and stopped by Hume's Hardware & Supply Store and purchased a new jump rope. The girls had been using some old piece of rope they'd found on the beach, but it was too heavy to swing right.

Boy-O-boy, they're going to love this. Who could have imagined me, just a month ago, that thoughts of ice cream and jump ropes would cause me to become practically giddy, a man of my age. Humph, what do you know, I guess I'm in love.

Sarah knew that man of hers was up to something as soon he pulled into the yard. He'd left for work this morning so serious and tense, he seemed wound up tighter than an eight-day clock. And look. Here he comes, mid-afternoon mind you, toting a bag of crushed ice and who-knows-what in those bags, grinning' like the Cheshire cat that just swallowed the canary.

"What's that silly grin on your face all about? What in heaven's name are you up to Bayard, and why are you home this early in the day?" Sarah asked.

"It's a beautiful summer afternoon Mother. We don't have many of them left before that darned train comes on Saturday, so I figured we better make each moment count, and I decided we should crank up some ice cream! The girls will love it. Doesn't that sound fun?" Bayard was trying to contain his excitement and while he was busting to tell her, he was more determined to make this a surprise for everyone. No, he just had to keep it to himself a little longer, until they passed around the ice cream.

"Yes," Sarah said flatly, "It will certainly delight the girls. But you're not fooling me Mr. Wharton, there's more going on here from the looks of you. All these years I've lived with you, and here's what I know for sure, *you* are a rotten liar and *you...*" Sarah nodded school teacher fashion, putting her hands on her hips, "*can't keep a secret* worth a pile of horse dookie!"

"Sarah Wharton! There's no need to get vulgar. You might be right. OK, you are right about that. However, in my defense, I believe those are great qualities in a man. I'm rather proud of not being a liar or deceptively good at holding in secrets. Just for right now, will you just play along with me? I'll give you one small hint my dear, you will know exactly what I'm up to before your head hits the pillow tonight. Can you wait for that?" Bayard asked, softening his face, fluttering his eyelashes and cocking his head, pleading.

Sarah laughed, rolled her eyes up and marched inside carrying the cream to mix up ice cream and to check on the chicken that was roasting in the oven, muttering the entire time and shaking her head. Knowing that curiosity had gotten the best of her made Bayard laugh out loud as he walked to the garage to fetch the crank freezer and some salt. "Oh boy, now, this is some kind of fun."

"Eilleen, after you carry the dishes to the sink honey, you

can go outback and help Dad do some cranking. And when the ice cream thickens up, run on down and invite Francis, Elaine and Gertrude to come over for some, too. If they're still finishing their dinner, wait outside until they are done, OK?" Mother instructed as she poured ice cream mixture into the metal canister.

"OK. So, this is liquid ice cream? It looks like chocolate milk with the Hershey's Syrup stirred in. Can I crank it first?" Eilleen asked Dad.

"Sure you can, why you can crank 'til you tell me your little arm's ready to fall off," Dad said teasing.

Out back, Sarah listened to Dad explaining, "First we pack the ice all around this metal container and start cranking the handle. You got to keep the paddles turning to stir around so it all freezes, not just what's on the outside next to the ice. We add the rock salt to make the ice melt and it's the melting that makes it extra cold, and that my dear child, creates the magic that turns our cream concoction into ice cream."

He was so patient and wonderful with her, never grew tired of her questions, and that little thing was full of them. But she was so bright she listened intently to every detail and never forgot a word. Why, taking in as much new information as she did every day since she'd been there, it's a wonder her little head hadn't exploded by now.

It was a hot evening for late June. Bayard brought the whole freezer inside and sat it in the sink to keep it out of the sun, removed the paddles and put a cork in the lid so the container could cure while staying immersed in the ice. Shortly, the girls arrived, and five small china bowls were filled with scoops of chocolate ice cream, put on a tray and carried to the front porch where they all found a seat to enjoy a warm land breeze that was coming straight up the beach while eating their frozen treats.

"So, girls, it appears to me, you all seem to be having a pretty good time with Eilleen being down here," Bayard said almost like a question.

"Yes, sir. We all are the best of friends!" Francis spoke first since Elaine had just spooned in a big mouthful of ice cream. "We always find so much fun stuff to do, making up jump rope rhymes and we all love swimming! Thank you again for our inner tubes! They're really swell."

Then Gertrude piped up, "Eilleen's the best friend, she never gets tired of playing. She thinks up the most fun games and she always makes me laugh. I just love her!"

"Good. That's nice to hear. You girls need to know, I've heard first hand that she thinks highly of the three of you. You're her best friends, too. Good friends are very important in life you know. They're not always easy to find, so, the friendship you all share, I believe is pretty-darn special. But, I have detected one slight problem." Dad stood and began rubbing his chin and looking at the floor in a corporate fashion. "You see, there's this train coming on Saturday, you know, the one headed to New York, to take Eilleen back? And when she gets on, it might just mess up the balance of the summer for us down here at Slaughter Beach. And it's surely going to put an end to Eilleen's fun. So, I got to thinking about this for a while, and I believe I've come up with a solution. Now, of course, you two girls and Eilleen, and this even includes you too Mother, you'd have to agree that this plan of mine's a good idea. But, I think it might be alright for us to miss that darned old train. Eilleen could stay on, right here with us for the rest of the summer and then, Mother and I will just drive her back to New York when summer's over."

The children became all eyes, sitting motionless, forgetting they were even holding ice cream. Eilleen's jaw dropped about a half inch as she leaned forward in her seat. Mother cocked her head with the slightest hint of a smile and squinted, waiting for what explanation was going to accompany this bomb shell of information. Miss Pennypacker would poop her drawers if Eilleen was missing when that train got to New York! And Grandmother Anna? Why she'd faint dead away! Dad knew that! *What was he up to?*

Dad continued deliberately slow, raising his palm, "Now, hold on, before anyone speaks, hear me out. I did happen to phone Miss Pennypacker the other day and we arranged a call for me to speak with Grandmother Anna just this morning. Oh, and I had a grand talk with her, too. Seems, it's all perfectly fine with all of them. So... I guess, the big decision is going to be up to you girls. What do you think? Should Eilleen stay the summer?"

Squeals of delight and laughter bounced off the front of the house and shot off flying in all directions. Wild jumping mixed with frantic arm motions began in unison. Sarah stood up and hugged Bayard shaking her head. "YOU RASCAL! I was right! I knew you were up to something... but this?" Sarah gripped his forearms, looked him in the eyes, and then gave him a big hug. "You are a wonderful man Bayard Wharton. I'll never know what possessed you to think of such a thing. Never mind, I'm just glad you did!"

"Hey, girls, does anyone around here feel like jumping for joy? How about this?" Dad was laughing at his own pun as he walked inside, reached under the living room sofa and retrieved the new jump rope with bright red wooden handles with a matching red thread intertwined through the cotton rope.

This produced even more squeals and bouncing, as if the joy contained inside these children was lifting them up from the surface of the earth! Their eyes sparkled as they inspected the brand-new rope, one actually made for jumping. They raced out on the beach to where the sand was damp and packed, to try it out.

Bayard sat down on the porch swing with a satisfied smile as he savored his ice cream and the huge success of his plan. "Take a good look at that Sarah. That's what a child's life ought to be like. By God, children were born to be happy and to be surrounded with love. And their bellies should be full too, and they should get a damn dish of ice cream every once in a while."

Together, they rocked on the porch swing watching the girls, content in their silence. The only the sounds were the swing's creaking chains against the hooks, small waves rolling in mixed with distant giggles and rhymes coming from three happy little girls and an occasional cry of a few gulls. What a day! They were going to have the rest of the summer to spend together. Thank God. It sure did feel right.

CHAPTER 13
JULY AND AUGUST

Saturday morning, after eating bowls of cornflakes and a few sweet slices of cantaloupe, Dad began to stroke his chin as he turned, furled his eyebrows looking at Eilleen and asked, "Isn't there something I promised you we were going to do before you went home? Seems to me I recall there was, in the back of my mind. Now, what was it?" He said looking up at the ceiling as though the answer might be painted on the rafters. "I think we talked about it soon after I picked you up at the train station. Hmm, let me think," and he tapped the kitchen table.

"I know what it was! The theater! You said you would take me to the movies! Are we going to go?" Eilleen asked, excitedly raising her eyebrows while her eyes danced in anticipation of the reply, which she'd quickly learned was never disappointing with Dad.

"That's right, it was. How about it? You feel like going? Look here in *The Milford Chronicle*, it says, 'Now Playing at the Plaza Theatre: Paramount Pictures proudly presents: Lewis Carroll's ALICE IN WONDERLAND, starring Charlotte Henry as Alice, and featuring Gary Cooper as the White Knight; Carey Grant as the Mock Turtle; and W. C. Fields as Humpty Dumpty. Don't miss this animated portrait of this Children's Classic book, brought to life as Alice goes through the Looking Glass and discovers what's on the other side. Ticket window opens at five o'clock; doors open at 6:30 for the music prelude; the show begins at 7:30 sharp.'"

Niece Dorothy thought it would be great fun to join in, so she had invited them over for supper with her and Mimi beforehand. She'd put on a pot of pole limas with corn and tomatoes and baked a batch of Bisquick biscuits she would serve with some carved baked ham. After dinner they'd make the short walk downtown.

To completely enjoy the theater experience, you had to arrive early enough for the music portion of the show. While the films now were almost always talkies, it was still marvelous to hear the talent of their organist play the Wurlitzer and fill the theatre with bold, bouncy, uplifting tunes and a few Classics. No one cared that this part was left over from the days of the silent films because the music sure made you feel good. "Happy" was the spirit most desired by folks around here right now. These dark, dismal days of the Depression had everyone seeking an escape to find a little happiness even if just for a few hours. It was as sought after as prospectors searching for gold. No wonder great books, films, music and those new radio "soap" programs were so popular. Seems one would choose their escape either through the arts and entertainment, or down at the local bar.

The ticket window was open when they arrived. Bayard got in line and purchased theirs; thirty cents for adults and fifteen cents for children for the evening show. They entered through the double, tall glass doors into a stunning lobby with its rich, decorative mosaic tile floor. Ushers, wearing double breasted, red jackets trimmed in gold braid and brass buttons, with pill box hats atop their heads were waiting to hold open the padded doors and escort patrons with flash lights, guiding them to their seats. Ticket holders could request which side of the theatre they wished to be seated in.

"Middle section please, and at least center way down will be fine for us," Bayard said. After they were settled, they got a kick out of how excited Eilleen became observing and taking in every detail, from the heavy gold fringe on the enormous crimson velvet curtain covering the picture screen, down to the rich feel of their plush seats.

Bayard excused himself and returned shortly carrying a large box of popcorn. "I know none of us are the least bit hungry, but we have to have some popcorn, it's part of the whole experience. Besides, it smelled so darn good. Pass it along, I'll share," Bayard said as he sat back down just as the pre-show recital was beginning.

"Look!" Eilleen said pointing over to the organist. "Isn't that Miss Mable who sewed my new dresses?"

"Yes, it is dear. She's played in this theatre since there were only silent films and back then she played a piano. That woman's going to play the keys on that organ like nothing you've ever heard. She plays by ear, that means any song she hears, she can play it on the spot, without ever looking at sheet music. Sit back and listen, you're going to enjoy this." Sarah said smiling. They were all smiling, and proud too. Proud to know Miss Mable, proud to be taking this child to see her first film on the big screen but most of all, proud that Eilleen was sitting right here with them and not on a seat on that train, the one that would be arriving in New York right about now.

After the final notes, everyone applauded, whistled and many stood to express their admiration for such talent. Then the lights dimmed, and the heavy burgundy curtain parted; the first stream of light from the projector hit the screen and the sound began, opening with a cartoon set to music. Eilleen pulled her head straight back in her seat as though gravity was pushing her back like lift-off in a plane, her eyes wide so not to miss a single moment. She never moved a muscle the entire evening and hardly ate any popcorn. Once the feature film began, she went straight to Wonderland.

After the movie, they gathered out in front of the Plaza and spoke with friends they knew and made sure to introduce Eilleen. Sarah saw the familiar faces of their friends from Clark Street, Bill and Matilda Murphy, who had brought their three children, Bob, Anne and their youngest, also named Eileen.

"Hi there neighbors. So, what did you think of *that* film?" Bill asked, knowing full well there couldn't be any adult who could be a fan of anything like the sights they'd just witnessed. Searching for appropriate words resulted in a few good laughs while they made crazy faces and shook their heads. When they introduced the children they soon noticed that both Eilleen and Eileen were the same age and instantly began sharing everything they loved about *Wonderland*, laughing like old friends while the adults chatted. "From the looks of it, I think our little girls might become good friends," Matilda said. Everyone in the group was thinking the same thing. Little did they know.

Walking home they asked Eilleen, "OK tootsie, tell us what you thought."

And she did. "It was magical and so wonderful! Maybe that's why they named it Wonderland. This whole night has been *the bees knees!*" She looked straight to the sky and you could see she was replaying every scene inside her head. "I loved the huge rabbit, and when Alice went straight through the mirror and found a new world. WOW. Wasn't it grand? I never could imagine such things. We never read *Alice in Wonderland* back home," Eilleen said, "Wait until I tell my sisters this story when I go home!"

Dad mumbled, "At least one of us loved it." For he had different feelings about buying a ticket to witness nothing but absurd silliness. "Those were the damnedest costumes I've ever seen. And to think, they were some of our topnotch, professional actors up there, play-acting in those ridiculous outfits. I sure hope they got paid enough. I know these are hard times and all, but it would take more than a few bucks to get me to wear some of that garb. I don't know what-in-all that crazy story was, but I'll tell you one thing I do know, I won't *ever* be able to look at W. C. Fields again without seeing Humpty Dumpty!" Everyone laughed. While the film had plenty of critics and never became a box office smash, Eilleen was a fan, she loved every minute of it.

The next few weeks rolled along with less excitement, but certainly equal in pleasure. Sweet days were filled with friends coming and going and plenty of lazy time spent on the beach during the sunny days or coloring and playing paper-dolls inside on the rainy ones. Inner tubes and sand buckets were always on the porch, ready to go. Thank goodness Eilleen never needed to be entertained, even if it rained. She'd get out her crayons and play or sit for hours on the sheltered porch swing and sing to herself and her bear, Tony, anytime she wasn't busy helping with chores. Oh my, how this child loved helping. Making the bed she'd remark about the beautiful colors in the bedspread. In the kitchen preparing vegetables, she'd talk about how nice it was they'd not be hungry plus how exciting it was to get to eat dessert, too.

Life here with Mother and Dad was ideal. Everything was so clean and pretty and the beach was beautiful, and everyone was kind and they smiled because they were happy. Eilleen felt safe and loved. How could she not be happy? Life was perfect in her little eyes.

But when Bayard drove off for work each day, it sure wasn't perfect, not out there in the real working world. Businesses everywhere were struggling or failing and closing their doors. Oh, Wharton and Barnard got plenty of orders, making a sale wasn't the problem, the problem was getting paid. No one had any cash. Credit had been extended to a few accounts they knew had a good history of paying on time, but now, even best of businesses weren't able to pay their bills anymore. The fact was, cash flow had totally dried up. Collections were piling up. What could they do? These companies didn't have any money for creditors, or themselves.

Wharton and Barnard stopped extending credit. But, it still made sense to do a few swaps and trades. They began using barter arrangements far more than they wanted to. That was OK to a point, but W & B still had to pay the light bill and a basket of tomatoes or a live chicken wasn't going to satisfy the electric company.

Wharton and Barnard was not alone. Every business, every company, each job was surrounded by the uncertainty of surviving for another day, let alone what in the world would tomorrow be like. Bayard knew he was luckier than most. They would probably be OK. Darn good thing they owned their building and didn't owe rent each month. If they had to help out a few other businesses to keep their doors open, well, then that's what they were going to do by God, even if it was financially painful. This town was full of fine, hard-working folks, many of them personal, lifelong friends. Bayard knew the worry and fear he saw on their faces was real. He'd sure want a little kindness sent his way if he were in their shoes. By gosh, life was treating him pretty good right now, in other ways of course. He knew automobile parts were a necessity to keep many businesses running, so they were just going to work the best they could, case by case, one day at a time.

The best part of Bayard's life sure wasn't coming from his business or his bank statements. He felt rich in other ways, satisfied in ways that counted far more than having money ever could and knowing this buffered the sting of reviewing their current negative finances. Maybe it's what helped him extend his kindness to so many, giving more than he might have in the past. He was grateful for his life and that gratitude sure helped him sleep better at night.

Most other businessmen he knew weren't getting much sleep at all these days, although, it didn't change a thing to fret. This problem was far bigger than their town of Milford, reached further than all of Sussex County or even the whole state of Delaware. Right now, it seemed like the entire United States was in some big trouble.

Cottage at Slaughter Beach

Sarah and the Model A

Gang Going Fishing

The Big Catch

Eilleen and Frances

Mules Tommy and Jackie with Eilleen and Frances

Eilleen on the Boardwalk

Picking Vegetables

Eilleen at S. Washington Street

Dorothy, Eilleen and the new 3-wheeler

Eilleen on mule

Eilleen on the beach, 1933

The Wharton Family

Eilleen ready for college

CHAPTER 14
THE KENT-SUSSEX FAIR

Everyone in the office instantly became excited when a whopping big order got called in to Wharton and Barnard Auto Parts for them to fill mid-July. And the best part—it was a cash transaction! Arriving next week by rail was the entire James E. Strates Shows®, the main attraction for the Kent-Sussex Fair. With them came numerous amusement rides powered by all sorts of motors, big and small. They brought along plenty of trucks and all sorts of engines and motorized equipment to power the carnival and the brutal use those machines got required a lot of engine parts, belts, plugs and hoses to keep them operational. The long-distance telephone call came in from Pennsylvania while Strates was breaking down and packing up before heading south to Delaware. They gave W & B a list of everything they'd need waiting for them the moment they arrived in Harrington.

Bayard and his men got right on it. Being well stocked, they expected to have most of it, but special-ordered parts needed to be put on RUSH delivery or forget it. This was a client on the move. They could be packed up and moved on to Timbuktu overnight. Acting fast and delivering a completed order on time would clench this year's sale and guarantee a telephone call next year too; not to mention... these guys paid in cash!

With a lot of scurrying and hustle, the W & B crew rounded up about ninety-five percent of the order. RUSH items arrived right on time, making them one-hundred percent ready. The Strates train was due to arrive this afternoon about 2:15 p.m.

The show cars would pull off on side tracks that were run just for them alongside the fairgrounds where they'd remain along with the set up of additional living tents that would function as home base for the duration of the fair.

The Kent-Sussex Fair Grounds consisted of thirty acres that was purchased in 1920 for a sum of $6,000. The first thing they did was build the racetrack and the Grandstand. James E. Strates Railroad Traveling Show arrived on the scene in 1923, adding tons of color and interest when they arrived bringing their huge Ferris wheel, a three abreast merry-go-round that blasted gay pipe organ music and various other colorful kiddie rides. Add in the carnival games, strings of lights and a few various eye-popping sideshow tents, and this crew could transform an old field of raw land into a sight to behold overnight.

Lots of local folks would also compete during the fair for blue ribbons, prizes and bragging rights on their best livestock and farm animals be it their horses and ponies, or cows, pigs, sheep or chickens. There were also ribbons to be coveted in various other categories too, like sewing, featuring hand stitched quilts or homemade garments and others for some prize-winning culinary specialties. After the final judging, an array of fresh canned goods and plenty of yummy baked goods remained on display for the fair goers to drool over. It could make you hungry just looking at those gleaming jars of pickles, canned peaches, rich colored jams, and all those scrumptious, crusted pies. Good gosh almighty, what man didn't love a good pie? It was almost impossible not to have your mouth water just walking through that department.

While browsing along the exhibit areas, you might be able to catch a pie-eating contest, take in a hog race, or see them shear a sheep or two. Plus, while you were on the grounds, you must stroll on over and view the latest in John Deere and McCormick farming equipment that was on display.

The big motorcycle race and all the harness racing events always packed the grandstands. Wharton and Barnard made sure they were there with plenty of motorcycle parts, belts and tires handy under a track-side tent they set up each year for the motorbike racers. Those were all cash sales too. Yes, Bayard was one man who looked forward to the Kent-Sussex Fair. What a wonderful event! And the cash it was going to generate was never needed more than it was this year that's for sure.

Boxes of parts, cases of oil, various hoses, belts and spark plugs were packed and boxed, and the delivery truck was ready to roll well before noon. Bayard himself would head over to Harrington and be right there waiting when that train pulled in. He'd grown kind of fond of waiting for trains these days, yep, good things seemed to come along with trains. Besides, he knew those guys from the Strates crew would be looking for his truck right away for what he carried was vitally important to keep their operation moving seamlessly. Those men had a fine system in place considering they moved from town to town so fast.

Not long after parking the truck, Bayard spotted the brightly painted advance car from a distance, done up in its bold yellow and red lettering that announced the STRATES TRAVELING SHOW was on the move and coming to town. It was a long train, made up of dozens of flat cars, stock cars and coaches.

The carnival folks didn't seem to mind living in tents as they traveled from place to place with their exhibits, rides and all the gear it took to run the big show. You had to be impressed with the precision with which these folks worked; it was organized chaos. Every piece had a place to go and a proper order to it. Nothing that was going on was haphazard with these guys and time was precious. They were experienced professionals and watching them was an amazing sight to behold—like watching worker ants build a complex colony—each one with a job to do; and they were out there busting to get it done.

Stan, the big boss, and his sidekick Charlie exited the Pie Car, where they served coffee and prepared the hot meals while traveling and Bayard caught the aroma of frying bacon and corn muffins drifting out the smoke stack. Both men came right over as soon as they spotted the W & B truck. Charlie was assigned to the boss car. His job was both housekeeper and enforcer of the law when necessary, keeping order and settling disputes of all types, and in short order, too. When he wasn't doing that, he got the mail and ran errands. It was fair to say Charlie was Stan's right-hand man.

Stan extended his strong, broad hand and said with a big smile, "Why, hello again Bayard my friend. I sure am glad to see you here waiting for us! How the heck have you been since last year, sir?" They vigorously shook hands. Stan had quite the grip.

"Quite well, I must say, sir! Thank you for asking," Bayard replied, smiling.

"Quite well? Now, there's something I haven't heard lately, not these days. Why, that's wonderful. Is business picking up?" Stan asked.

"Oh no, not 'well' in business, I'm afraid. No, we're just hanging on by a thread, like everyone else. Guess I'm referring to me. I'm a happy man Stan. My wife and I have a new daughter for the summer, little Eilleen, she's only five and came for a visit from the Fresh Air Program, and I must say, she's a pure joy. We're having a wonderful time and by God, no damn old Depression is going to ruin this summer for us!" Bayard said laughing.

"Now that's the spirit. Hell, there's not much a man can do about a bad economy anyway except hold his head up and keep on going 'till it's over. Wonderful to hear. Aren't children simply the best? Why, I wouldn't be in this line of work if I weren't still half kid-at-heart myself." Stan added, laughing in his big booming voice as he firmly patted Bayard's shoulder. "Hold on, wait right here a minute. I'll be right back."

Stan shortly returned carrying three ornate VIP passes he handed to Bayard that were engraved "James E. Strates" in fancy script, gold foil letters. "I'm sure you're planning to bring Eilleen to come over to see the Kent-Sussex Fair, so here are some passes, from me to you and your family. These VIPs will get you in the gate, into the grandstand and on all the rides too. But, you gotta promise me you'll take her on the Ferris wheel, it's a real doozy! Lands sake alive, I'm telling you, riding the wheel, and the views you'll take in way up there on the tip-top, well, it will be a thrill she'll never forget! Now, you keep on having fun like this Bayard," Stan said, as he patted his shoulder again. "It's the only way to get through this life. When you come to the fair, leave your miseries outside the gate. That's what I always say, 'cause it's another world here on the grounds of the carnival. Making folks forget their troubles and have some fun for a change... well we're happy we get to make that happen for these good, hard working local folks, and it makes me proud to say, that's our job. Speaking of work, you got those special-order wheel bearings and belts with you?"

"Sure do." Bayard said with pride.

"Hot-diggity-dogs, now that's some sweet music to my ears. Our Ferris wheel was originally powered by a No. 5 Eli Bridge, but now, we got her running on a cast iron McCormick-Deering engine. She's been real reliable and running much better than with them old steam engines we used to have. Looks like it's easier to get the parts we need for her too. Thanks Bayard, you're a life saver."

"And thank you sir, and my wife and Eilleen thank you as well. We will try out the Ferris wheel and I promise you, we'll have a grand time doing it too, I am sure of that."

The parts were exchanged with an invoice that got paid in full, with a big 'ol wad of cold hard cash. *Boy, does this ever feel great*, Bayard thought. To think, most invoices used to get paid in cash all the time and I never thought a thing about it. *I might have taken it for granted back then, but not today. No, I am a blessed man to have this sale. And look at this, gold VIP passes to boot, what do you know.*

Eilleen came running towards Dad's car that evening when he rolled up the clam shell driveway. "Dad, you *have* to come to the beach and see the shark that washed up. It's a *hammerhead*! His head really does look like a hammer too, with *eyeballs* way out on each end! Come on. You gotta see this!" She said as she grabbed his hand and started pulling him along. "It's huge, too!"

Dad slipped the fancy passes into his pants pocket, no sense trying to compete with all this fuss going on. He'd save the tickets for later. Who needs to think about a fabulous trip to the

Fair and riding a world class Ferris wheel when you have some old, washed up, dead stinking shark with eyeballs, lying on the beach creating this much excitement? He had to laugh.

Together they crossed the dunes and continued down the beach to view this wondrous site. Hmm, maybe he ought to talk to Stan over at Strates Shows about adding a hammerhead shark in a tank of formaldehyde as another attraction to the freak show. Seems it's quite a hit here at Slaughter Beach. A crowd of kids and parents circled around, observing the unusual fish. It was a really big one, maybe fifty or sixty pounds. Must have died out in the deep water of the bay and washed ashore. Most unusual indeed.

All through dinner there were discussions about the day's events, what the girls thought and by whom and exactly how the shark was first discovered. Bayard was going to wait for things to get quiet if it killed him before he revealed the passes. He had been home almost three hours now, and the conversations were still flowing. Come to think of it, they did most nights. That's probably what he enjoyed the most, having the place filled with this type of fun and chatter. Why, this old cottage must have sounded like the tomb of the dead before Eilleen arrived because Bayard couldn't think of anything he and Sarah said to each other that ever filled an entire evening. And they got along fine too, but it sure must have been quiet.

After Eilleen got her nightie on, they all went out on the porch to swing or rock for a while and enjoy the cool evening breeze; and relax listening to the waves. *Ah... listen to that silence,* Bayard thought. While that's what he had been waiting for, but now Dad had a new concern—should he stir up the pot adding a new layer of excitement, right before bedtime?

Would Sarah want to kill him if he did? Would Eilleen ever be able to get to sleep after this news? He made a fatherly decision to just enjoy this quiet time tonight at the end of a wonderful day and let it be. He patted his pocket, knowing when the time was right, he'd tell them, but for now he'd be the keeper of a most wonderful surprise. Besides, this time on the porch was positively wonderful--all on its own, no gold foil passes required.

Eilleen started singing: "*A hammerhead shark... washed on the beach before dark... it lay dead in the sand... way too big for a pan... it was a surprise... you should have seen those eyes!*" Everyone laughed, what an imagination.

What a great day. Nope, you don't need to add a thing to an evening that's already absolutely perfect.

CHAPTER 15
A BLUE RIBBON DAY

Those impressive James E. Strates passes were about to burn a hole in Dad's trouser pocket he'd held off so long, waiting for the right moment. But this morning, he was bound and determined to reveal them. By golly, it was high time to make some plans.

Sarah flipped the last flap-jack off the cast-iron griddle and onto her mother's floral platter and they all sat down and said grace. While they were passing the butter and maple syrup, Dad spoke up, "Girls, I have an announcement. How'd you like to experience a grand adventure and go with me over to the Kent-Sussex Fair? I think tomorrow would be the perfect time, and.... right here... happens to be... " Dad said, as he reached deep into his pocket, "Golden VIP tickets for me and my two best girls. Yes sir, from Stan, the main man himself, big boss man of Strates Shows. Now, what do you have to say about them apples?"

"Ah!" Sarah inhaled quickly, surprised, "That will be such fun! Mable's competing for a blue ribbon in sewing and she entered a beautiful wedding gown, we'll have to look for it," Sarah said.

"What's ... *the fair?*" Eilleen asked, not knowing enough to even be excited.

"My-oh-my, let me think, kiddo." Dad continued imitating in his best carnival barker style, "It's an EX-trava-ganza of Mammoth PRO-portions, SPR-inkled with the local talents from all of Kent and Sussex County, showing off the BEST they can sew OR bake. And livestock! GR-OOMED to perfection. Goats, pigs, horses, ponies, cows and sheep, oh, the BEST you'll ever see! Not to mention the hens, roosters and ducks! The NEWEST in farming equipment this side of the Mississippi will be on display too. THEN, if that is not enough, there's peanuts, popcorn, ice cream and hot dog stands to tempt and treat you as the flags fly high over the one and only TRA-veling CARnival, complete with RIDES, and wild side shows packed with sights to behold!"

Back to talking like Dad again, he asked his audience, "How'd I do? You know Eilleen, folks travel all over and even from out of state just to walk around and take it all in."

Mother was still laughing at Bayard's theatrical performance. "Well you gave quite the colorful description, except you left out *your* favorite part, the race track," Mother added, turning to Eilleen. "There is a big Grandstand where you go to watch them race, oh gee, just about *anything* a crazy bunch of grown men can think up. They race horses, motorcycles and even cars." Mother continued, "We'll be able to get up real close to all the animals on exhibit, you're going to love it! We'll pack a basket and eat before we get to the grounds. I know, we can stop by Abbott's Mill Pond on the way. I think the big thermos for lemonade is out in the garage. Oh, this is going to be marvelous. By the way, Dad, may I ask you one thing? How long have you had those passes in your pocket, anyway? It certainly is a darn good thing I didn't wash those trousers this morning!"

Their first fair surprise arrived when they had to park. "What the Sam Hill is this? Did everyone from three counties decide to come here today? Oh, drat, look at all these cars would you.

Applesauce."

Automobiles slowly merged from two directions. The parking charge was twenty-five cents with a five cent War Tax. "I suppose organizing is vitally important with this many cars," Dad said, as young men directed automobiles to line up in open spaces on the packed dirt farm field.

From the parking lot you could see tops of tents with flags flapping and flying as if they were dancing. The Ferris wheel was in full motion, towering above the rest of the fair, traveling its smooth loop with every seat filled. In the distance, they could hear a mix of music and carnival barkers and the sound was a festive promise that excitement was indeed waiting behind those gates. The VIP passes got them right in.

"Let's head over to the animals first, then we will go look at the exhibits," Mother suggested. We'll save the carnival for last since it looks far more spectacular after dark. Once the lights come on Eilleen, it's all simply magical!"

The swine barn was first stop with dozens of pens for hogs and piglets. Eilleen reached through the fence and felt a huge hog's hairy back as he laid on his side. "Ooh. He isn't soft at all! He feels like broom bristles." she said, laughing out loud. "But aren't all the little piggies so cute! Too bad they have to grow up."

The full barns smelled of hay, grain and animals, sweet and warm, just like a farm. Eilleen loved the animals and reached in to touch every one of the sheep, the smooth, freshly sheered ones and still thick wooly ones. She petted the goats, rabbits, and horses and discovered horse noses felt like velvet. Lovingly petting a Holstein, she remarked, "Don't cows have the kindest eyes of all?" Dad decided her fondness for the black and whites must be because she saw them first, fresh from the train.

They held some newly hatched fuzzy, bitty chicks and continued from building to building observing it all. Bayard looked around and saw dozens of other families doing the same thing, but this experience was entirely new to him. Oh sure, he stopped by the fair plenty of times and loved to catch a race, but he'd never explored the barns or looked the animals in the eyes, never petted them, taking the time to feel their textures, or notice their bodies warmth like he was doing today. How interesting and enjoyable it was, but something he would never have done... without a child in tow. "I guess you can grow up and be an adult or even become a married couple, but you're just not a family without a child."

It dawned on him that was it. They *were a family!* The Wharton family, doing what other families do, something he'd never experienced before, and he liked... no, he loved it! He'd have to think more about this, later. Right now, they had to walk these grounds and take in every undiscovered inch of the fair.

After visiting every barn, every stall and every cage, they moved on to the exhibits, starting with the Sewing and Needlework pavilion. Yep, there was a blue ribbon, pinned on the front of Mable Murphy's beautiful wedding gown. After the judging, the stapled identification tags were opened. Sarah loved to wander the isles reading them and always knew many of the local women. What beautiful hand work these ladies could do.

Motorcycle races were to begin at 6:00 p.m. sharp. They had just enough time to stop by the Grange Pavilion to get fried chicken platters served with corn on the cob, rolls and a slice of garden ripe tomato; famous with the locals and the 'must have' meal during your visit.

After they were full and had wiped the butter off Eilleen's face, it was time to use their VIP passes again for some super, front row box seats in the Grandstand.

By 5:55 p.m. the motorcycles and riders were positioned at the starting line, revving their engines. With a firing of the gun, BAM... the race was on! Those bikes took off with such a burst of speed, some slid and others fish-tailed, losing precious time. As soon as they all gained full traction, they began flying around the dirt packed track, leaving a whopping cloud of dust behind. It was fast and dangerous. Thank goodness the riders were wearing leather helmets strapped snug under their chins.

A few laps in and there was a spin-out on the far side of the track in the back turn when three bikes clipped each other and skidded off the main pathway. One bike fell over completely on its side sliding and dragging its trapped rider many feet before stopping. Everyone in the grandstand gasped. Some looked away, others stood up to see more. The yellow flag went out, stalling the race. Medics raced over to assist bringing a stretcher as the ambulance drove across the track. Holding their current order, the racers stopped and kept their bikes idling until they got the crashed bikes and the fallen riders off the track

Everyone in the stands was relieved and started cheering as two of the men were able to walk off the track under their own steam. Medics waved and gave the crowd the thumbs up, seems the third man on the stretcher would be OK too.

"Whew, that was close." Sarah said, "They were lucky. Good grief... Bayard, that could have been awful, and you thought Eilleen would like this?"

"Look at her Sara. She loves it!" Dad said, as he cheered for the men too.

Eilleen was hardly in her seat, leaning so far forward she was draped over the rail in front of her, waiting for the race to resume. The cheering in the stands soon turned to hollering and whooping, demanding the race to begin again, with Eilleen joining in. It was thrilling! Then stomping began, in unison... bang... bang... bang... what a noisy bunch this rowdy crowd was, it was clear, they loved racing. Within seconds the green flag waved, and they were off... speeding around the track until the final lap. The fans cheering support never stopped.

As they exited the grandstand, it was becoming twilight and lights were beginning to come on. They decided to find the Big Top Menagerie Tent and use those magic passes again and soon found VIP seats, roped off, near the center ring right as the Master of Ceremonies announced: "Ladies and Gentlemen, I am proud to present, straight from Paris, France, Ooh-la-la! The Prancing Poodle Review!" Swinging his arm out in a swooping half circle, he beckoned in the act. Out bounced three curly poodles who could balance a ball on their noses, walk on their hind legs and jump through hoops of fire before forming a Congo line to exit; right as painted clowns, a juggler on a unicycle and a tightrope walker raced in. That act was followed by three beautiful, pure white dancing horses wearing red feathered plumes behind their ears, twirling circles to music and when it ended, they placed their front hooves on the raised ring to take a bow in unison before prancing out in a line.

The ringleader took to the center circle, stood beneath a strong beam from the spotlight hung overhead and announced: "Ladies and Gentlemen. Boys and Girls. Are you ready? It's the moment you have been waiting for. Here come the Pachyderms!"

Sure enough, three real elephants appeared from behind a side curtain that suddenly lifted, and they entered the tent and began to parade around the ring. They were gigantic with huge ears and a small baby trailed in staying close behind its momma. It was a sight to behold! One elephant picked up the woman in a sparkly gold outfit with its trunk then hoisted her to settle in sitting right behind his ears as she led the group while they turned and moved in unison. Eilleen cheered and giggled with delight as she watched.

The Wharton family exited the tent with their heads full of spectacular sights that would be tucked away in the memory folds of their brains that would last, oh, probably forever! Real live, giant wrinkly, gray Elephants, up so close you could almost touch them. Boy, you sure didn't get to see that every day.

Walking out, they passed a row of tents filled with the strangest things you could imagine, tempting you to spend an extra ten or fifteen cents to come in and see for yourself. The Sword Swallower and the Fire-Eating gentlemen shared a tent. Bayard whispered over to Sarah, "What do you suppose those fellows have for supper before coming to work?" There was a tent for Tiny Tim, the world's smallest man, whom they claimed put Thumbelina's smallness to shame. Then a main event tent wore a large banner boasting "Oddities of All Types, From All Over the World," featuring a TWO-HEADED CALF; a living WOMAN with NO ARMS and SNAKEMAN, with the skin of a snake and a reptile's forked tongue; along with many... many more freak, odd and unusual things you'd be talking about for years to come.

Sarah made sure they kept walking. "No, Bayard! I don't care if the VIP passes work or not. NO! Eilleen would be upset seeing a woman with no arms, not to mention the nightmares she could have from the image of a two-headed calf burned into her little mind. She loves cows... you know that, they have kind eyes. Use your head man!" And she gave him a swift whack.

They kept walking.

Mother changed the subject. " Look Dad, Eilleen's over there watching them spin cotton candy."

With her face pressed to the glass, Eilleen watched as they sprinkled crystals of a colored mixture into a tub that magically spun and produced a light, spiderweb, see-through fluff that got scooped up and swirled onto a paper cone with just a couple twists of the wrist. What was this stuff?

"We'll take one." Dad said as he stepped up behind Eilleen smelling the hot, caramelized sugar. "You gotta try this at least once in your life Eilleen, why it isn't even a fair without some cotton candy. Here you go." Dad gave the man a quarter and handed the paper cone loaded with swirled pink confection bigger than her head, to Eilleen.

"Oh-my-stars. It looks just like a pink cloud!" Eilleen said, her eyes wide and dancing observing this treat's beauty, and she took a bite. "It's so sweet, but it disappeared before I could swallow." She giggled. It surprised her, so she tried another bite that also vaporized on her tongue. Sticky sugar droplets formed along the eaten edges of the cotton candy from her moist little lips. As they continued walking along, Mom and Dad both tugged off a few pinches of fluff too, just to remember what it tasted like. Dad noticed Eilleen's face had numerous pink sticky spots on her cheeks and on her chin, but she was unaware as she walked along in a trance, looking across at the lights and the carnival rides, eating her pink cloud. She was so stinking cute and innocent; his heart was melting faster than her spun sugar.

Carousel horses came into view prancing to the gay pipe organ music. The three of them got in line and were soon choosing their mounts for an imaginary race Eilleen said they were about to take. Eilleen chose a white horse, always her favorite; and around they went as lights, sounds and colors spun past them giving them the speed they needed for the pretend race to feel real. As each horse reached its height, it lunged forward on its descent, indeed out in front a few inches for a moment. They wouldn't know the winner until the ride came to a complete stop. They all leaned forward, hoping to coax their horse ahead of the others as the ride stopped traveling, inching to a halt in slow motion. How much more fun were they having than the other riders? When the horses finally stopped, Mother and Eilleen were in a dead tie, but if wild bouncing could change the outcome even a smidgen, then Eilleen was going to win for sure.

"Let's get her out of here before they throw us off, Mother," Dad said still laughing, scooping Eilleen up to help her dismount. "Maybe she's had enough sugar for one day."

Still giggling, a wall of colored balloons behind a booth caught Eilleen's eye. But, better than that, men were throwing darts and if they broke a balloon, they won a prize.

"Look Dad! You can do that! Come on, win me a Cupie Doll, please?" she said, jumping up and down, bubbling over with energy.

"Oh boy, hold on now. I can't promise you I'll win, but would you cheer me on if I give it my best try?" Dad asked, already knowing the answer.

"Of course! I'm a great cheerer! Hot-diggity-dogs!" Eilleen

said shrilly, still jumping.

The sign read: "Your choice, 3 DARTS FOR A ¼ DOLLAR-OR-3 DARTS FOR 25 CENTS. Dad shook his head and exchanged his coin for the darts. He took a stand, aimed carefully for his first throw, but missed. His second try was a direct hit popping a balloon, earning a small prize, but with one dart to go, he could still win a medium prize which happened to be, (da-da-de-da!), the Cupie Doll. Good grief, what pressure. He took aim and closed his eyes and tossed the dart. Pow, it hit! The man in a striped shirt hollered out, "We have another winner! Here's your Cupie Doll, sir."

Eilleen was delighted and right away announced, "I'm naming her Cotton Candy! See her pink dress and pink hair? I'm going to call her CC for short!" and she hugged her prized doll.

"Well gang, we've been on a roll, but my old dogs are beginning to bark. How about we head over for a spin on that world-famous Ferris wheel, then call it a day? We saved the best for last, the view from up top is going to be spectacular!" Dad said.

"I'm not so sure about that," Mother said shaking her head. "Why on Earth would sensible folks, with two feet planted safely on the ground, pay good money to be hoisted up—backwards no less—to ascend to great heights only to roll over the top zooming straight for the ground! For the fun of it? Mmmm, you might have to count me out for this ride."

"Now, Sar..err... Mother, look at all those happy faces. Don't they look like they are having the time of their lives? You don't want to miss the best part of the fair, do you? Heck no, why, we wouldn't want that to happen. How could we enjoy taking in the breathtaking aerial views of the whole fair knowing that you remained here on the ground and missed it. Isn't that right Eilleen?" Dad prompted with his little boy smile knowing full well without Eilleen being here, Sarah would NEVER ride the likes of a Ferris wheel.

"Yes. Dad's right. You must come! It's what we've been waiting all day for. YOU said it's magical out here with all the lights. You're right. We've done everything together this whole day. We can't stop now. Be brave, please? You will be fine. I'll sit in the middle, right next to you," Eilleen said as she tilted her head to one side looking straight into Mother's eyes, pleading with sticky pink droplets still stuck on her cheeks. How on earth could she say no to that little face?

"Oh, OK," Mom sighed, adding in a less than enthusiastic voice, "I guess everyone is walking off in one piece. No one's fainting or throwing up."

As Eilleen danced in celebration, Sarah leaned her head on Bayard's shoulder and muttered under her breath "Oh... you are going to owe me for this one... Dad. I saw how you set me up. You think you're so clever. Some things never change, you are such a rascal. Sometimes, I don't know why I love you so."

The line was advancing, not fast enough for Eilleen, but plenty fast for Mother who was still deciding whether to get on or run. Again, she leaned close to Bayard's ear and told him, "If Eilleen wasn't here right now, I'd have a few choice words for you buster, and they wouldn't be ladylike!"

"That's funny," Bayard said chuckling, "Sarah, if Eilleen weren't here, can you fathom either one of us being in this line right now? Or even stepping foot on a carnival grounds?"

Sarah cut her eyes over and gave Bayard a nasty look, but

she was at a total loss for words on that one. He was right. She burst out laughing and wished for a better comeback to top his. Not only was she out of her element, he was making her feel rather stupid to boot. "Well, they've always said children keep you young. It doesn't get much younger than this, do you think?" Sarah asked. "I was about seventeen the last time I rode a Ferris wheel."

"We're both still young, Sarah. Probably a whole lot younger than we even knew. Look how much fun we've had today. Why, we're younger right now than we were five summers ago." Bayard said, and Sarah knew he was right.

As passengers exited left, new riders boarded from the right. They were next. Dad noticed that Mother and Eilleen were holding hands as they climbed the ramp to the Ferris wheel seat. The second the three of them were seated, the carnie snapped the bar across their laps and they were off... for a short jolt. While the wheel was being loaded, it was jolt and rise, stop and start, but soon they made their way smack dab to the tip-top and halted, as their seat rocked. "Wow! Look how far you can see from up here girls." Dad marveled.

"I think I can see the whole world! Look at all the little cars parked way back there. And the race track. People look so small from up here!" squealed Eilleen clutching CC.

"Holy cow." Mother added as she looked in all directions, "It certainly does look magical."

Bayard scooched behind Eilleen and planted a kiss on Sarah's cheek. He was so proud of her for riding, he wasn't sure she would, knowing this wasn't her cup of tea. After all these years that woman could still surprise the tar out of him.

After a few more starts and stops and the wheel loaded with

a fresh batch of riders, the engine backfired, grew loud, and they were off and running. Rising at a good clip, they arched over the top and began free falling, leaving them feeling weightless. Both Mother and Eilleen screamed the first time over. Only mother the second time, as she hollered, "I have butterflies in my stomach. I feel like I'm f-a-l-l-i-n-g!" she called out after they rounded the top, heading for the ground again.

"No. We're not falling, we're flying!" Eilleen insisted, still giggling, "Feel the difference? We never hit the ground."

"No, we didn't. Thank God." Mother said, and this time as they rolled over the top again and as they began falling Mother screamed," It IS like flying! Aaaaahhhh!"

"Magical indeed." Bayard was grinning from ear to ear thinking, what a woman and what a perfect family they made.

Chapter 16
Lazy Days of Summer

Before you could brush beach sand off your toes twice, it was August. Temperatures soared into the nineties, making for some scorching hot days and it hadn't rained in weeks. By late afternoon it was stifling, but usually on an in-coming high tide a little breeze would blow in from the bay—if you were lucky—and cool things down a bit. There was always some kind of air moving along the shore, even if it was nothing more than a stinking old hot land breeze.

Every day the girls cooled off splashing in the bay, an activity they never tired of. By sunset, evenings turned lovely, even with the summer humidity, folks returned outdoors to stroll the boardwalk or to rock in their screened porches, until it was time for bed.

One morning after Dad left for work, Mother asked, "Hey cutie pie, want to take a walk with me and help me look for beach plums?"

"Of course, I do. And I know where we can find a whole bunch of them, too! Frances showed me. They're growing in some bushes just off the road, I'll show you." Eilleen shared.

"Here's a little basket for you and one for me. Let's go pick some. If we get enough, we may be able to cook up a few jars of jam today." Mother said, "I've got plenty of sugar and pectin and you can help me."

Both wearing sun hats, they walked along on the sandy road behind the cottages, smelling the salty low tide of the back marsh, listening to gulls calling out overhead. Sure enough, they discovered bushes that were loaded with beach plums.

Mother instructed, "Pick the dark purple ones. Green ones aren't ripe yet, we can come back for them later, but if we don't pick these ripe ones now, the birds will eat them." Before long they'd gathered plenty.

"Good thing we came early," Mother said, wiping droplets of perspiration from her forehead, "it's going to be a hot one." She could feel the intense sun on the back of her hands.

Back in the kitchen, they ran the sink full of cool water and dumped the fruit in to wash. Clean plums were put in a pan with a little water to boil. Once cooked and cooled, Mother took a metal potato masher to them, crushing out the seeds and smashing the meat of the berries, pressing out all the juice. Next, the liquid mash was strained through folded cheese cloth since only clear juice would be used. She measured juice and Eilleen added scoops of sugar and they brought it to a boil, stirring non-stop so the sugar wouldn't scorch. When the steam began rising from the pan, Eilleen added a bottle of pectin and soon it was boiling away, scenting the kitchen with fresh fruit. They scalded jelly jars by dipping them into a pot of boiling water, lifting them with tongs, then placed them on a cotton towel to be ready. While the mixture boiled, Mother broke off chunks of white wax and placed a few in each jar.

"What's that for, are we going to eat wax?" Eilleen asked.

"No silly, it works like magic. Watch... you'll see." Mother said.

A long metal spoon was dipped in the boiling fruit juice a few times before liquid began to cling, a few minutes later, drips hung, draping from the spoon and Mother knew it had thickened into jelly. She turned off the burner, made sure Eilleen was standing back, then wrapped a towel around the handle and poured the molten jelly into the glass jars. Instantly the wax melted, rising to the top. "See, when this cools off, the wax will harden on top and seal the jars."

The remaining hot jelly, Mother poured into a jar with no wax. "This is the one we get to eat right away. But the rest of them will go back to Milford and they will be wonderful to enjoy this winter when it's cold and snow is falling. I love serving some with hot biscuits for Christmas dinner."

Eilleen nodded, but her smile instantly faded since she couldn't remember a time when the snow fell back home when she wasn't just plain old cold and hungry. There were no shiny glass jars of homemade jellies in Grandmother Anna's cupboard waiting to be opened for Christmas.

For the first time since her visit, she worried about going home. Life was so good here and she wanted to eat beach plum jelly this winter. She loved Mother and Dad and absolutely knew now, by comparison, how awful her life had been. Far worse than anyone here knew, and it scared her.

Before she could process the dark thought that was just about to cause her to cry, there was a knock on the kitchen door and Elaine and Frances came bouncing in with smiling faces. Mother unwrapped a few soft slices of Wonder bread and smeared on some of the warm jelly. The girls gobbled them while making plans to do whatever it is three little girls think up on a summer day. Eilleen grabbed CC from the living room and out the porch door they went, off to play, chattering all at once.

Summer continued like this, full of long, lazy days. Highlights might be catching an unsuspecting plump bumble bee who had been busy sucking nectar from white clover blooms or some yolk yellow buttercups; or hurrying down the beach to witness a fresh catch still flopping on a fisherman's line; or seeing firsthand by bending down and getting your face up close to discover what minnows, crabs or sea life might be mixed in the seaweed inside the seine nets that were pulled up on shore from their drag through the bay. At night the same bumble bee jar was used to house a few lightening bugs that looked like trapped stars as they twinkled inside the glass, (but the rule was they had to be released before bedtime). Other nights they'd spot a shooting star while sitting around a small campfire that glowed away a small spot of darkness from the beach. August was a relaxing time, full of days of peaceful living for the folks on this quiet beach, for there was not much going on that could rile up anyone who was living down here. There was no traffic to speak of, only the mailman making his rounds and every few days visits from Jackie and Tommie, the two plow mules who pulled a flatbed wagon filled with ice blocks covered in heavy canvas down to the beach for their scheduled deliveries, making sure they kept the local iceboxes stocked. Both mules were quiet and kind animals who always had time to enjoy a few hugs from the kids.

The screened porch door slammed shut. "Mother, you must come out to watch; we just made up our own jump-rope song." Eilleen rushed into the cottage pulling Mother's hand to come out to the beach.

"Yes, Mrs. Wharton, please, come out." Frances said, "Our

mothers have come to watch us, too. Hurry! It'll be fun."

Sarah joined them under her umbrella that was set up over a couple canvas striped beach chairs and a blanket. The girls carried their jump rope down to the harder damp sand for the performance.

"We call this: *The Three-Gals Song,*" Elaine announced as she was beaming at their accomplishment. "Ready girls?"

The rope started swinging with Eilleen and Elaine looping it for Frances who hopped in as the first designated jumper. They sang in unison:

When three-gals meet
on a day so bright
We laugh, sing and play
from morning 'till night,
We have a lot of fun
playing with everyone!
Frances...Elaine... & Eilleen!
1-2-3-4-5-6-7-8-9-10....

Frances missed her step on count number eleven, Elaine missed on count number eight, and Eilleen made it to number ten. They all took a bow at end their performance. As the mothers clapped, the girls added a pretend curtsy too, holding out imaginary hems of dresses they weren't wearing, and the mothers clapped more. What these three couldn't think up.

"Girls, I believe we're going to need a repeat performance tonight, when the Dad's get home. How about after dinner?" Mother asked, sincerely knowing how much Bayard would love it.

"Yes! Of course!" They replied in unison, pleased and clapping.

And so, after dinner, they jumped again. It was a second grand success!

Days rolled into weeks in an easy-peasy summertime fashion with plenty of time to lollygag until one August afternoon. Sarah had just washed the lunch plates and was putting away the glasses when Bayard rolled up the driveway. It was far too early, what in thunder was he doing home so soon? Sarah hoped he was feeling OK. Out the kitchen window she noticed a look on his face that she didn't like. And he'd changed out of his suit too and was wearing old clothes. She hurried to the back door and opened it for him to come inside when she saw Tom from Wharton and Barnard, drive up in the W&B pickup truck.

"Sarah, my dear," Bayard started speaking before Sarah could even begin with her questions, "seems we need to pack up and head back to Milford today. We have enough time, so I don't want you to panic, but there's a hurricane heading our way, and it's going to be a real doozy. Storm warnings have been posted from Miami to Boston on this one. They're saying it's going to make landfall somewhere between Cape Hatteras and Atlantic City, NJ and it's going to give our coast here a real pounding, so it won't be safe to stay here. Tom's going to help me nail down a few things. See if you can round up what you want to take back to Milford, I brought some boxes. I imagine we won't be able to be back here for about a week, the roads are sure to flood from the back marsh.

"The fire department's been alerted, so fellows will be going door to door shortly to make sure everyone has time to skedaddle. It's a mandatory evacuation for Slaughter Beach, Sarah. Milford folks are preparing for some big flooding in

Milford around the Mispillion River too. Could cause a lot of damage downtown, but that's to be expected from a storm like this one."

"Should I round up Eilleen, now? She's down playing at Elaine's," Sarah asked with concern in her voice after hearing the unexpected news.

"No, we have most of the day before it gets here, and I'll be working for a while, just let her play. I want to clear out the porch furniture, put everything either inside the cottage or out in the garage. I'm going to nail the porch door shut and the out-house door too, it might not be fancy, but without indoor plumbing down here, I want it to stay in one piece if I can and try to keep the doors from banging loose and blowing off. We'll take whatever steps we can to prevent damage, but that's all we can do. Sarah, I don't want to scare you, but anything you don't want broken better come home with us. We can't take it all, but pack up anything you especially treasure."

"I guess you mean after you and Eilleen?" She flashed him an encouraging smile. "As long as the both of you are all alright, I'll be fine." She was teasing but he knew exactly what she meant.

Out the kitchen window, the sky looked gray, but no different than maybe an ordinary summer shower was heading their way. Thank goodness for today's radio communications. Sarah was glad Eilleen was off playing, they wouldn't have to worry her while they prepared.

"Bring me Eilleen's suitcase when it's packed and don't forget Tony, but leave things like her sea shells, they'll be fine," Bayard said.

They packed up clothes and boxed their fresh food and groceries. Sarah covered the furniture upstairs with extra sheets to protect what she could from the grit that would surely find a way past the windows as it did every time they had high winds. Clean up was always a mess from a big storm like this, hence the downside to the joy of living on the beach.

A few hours later, Eilleen came walking back and noticed the front porch was totally empty and screen door was nailed shut. "What the heck is going on? Are we moving?" She asked, "Were you going to come and get me?"

"Yes ma'am, I most certainly was, if you didn't get back here very soon," Dad said as he knelt on one knee to look her in the eyes. "Sweetie, we're going to relocate back to Milford to ride out a big storm that's heading our way. Kiddo, it looks like we're in for a hurricane. Your Mother and Dad are going to get you to the safest place we can, and in a storm like this one's supposed to be, it sure as heck isn't here. But, we'll be back after it's all over and you can help us sweep out the sand. OK?"

They finished packing Bayard's car and put the rest of the boxes in the back of Tom's truck. They were about to follow each other to Milford when Bayard hollered out his window, "Hey Tommy, go on ahead and swing by my house, will you? The back door is open. Just unload the boxes and leave everything in the kitchen, OK? And thanks! I'm going to drive down the beach to make sure everyone got the news about this storm. Take the rest of the day off too, Tommy. We won't be working tomorrow, so stay safe my friend."

"Will do, Mr. Wharton, and thank you too, sir." Tom replied, very happy with the tip Bayard had slipped him for his help.

All along the beach, folks were scurrying around their cottages, battening down the hatches preparing for the harsh storm that was on its way. So, the word was out. Bayard thought it would be a good idea for Eilleen to say goodbye in person to her friends, so she'd know they left the beach with their families and were safe. No telling what the radio reports were going to sound like in the middle of this event as they listened from home while they still had power. Yes, seeing them in person might help keep her worries on the back burner.

It was raining a steady downpour with branched lightening flashing across the sky in the distance by the time they arrived home to South Washington Street in Milford. They saw how folks had been preparing all along their route. This wasn't like the old days when storms like this could surprise you. No, today they have modern ways to forecast storms, thank goodness for radios.

Rain was solid most of the next day before the winds picked up. But, when it did, it really did. Of course, the power went out, but they were ready for that. Candles and oil lanterns stood ready on the kitchen table with matches right there, so you wouldn't have to go looking for them in the dark. It was always dark as pitch when they lost the power, or so it seemed as soon as the street lights went out.

Bayard had stopped by the ice house yesterday and brought back a big block of ice so their food wouldn't spoil; and the bathtub was filled with water so nothing was left to do now but ride it out. From the sounds of things outside, there was going to be a lot of damage, strong gusts shook the house and the wind whistled around the windows and really howled outside.

Eilleen went upstairs to get Tony. "I was worried the sound of the wind might be scaring him. Where is C.C? I couldn't find her in my room," Eilleen asked as she squeezed her bear each time the lightening flashed, or she heard limbs cracking outside.

"I didn't see her when we packed. I remember you took her to Elaine's this morning. Did you bring her back with you?" Mother asked.

"Yes, I did. I know, I sat her on the davenport. That's where she is." Eilleen said.

"Well, guess what sweetie, the center of the house is the safest place she can be," Dad said. "We'll be back in a few days and she'll be sitting right there. We've seen quite a few of these storms and that's one tough old cottage. She'll be right there, waiting. You'll see." Dad said.

"OK," Eilleen said in a small, tired little voice. Dad never steered her wrong before, it would be a waste of her emotions to worry, even a little bit, if he was confident.

Walnuts, twigs and random things were being hurled, hitting the side of the house. Every now and then they heard a sharp snap or powerful crash and they knew another large limb or tree had gone down. The ground became too soft from so much rain pounding down, even deep tree roots couldn't hold on any longer against such high winds. Some trees broke off sharply, others came out of the ground, huge clusters of roots and all.

They stayed together in the kitchen, found things to eat and played a few card games until it was very late, then decided they'd try to sleep together in Mother and Dad's bed upstairs, if they could sleep at all. Sarah closed all the drapes in case any of the windows were to get broken by a limb or flying debris. The entire two-story house shook so hard at times, Sarah's perfume bottles rattled on the dresser and picture frames shifted on the walls. Sarah and Bayard exchanged worried glances but refused to show any concern in front of Eilleen, who snuggled between them. The driving rains pounded the house and the wind roared fiercely, like nothing either of the Wharton's could ever remember hearing before. There would be no sleeping for them.

It was one wicked and powerful storm that ripped through Milford that night. It went down in the history books to forever be known as the *Chesapeake-Potomac Hurricane of August, 1933*.... a storm that wreaked utter havoc up and down the entire East Coast.

CHAPTER 17
AFTER THE STORM

The worst was finally over. The ferocious hurricane had passed, and now only a light rain and a few blustery gusts remained.

Eilleen opened her eyes and said, "Morning Mother. Wasn't that the most awful storm you've ever heard? I'm glad we left the beach. It's a good thing this house is strong."

"Yes honey, we're all in one piece, but oh my goodness, is our yard ever a mess. Come over here and take a look," Sarah said as she pulled back the draperies. They saw no losses of their trees from what they could tell from the window, but some very large limbs had broken off and leaves and debris were flung and plastered everywhere. Entire trees were down across the street and the road out front looked like a muddy river with flooding from both the rain and the rising waters that overflowed from the Mispillion River. The power lines were down, and all the telephones were out and would be for a while, but after scanning the aftermath from all the windows upstairs, Sarah felt grateful it wasn't worse, they were lucky.

Eilleen was happy to be safe and as they started downstairs said, "It sounded just like a freight train came through our yard last night. Did you feel the whole house vibrate? I felt just like a little bird, shaking in my nest up in the top of a tree."

"Good morning girls! Seems you two finally got a few hours of sleep in the wee hours after all." Dad greeted them coming down still in their nightgowns. He was closing the closet door from under the staircase wearing buckle-across galoshes and his yellow rain slicker, holding a large black umbrella.

"Now, don't worry," he said seeing concern on their faces, "I'm just walking downtown to see how bad the flooding is and check on how things held up inside the shop. We sit on the river and sure have seen our share of flooding from way smaller storms than this one. Plus, I want to pick up the newspaper, then we'll really find what the storm's been up to around here. If I don't get to the news stand early, they'll be sold out. Put some coffee on Mother, I'll be right back in two shakes of a lamb's tail." The girls felt a breeze strong enough to flutter their nightgowns as he passed through the kitchen and out the back door with a gait that matched the forceful purpose of his mission.

Sarah was able to put the percolator on for coffee since they had a gas stove, but they wouldn't be using the toaster anytime soon. She fried up some bacon and decided to wait to cook the eggs until Dad got back.

While that was the original plan, he'd been gone awhile now. Either things were very bad, or he had gotten too involved in conversations with the other men who couldn't stand it either and had to get out there to be right in the middle of it all, walking around, knee deep in this flooded mess in their galoshes. Men were just like that. She certainly had no desire to go out there, not until the rain stopped.

"Have a seat Eilleen. I'll scramble up some eggs for us sweetie, we'll eat now, and I'll cook Dad's eggs when he gets back. Then we can hear all about what he's found out."

It was quite a while later when the back door opened, and a drenched Bayard entered the mud room. He removed his rain gear, stomped his wet boots before removing them and came in the kitchen, ready for a cup of coffee, and yes, he had the newspaper under his arm, his trophy from the morning mission.

"How is it out there?" Sarah asked.

"It's one big mess, that's all I can say. A huge mess! Trees have fallen across power lines everywhere, some ripping the wires right out of the poles. We could be without power for days. The Mispillion's flooded downtown all the way north and south on Walnut so far it reached both of the banks. Guess those old bankers knew just how far away from a river to build, not wanting the currency to get wet, not that there's much of it left inside any of them right now, anyway. The American Store, well, if they were open, you'd need a boat to get to them. Our office is under water, about two feet but we know flooding happens, so we always keep all the parts up on shelves or hooks, but it's like walking through a lake in there. I swear Sarah; if the water was any higher, I wouldn't have been able to push open the front door. Aaah... it'll be OK, everything will dry out once the water recedes. Nothing we can do about it but wait. I'm glad we set the store up the way we did, always thinking about 'what-if?' Rem's good like that, guess that's another reason why he's such a great partner. Even our files were up high enough. Once again, we're better off than some other businesses and stores closer to the center of downtown. Those poor folks have a real mess on their hands."

As Bayard drank his coffee, Sarah cracked two fresh eggs that sizzled and popped, frying in a coating of bacon grease. "Hmm, that sure smells good, I'm hungrier than I thought. Thank you my dear.

"Look at these headlines," Bayard said as he shook off and unfolded the damp newspaper, "On August 22, 1933, the

Chesapeake-Potomac Hurricane damages most of the Mid-Atlantic. Says here, The Coast Guard rescued over two hundred people who were in boats that capsized along the coast. Flooding has affected a larger portion of the northeast than any storm in the 1900s.

"Goes on to say," Dad read between bites of hot eggs and bacon, "Delaware has lost three bridges along the DuPont Highway and terrific road damages have occurred. There are reports of 13.24 inches of rain in Bridgeville! Good Lord! Mix that amount of rain with these winds, and you have some big trouble. Umm, here it says, Delaware beaches made out better than Maryland, however it appears that Delaware has had one square mile of beaches wash away.

"Listen to this," he continued reading, "Ocean City, Maryland was hardest hit by this powerful storm. The winds caused the ocean to wash away entire streets and burst through a low spot on Ocean City Island, taking out the railroad and the fishing camps. It seems the Atlantic Ocean and the Back Bay have now been forever joined with this storm washing away the last of the solid land at the narrowest point, creating a new inlet. Homes have been swept off their foundations. Entire cars have been buried under sand. The auto causeway is impassable.

"Salisbury, Maryland was under full siege by this storm as well. A short-wave radio message proclaimed the city's desperation. 'We have lost all power, we are cut off from outside aid. Please notify Baltimore.'"

Bayard lowered the paper to his lap. "Guess we're lucky up here in Milford. I had no idea. It goes on to say, 'In Ocean City, for the time being, rail, boat and street traffic is crippled. Persons who never as much as owned a row boat returned to

Ocean City to find yachts resting almost on their front steps. Automobiles left standing in the flood, were found covered in sand. This is the single worst storm since 1896, reported The Sun newspaper.'"

Everyone was thinking it, but no one dared ask, what about Slaughter Beach? Bayard sat down the paper and there were a few moments of silence before he picked up his fork to finish his eggs.

"You know, Slaughter Beach is well over an hour north of Ocean City, not to mention it's a bay beach. Bay beaches never get the pounding like beaches directly on the ocean do. Why, we are almost in a harbor area if you look on the map. Those old cottages have been standing there a long time, if they could talk, I bet they could tell us about many a storm they have ridden out, and, here's the truth, if we have to make a repair or two, then that's what we'll do. Almost time to paint the trim, anyway. No, from the sounds of it in the paper, we're lucky. The three of us are safe and sound and that's what counts. Look around, here we are, sitting together, house intact, gas stove working so we got a hot breakfast and a fresh cup of coffee, yep, and I have two beautiful girls, and the business. Aaah, yes, it's flooded and all, but it's still standing. I'm a lucky man I tell you, with plenty of blessings to count, that's for sure."

As soon as he took his last sip of coffee, Bayard folded the paper, put his napkin in his plate, pushed back his chair as it squeaked on the linoleum then headed for the back porch to suit up again. "We have to stay open and help out, Sarah. Rem's down there now. We posted a note that we will fill orders until 7:00 p.m. tonight. Farm trucks are running supplies, emergency trucks are out there, and this much mud is always tough on these vehicles. Lots of them are breaking down trying to run rescues. All this water on the roads is covering spots where the road's washed away and they're driving straight into deep holes they can't see. With no phone service, neighbors are going door to door and volunteers are helping to move the elderly to places that can care for them. You realize, if we can get some parts to them and help to keep broken down vehicles running, more folks can be helped. It's the least we can do. I'll be back when I can."

Eilleen watched Dad give Mother a kiss on the cheek before coming over to give her one too. "You're my two best girls!"

"Be safe Dad and tell Rem I said hello."

The next day, Bayard was off early again trying to fill orders, or figure out how to help by getting tires and parts to stuck and stranded trucks that desperately needed them. The rain had stopped, and the sound of chain saws was heard in the distance while crews cut up downed trees and limbs, but there was still no power.

About 11:00 a.m. there was a knock and Sarah opened the front door and happily discovered Matilda Murphy there with her daughter, Eileen, on the front stoop. Those two had been out walking to see how the neighborhood was holding up.

Sarah invited them in. "Would you ladies like some iced tea? Tillie, please have a seat and I'll call Eilleen down. She'll be so happy to see someone her age for a change. Eilleen, you have company!" Mother called and Eilleen came bolting down the staircase, excited to have a playmate.

"Yes, tea sounds nice, thank you. We stopped in because I just was wondering if it might be OK for Eilleen to come back to our house for a visit. My Eileen's going stir crazy not getting outside, but power lines are down and with broken trees, all this mud and such, I want her to play inside. We have a new book of paper dolls and it sure would give me a break if she had a friend to play with and keep her busy for a while."

"I think that would be nice. Want me to walk down later for her?" Sarah asked.

"OK. Say about 4:00?" Tillie suggested.

"I'll plan to walk over about then. It will get me out of the house. Thanks for thinking of her, Tillie. I'm so happy there's a new girlfriend for her who lives close by."

Tillie said, "I don't know about you, but I feel like I'm missing an old friend with the power out and not being able to listen to *The Breakfast Club* with Arthur Geoffrey these last few days. And what do you think about that new program on NBC, ...*Ma Perkins?* Did you happen to catch that one a few times? Oh boy, I really like that program. I bet we're missing out on some big things that are happening on that show."

"I agree, I really like that one, too. You can't help but get caught up in the story and when the music picks up, I get in such a state of suspense, why I can't even keep washing the dishes, and then every single day it cuts off right at the most exciting part! The story leaves me hanging on pins and needles waiting until tomorrow," Sarah added, "I must confess, I even watch the clock to time it just right so I can run outside to hang out the wash and get back in, just so I don't miss a word of the story. Isn't that awful?"

"Bayard, on the other hand, wants nothing to do with the new Red Network shows. He thinks radio should be commercial free, so he sticks to Blue Network, nothing but stinking news and documentary broadcasts, you know how men are. But me?

They can talk about a new soap powder all they want as long as they give me a good story to listen to." Both women laughed knowing they'd be glad when the electricity was back on.

Tillie left with the girls walking toward the Murphy's house as Sarah watched from the doorway. She felt a wave of contentment and deep satisfaction, feelings that mothers have when they're proud of their children. Watching two little girls skipping on the sidewalk with muddy brown flood water rushing by in the street on one side, and yards full of mangled debris, uprooted trees and storm devastation on the other, was a beautiful sight.

About 1:30 Bayard came in for lunch and noticed how quiet it was.

"Hey, something's missing around here, where's my other best girl?"

Sarah told him she was off making a new friend as she placed an egg salad sandwich with a slice of fresh tomato on the table for him.

"I heard the phone lines could be back and operational sometime later today. I'm going to have to call Grandmother Anna and let her know Eilleen is fine. I'm sure she's heard about this storm. I wouldn't want her to be worried." Then Bayard sat perfectly still not talking or eating his sandwich.

"Sarah, Anna is expecting us to bring Eilleen back soon you know. When I call, she is going to want to make the arrangements. September begins next week."

"I know Dad, it's all I can think about." Sarah said as she felt her chest tighten. She slowly slid out a chair and sat down next to Bayard with a glass of iced tea but found herself nervously chewing at her nails.

"I can't do it. I can't!" he declared, "It's just that simple. How can we, in our right minds, believe that taking her back is good for anyone? Can you tell me? The child's mother has just died. Her father has been missing her whole life. Grandmother Anna is far too old for raising a young child, although her heart is in the right place, I'll give her that. They don't have any money, Good Lord, the child sings and begs so they can eat! And, if something happens to Anna, what's going to happen then? Eilleen goes straight to an orphanage?" The kitchen chair scraped across the linoleum as Bayard abruptly got up and started pacing. Both his hands were running across his head while applying pressure to his temples as if to keep his brain inside his skull and the look on his face was one of sheer agony.

"As I live and breathe, Sarah, I believe she belongs here with us, where she can have friends, wear nice clothes and drink real milk for God's sake. House cats around here get real milk. I want her to live where she's safe. How could I ever sleep again with visions of her going hungry this winter surviving on powdered milk? I don't ever want her to think of her being cold!" He hung his head and his voice cracked as tears sprung from his eyes, as these thoughts were too much.

"Lord knows, I'm not the richest man, but that child deserves a good life and we can give her that. Having her here, it's been so easy. Hell, it's been nothing but a joy. And, Sarah, you're such a good mother. Am I crazy? You feel this way too, don't you? What the Sam Hill are we going to do? We're a family, and you can't make up a thing like that, but it happened for us and not because we thought it would be fun, but I don't know, I believe it was meant to be. Just like when I had to change the tag, because I knew," Bayard grew more upset, his eyes filled, brimming with tears," the minute I saw her little face. And right now, I still know it, deep down in my soul. We were meant to be a family."

Sarah's chin quivered watching Bayard standing there starting to cry. In nine years she had never seen him cry. They hugged in the kitchen, both agreeing with what they felt. Hearts never break unless you care, and both of their hearts were breaking from the love they'd found, it was that pure and simple.

Sarah got some clean hankies straight out of the laundry basket and walked back saying, "Come on over here and sit down, Bayard. She handed him a hankie and he blew his nose. Here's what we need to do. I think, when you place the telephone call to Anna, you need to state what's on your mind and in your heart. Tell her about us exactly the way you just did to me. After all, it's the honest truth. Nothing is ever clearer or more straight forward than speaking the pure truth. Who knows, maybe she is secretly hoping for such an outcome. I know I might be delighted by such an offer if I were in her shoes. She loves Eilleen, but she knows what a hard time they have, Anna can't wish her to live a life of such hardship. When you love someone, you want what's best for them, so this might just thrill her to learn Eilleen has such a chance for a better life. Think about it. Anna might be very pleased. We know how we feel and Eilleen must agree of course, but Bayard, she hardly speaks of New York anymore and I believe every time she does, it makes her terribly sad. So, all of us could very well end up living happier ever after."

"Maybe you're right. You could be on to something mother. I'm sure Anna wishes she could do more and you do have to face the facts when you're her age. Yes, I see what you mean, this type of offer, not that this is any sort of business deal or anything, but, life often brings us plenty of sorrow and tons of hard times, but how often does life turn around and deliver an answer to a tough problem or offer a permanent solution for a big problem, from a single telephone call? You're right, I need to be more confident this will be a good call, with a great outcome. No more fearful ideas.

"Tonight, let's say our prayers, Mother. Anna is a smart and resourceful woman. I think you could be right. I have to believe everything's going to work out and be just fine."

CHAPTER 18
THE CALL

"Delores, I want you to get on the horn and call the Fresh Air Foundation and have them put Miss Pennypacker on the line for me. The telephone number is on this letterhead." Bayard handed the envelope with the letter inside to his secretary. It took several telephone calls before finally connecting with Miss Pennypacker, for it was late summer now, weeks after the Fresh Air Fund had concluded their summer trips, and this was their down time with much of the staff vacationing until mid-September. The Fresh Air Foundation finally did reach Miss Pennypacker, and she and Bayard were able to talk. Into the conversation, she agreed she would speak with Anna and afterward, got back to Bayard to confirm an appointed time for the two of them to speak on the telephone at the church near Anna's home. Miss Pennypacker was happy to help with this arrangement since she sincerely believed results from their conversation could turn out to be vitally important.

"Today's the day Mother. What happens next will permanently change our lives." Bayard said, looking out the kitchen window while he finished his coffee. "You're sure you're ready for this?"

"Yes indeed, I most certainly am," Mother said, naturally smiling but forcing some of the confidence she added to her voice. While she dearly loved Eilleen and desperately wanted her to become their little girl, without a question, she felt a nagging mother-like reservation in her gut she couldn't shake. Exactly what would Grandmother Anna's decision be on giving the child away? That's no easy choice, no matter how dire your circumstances. While it would break her heart if they couldn't keep Eilleen, her biggest fear right now was for Bayard. She'd never seen him like this. Not ever. Even optimism has its limits.

They talked about whether to speak to Eilleen about their idea, to see how she felt before today's telephone call, but Sarah discouraged it. "Her feelings are most important, there's no doubt about that, but the last thing we want to do is falsely get her hopes up. Let's know exactly what our options are first, then we can speak to her." They both agreed that was best.

Rem knew the call was arranged for 11:15 that morning, so he stopped by Bayard's office first thing and closed the door. "How you holding up old man? Look at you… about to have a baby at your age... what's she weigh in, about forty pounds and three feet tall? We'll have to get you some cigars to pass around!" He was laughing, attempting to break the tension before changing his tone.

"I'm just joshing. Truth is, I can tell you're nervous, but hells-bells Bayard, if you take a piece of paper, draw a line down the middle, list the pros on one side and cons on the other, there are at least fifty pros for a life here in Delaware and only one con I can think of... missing her grandmother and sisters. But that life of hers in New York? You gotta flip those numbers and that one pro sure doesn't fill your belly or improve the quality of life on any level, not when you live like they do."

Rem scooted his chair closer and put his elbows on his knees, looking straight in Bayard's eyes. "You're doing a great thing here my friend. I believe it's the right thing too. The three of you really have something; I see it as plain as the nose on my face every time I see you all together. Now, any woman in this grandmother's position, who loves their child, should jump at an opportunity like this. Just be sure to stick to how good this is for Eilleen when you're speaking to her. Don't mention how much *you* love her or how *you'll* miss her, she won't give a rat's ass about how you feel, so don't make it a competition about who loves her most, or she'll get defensive, as she should, that's only natural and besides, no one is questioning who loves her the most here. No, you keep selling benefits for the better quality of life you can offer, bottom line is you're offering security and a bright future." Then Rem gave him a couple of strong pats on top of his shoulder. "By the way, keep it short. I'm not sure what's going to do us in around here, this darn Depression, that disastrous flooding, or these damn long distance telephone calls to New York!" He broke into his booming laugh as he left the office.

"Thanks Rem." Bayard nodded agreeing with the wisdom, Yes, he'd do just that, stick to the benefits. Bayard needed a glass of water.

Right on time, Delores put the telephone call through to New York where Anna was waiting and picked up on the other end.

"Good morning Anna. I want you to know first thing, we're all doing fine down here. We weathered that storm okay," Bayard assured her.

"Oh, that's very good to hear. I must say, I'm relieved."

"How have you and the girls been up there?"

"We're all right. Thank you for asking, but we sure have missed our little sunshine. We're looking forward to her coming home and so we can hear all about her summer in Delaware.

What day do you plan to drive her back?" Anna asked in a light voice, about as excited as she could remember anticipating Eilleen's return. Boy, had they missed that child.

"Now, we can talk about that in just a minute. But first, I want to speak with you about something that's most important. You need to know, my wife Sarah and I, have discussed this at great length and we've come up with a serious proposal we'd like for you to consider, a very good one. Good for everyone in our estimation.

"Eilleen's been happy this summer and quite simply, she is thriving being down here with us. And, with her parents gone, naturally we're quite concerned about her future. I'm sure you've asked yourself, what on earth will lie ahead for the child if anything were to ever happen to you? Now Anna, no one doubts your love for the child. We know you couldn't love her more, but a child needs two parents growing up. Sarah and I would like to offer our love and our home to Eilleen. She'd have nice clothes, plenty of food, a nice room all her own and never again would she have to worry about a thing.

"Anna, we can give her security and you could be certain she'd have a fine life, with friends, and fun and the love of a Mother and Father and she'd go to good schools, too. I thought you might find this solution to be an answer to your prayers. I'd like you to please take some time and give this idea some deep and serious consideration."

"*What* are you saying here? *Aren't* you planning to bring her back?" Anna asked in a panicked tone.

"No, no, that's not at all what I'm saying," Bayard replied, defending his position. Wasn't she even listening?

"You want to give her... *a life?* She has a life. You were

supposed to give her a vacation! A break from the city, not some sort of *rescue* from her life with a grandmother who loves her and her two sisters who couldn't love her more if they tried. Eilleen has two sisters who miss her! Don't they count? These girls love each other! How is your proposal supposed to help them? Can you tell me that?" Anna responded with a shrill pitch to her stressed voice. This was not at all what she expected to hear. In the back of her mind, she wondered if she should contact the police.

"I know... this is a very big decision and..." Bayard was cut off.

"AND? ... You listen to me AND be sure to hear it buster. This is merely your idea. Not a decision. There's not a decision that needs to be made at all! This is some crazy notion you've dreamed up...all on your own. You rich folks with no children. Oh, you must have had fun and now you want to keep her... like a... *like a puppy you found!* "Anna blurted as she began crying, "Eilleen is my *daughter's child!* She is my granddaughter! *MY decision* is this: I want you to bring my granddaughter home right now! Is that clear enough? Do I need to contact the authorities? The staff at the Fresh Air Foundation has your address you know! I could have you arrested for kidnapping if you don't return her! And, the Fresh Air Foundation will have your hide for this as well!"

In a split second, her fear was replaced with a surge of spitfire anger. Grandmother Anna was riled up and fighting mad. "I will promise you this, *IF* that child is not on our doorstep in two days, I will call the police. Furthermore, IF she is not home on time, just like we agreed, I'll make sure she never returns to your home for a summer... *ever again!* I thought it was a wonderful option, for her to spend summers with you and your wife. I need to know, *right this minute*, are you a man of your word? Are you the honorable man they say you are Mr. Wharton? Now, *you* have the decision to make! What's it going to be?"

Bayard's head was spinning as his thoughts swirled and his brain buzzed like a beehive that had been whacked with a baseball bat. He knew this was not the time for any further discussion.

"I am a man of my word. We will make arrangements to leave first thing in the morning. I think we will stay over in Philadelphia for one night and then proceed north. They say several bridges are out, so we may encounter some unexpected delays, but barring that, your granddaughter will be home exactly as we discussed.

"I do want to assure you Anna, while you may not like my offer, it was made with nothing but love and concern for Eilleen and for her future. And for yours too! Somehow, I figured it would give you comfort. Please accept my apologies for upsetting you. That was not my intention. I will keep my word and I hope you'll stand by yours too and allow us to see Eilleen next summer. This was merely an offer, certainly not any kind of threat. You need to know, Eilleen knows nothing of this conversation. She's excited to see you." Bayard said in a voice so flat and monotone he didn't even recognize it. He'd said the right thing at the moment, that didn't feel the least bit right. What other choice was there?

He hung up the phone so numb he couldn't feel his body. It was like his soul was ablaze inside his chest with feelings that raced and ricocheted going nowhere, trapped and stuck inside a body that was like a blob of damp, heavy, clay, weighing him down, making him unable to move. It was like his body wasn't even a part of him anymore, just an entrapment for stifling his emotions, rendering them useless and squelching his joy. He was witnessing the extinguishing of a vital flame while its precious fuel was disconnected—pouring and sinking into the ground, gone. All his good energy, hopes and dreams were going up in smoke. All those plans, wasted and worthless, disintegrated into ash. Just like that, his hopes vanished, and all his big dreams were over... leaving his future empty and bleak.

He plopped down beside his desk so hard his chair creaked from the dead weight of his descent as he covered his face with his hands. His thoughts raced, *Oh God, this life is too hard.* When does it end? You keep going and trying... and for what? There's always a strong wind to knock you back or a raging current to sweep you away despite your best efforts. Finances? They are all going down the drain. I can't stop that. Heck, everybody I know is broke, he thought. Nothing I can do. Storms and floods washing out roads, destruction's all around? Not a blessed thing I can do about that either, but THIS? Now this is a whole different story. One little girl who's living in poverty, whose future is so bleak I can see the darkness coming sitting right here, but look at me, I have the power to fix that problem... easily too, in the blink of an eye, without the least bit of effort, but NO. I'm denied? What is this about? All my love and caring doesn't count? My plan is not enough? So, is that it? More of the same old story, my best efforts mixed with the most wonderful of intentions are not ENOUGH? Then let me ask, when is it enough?"

Feeling more defeated and overwhelmed than he could

remember being in his entire life, Bayard began softly praying out loud in his office while still slumped in his chair. "OK God. I give up. Go ahead. Take my business, you can have it. Take my money too, or what's left of it, it's all yours. Let the surf pound down the cottage into a pile of rubble, I really don't care. Haven't I shown you by the way I live? I try to do what's right and I do think of others? But this? NO! I'm going to draw the line here! Eilleen's merely a child! None of this is her fault." Bayard's balled up fist struck his desk with a powerful thud.

"No! You're supposed to be my God. Well, I pray to heaven you're listening to me now, 'cause buddy, I'm filing a complaint with you on this one! This isn't just some paper money, or sticks and shingles, or car parts and pieces. Dear God, we're talking about a little girl's life! You gotta give me some answers, right now, starting with *why?*" As Bayard continued, he began to cry as he quietly spoke.

"Dear God, I have to ask, WHY did you have her come into my life? Only to have me love her this much? So life could take her back and leave me here, thinking of her everyday out there suffering in poverty? She had a taste of how better life can be during this summer, and now, she's gotta go back to wearing tattered clothes, be cold and hungry, begging in the streets? Do you want to leave me with a hole ripped in my heart that will never mend? This is senseless!" Bayard slammed the top of his desk with his fist again then paused before continuing in a soft murmur.

"I believe you to be a God of love. So, please God, will you love me a little right now? I pray you give me the strength I need to do this. Oh, I'll drive her back, just like I promised, we'll leave in the morning. But, please, don't you quit on me after that, because after I do this, you're going to have to give me the strength to go on. I don't see how I can. So, it's going to be up to you. I need you to do this for me. I don't know how, but somehow I'm going to trust that you will. Amen."

Quite some time passed as Bayard sat at his desk lost in his thoughts. It was exhausting just thinking about the trip he needed to make and all its implications. Suddenly he felt much older than his years.

CHAPTER NINETEEN
THE RETURN

"Guess that's it. Nothing else for me to do," Bayard thought, as he sat there numb as a stump, thoroughly exhausted. "Can't fuss about it 'cause there's nobody I know wants to listen to me belly ache about my problems, hell, they've got enough of their own. The call's been made. Eilleen has to go home that's clear. I've said my piece to God so, I guess it's time for me to dry my eyes, be a man and get on with it."

Bayard took a deep breath, trying his best to pull himself together the only way he knew, by focusing on any positive crumbs that remained when most of the good stuff is gone.

As for Eilleen, thank goodness she had no idea of our intentions, Bayard thought. For all she knows, it's simply time to go back home. We're going to make this a positive trip back for her. I refuse to let her see me the least bit upset. We'll talk all about next summer and make some grand plans to give her something to look forward to. It's a long trip, so we'll stay over in Philadelphia and do some shopping in the stores up there. Yes, I'll take her to John Wanamaker's. We'll buy her a warm coat and a hat at Wanamaker's and, yes-sir-re, some warm gloves too, maybe a pair lined with soft rabbit fur! She's going to stay warm if I have anything to do about it, and let's throw in a pair of flannel pajamas, she'll need them. Plus, a good woolen blanket for her bed and maybe long johns too, if Sarah thinks we need them. By God, *I can make that happen...* see if I don't!"

Inspired by his plan of action, one he'd carry out to the letter, he stood up. If he began to feel emotional, he'd simply revert all his attention back to "the plan," for he certainly wasn't going to allow himself to break down, not in front of the child. One small crack and he knew it wouldn't be pretty. No, he vowed not to have that happen under any circumstance.

Sarah was in the kitchen when he parked in the driveway and one glance of Bayard's weary walk toward the back door with circles under his swollen eyes said it all. He looked up at her through the window and gave his wife a brief "no" shake of his head with his lips pursed, indicating the outcome, one she already knew. Her stomach clenched, but she never said a word, she'd wait to see how Bayard wanted to handle it.

That night at the dinner table, as cool as a cucumber, Dad simply stated, "Ladies, I've got a little break at work since the flood waters have almost receded back to normal, so I thought tomorrow would be the perfect time to head north, maybe in the morning. What do you think of doing some shopping in Philadelphia, for a few winter things before we take you home? I spoke to your Grandmother Anna today, and they're all tickled pink you'll be home in a few days and your sisters can't wait to hear everything you've been doing."

"Oh, *please...* can't we wait until next week, just a few more days? Pretty-pretty-please with sugar on top?" Eilleen asked as she tilted her head, for she had learned by now what usually worked.

Mother picked up her role perfectly as if this were a well-rehearsed act in a play. "Oh no sweetheart, Dad's telephone call made arrangements with your grandmother, she's expecting you. It's a long trip and we'll get to stay over a night in Philadelphia in a hotel. There's another new experience for you. The stores are beautiful up there and full of the latest goods and we'll take you shopping. We've kept you here far longer than anyone first planned, so we better get you back, so you'll be allowed to come again next summer." Mother said, her voice void of any trace of sadness, the actress in her knew how to convey the plan as though it was another normal part of the visit. "When Dad and I get back here, we'll have a lot of clean-up work to do down at the beach. No, it's the right time."

"OK," Eilleen said, sounding a little disappointed.

By 7:30 the next morning the car was packed with all of Eilleen's things. Bayard removed the spare tire and attached a trunk box to hold her suitcase and an overnight bag. He stowed a lunch bag with fresh apples and ham sandwiches along with their good old traveling thermos of lemonade tucked behind the back seat. Bayard could only half feel his body that was already weary from dragging the weight of it along just to pack the car. But soon, they were on the road, Eilleen in the back seat with Tony in her lap.

Heading north, outside Frederica, Eilleen spotted a farm's open field full of black and white cows with a young calf pressed close beside it's mother near the fence. "Look Dad, there's the cows I love with a baby, oh, can we stop? Please, I just want one more, close up look at their faces."

Bayard shook his head no but of course it was no use, his words responded differently, "Just for two minutes, Missy. And we can't pull off the road after this or we'll never get to Philadelphia before dark." Dad said.

Eilleen hopped out as soon as the car rolled into the grass along the roadway. "Look at the baby calf! Aren't cows just the sweetest? I even love smelling them."

Bayard watched her admire the animals and noticed when her eyes looked up from them and searched off toward the distance as she scanned the entire horizon as if to save the image to bring it back with her, then she inhaled deeply. Such an adult thing to do for a five-year-old, who would turn six in a few weeks.

"The smells of a farm and the saltwater and beach smells are some of the best things in Delaware, but I don't really know how I'm going to be able to tell my sisters about them," Eilleen said as she leaned on the whitewashed rails, reaching in to touch the mother cow as the Wharton's watched.

"This is what we did the first day Mother. We stood like this, looking at a bunch of old black and white cows as if we were witnessing a field of exotic giraffes or something." Dad whispered, but he was done talking for his throat grew tight and he felt his eyes begin to water, his emotions wanted to surface. Nope... no cracks, he thought, it was time to stick to the plan or fall out and blubber like a baby. "Back in the car gang! What do you say? We have places to get to and things to do!" Mother turned her head so Eilleen couldn't see her quickly dab away a few tears with her hankie.

They continued on the drive north. After a few detours they made it to the north side of Wilmington, where they stopped to eat their picnic lunch, then continued to Philadelphia. They checked in to the Bellevue-Stratford, located at 200 South Broad Street, a beautifully stunning hotel fashioned from the French Renaissance, built in 1904 with lighting fixtures designed by Thomas Edison. The bell hop took their bags and Tony up to their spacious and lovely room, but in short order, the Wharton's were walking through the lobby and out the revolving door, off to do some city shopping.

It was around 3:30 they got to John Wanamaker's, a magnificent building with marble floors and grand, high ceilings so ornate, why the place looked more like a palace than a store. At 4:00 there was a pipe organ performance in the marble Emporium. This very organ was once featured at the St. Louis World's Fair and was one of the largest organs in the world. Every square foot of the stores huge space became filled with music and the sound of it was simply overwhelming and rich to the bone, just like a formal concert. Shoppers gathered along the railings at each of the many floors that all overlooked the main level, creating a dramatic spectacle with such a vast open center. What a magnificent place to be. Eilleen was speechless for most of the musical event, then she would giggle and pull Mother's arm every time she wanted to show her another wonderful something she'd spy, her eyes bright and shining.

There were nine floors to shop, reached by elevator and the operator would recite the goods on display at each floor. Soon the doors opened as they stopped on the fourth floor: "*Children's Accessories, Sleepwear, Little Girlswear, Girlswear and Boyswear,*" was announced. They stocked up on the important winter clothing a little girl might need, including undershirts and winter socks.

Eilleen looked absolutely darling when she tried on a marine blue wool, double-breasted coat. "Mother and I want you to have this coat Eilleen, it's for your birthday. Anyone who's turning six and is as cute as you are needs a fine coat like this. Why, the color's perfect, it brings out the blue in your eyes." Bayard struggled again but refocused quickly by asking the salesperson to please remove all price tags on their purchases while at the counter. He didn't want Anna seeing what was spent. They also purchased Grandmother Anna, Marie and Jene each a winter scarf and a pair of gloves as a surprise. Mother sensed Eilleen was more excited about those gifts than her own new clothes. That child had such a genuine, big heart for others.

In the morning, they ate breakfast downstairs in the hotel where Eilleen ordered French toast she loaded up with soft butter and warm syrup and enjoyed a glass of fresh-squeezed orange juice. Dad couldn't help himself... silently questioning how long it would be before she would ever eat a breakfast like this again. Just looking at her healthy coloring, her bright eyes and shiny hair, she looked so radiant and beautiful, nothing close to resembling that shabby, pale little child that got off.... "No! Stop it... stick to the plan," he thought.

"That was delicious," Dad said as he put his napkin on the plate and pushed back his chair. "Let's hit the road again Ladies, shall we?"

Surprisingly, most of the road repairs had been completed along the route making the drive better than expected, but this was still one long trip for sure. Using their Esso Eastern Shore Road Map, making one U-turn and stopping to fill up with gasoline a couple of times, they finally arrived in front of the old brick and brownstone building Eilleen called home. Bayard felt himself clench the wheel. If he could just grip it hard enough, maybe he could stay in control and hold down those emotions that bounced from despair to anger to an overwhelming feeling of utter sadness, all trying to get out from somewhere in his gut, it was a horrible moment for him. He felt on the verge of needing medical attention.

Grandmother Anna was the first one out the door and Bayard looked at her and for a split-second thought, *Look how old she is... it won't be long before she... NO... stop that man! What on earth are you thinking? Dear God, please forgive me, I never want anyone to die for my gain, or Eilleen's.* That was the very moment when Bayard realized that crazy thoughts lived only a heartbeat away from an otherwise sane mind, given the right circumstances.

Time to stick to the plan... nothing else. Unload the car. Give hugs and kisses, like this was a normal day. Then drive back, to live an empty life. No thinking until tomorrow, that's the new plan. No thinking, at all.

Eilleen bounced out of the car and ran to Grandmother Anna, Marie and Jene. They were hugging and delighted, crying happy tears just looking at her. She looked wonderful and indeed, far different from the child that left them in June.

"Thank you so much, Sarah and Bayard, for having her in your home." Anna said, "She looks marvelous, a true sight for my old sore eyes!" Then in a softer voice, Anna turned her back to the girls and said, "Bayard, I want to apologize to you. I'm sorry for my outburst and my terrible behavior on the telephone. I panicked. There was no need for me to speak to you that way, of course, I know that now. I just never anticipated an option like that from you. It caught me off guard. But, I know your heart was coming from a place of kindness. We are so happy to have our little girl home. Next summer will be here in a flash and I know Eilleen will be looking forward to it." Anna winked at him, reached for his hand and gave it a few soft pats, beaming with happiness without noticing both the faces of the Wharton's looked like they were witnessing a funeral, a far cry from seeing any kind of celebration.

Stick to the plan, man, this is it. Stick to the plan. "OK Eilleen, give Mother and Dad a hug, we love you, sweetie. We've got a long drive ahead."

She quickly ran over and embraced Mother giving her a giant hug saying, "I love you, Mother!" Witnessing that display of affection almost opened the crack for Bayard. Then she looked straight into his eyes and said, "I love you *sooo much*, Dad!" and she attacked him, wrapping her arms around his waist and giving him a hug so big, it used all her might! While he ached, wanting desperately to melt into that hug, feel all of it, then collapse and have a complete crying jag, the kind with gasping sobs and lots of snot, he knew he couldn't. He held back, trying not to feel the pressure of the hug and so he went through the motions, feeling enough to send his love to her without letting anything seep back into him. It was the only way. She could never know that her precious hug was practically killing him.

After that embrace, he was done. He couldn't remember a single thing; shutting the car doors, starting the engine, looking for oncoming automobiles?... nothing. Did he even wave good bye? He couldn't say.

It was over. They drove away.

CHAPTER 20
SISTERS

Jene and Marie fired off questions, one right on top of the next, as they helped lug the bags and belongings up the six flights of steep stairs to their apartment. Grandmother Anna draped her arm around her long-lost granddaughter and squeezed her shoulder, so happy to see her.

Eilleen was excited to be home, but her mood quickly changed as soon as they opened the door to the apartment and crossed the threshold. The old place looked so much worse than she ever remembered. It startled her. Looking around with unaccustomed eyes, everything she saw was colorless, faded, bleak and ugly, for it seemed as if Webster's definition of dismal was staring her in the face. Had it always been this bad, she wondered? How could she not have noticed?

Her sisters gathered around, and she began telling them about her adventures, beginning with getting off the train, meeting "Dad" for the first time, going for ice cream and how exciting it was to see a wide-open field with black and white cows. She was beginning to describe Slaughter Beach as she opened her dresser drawer to put away new pj's, and noticed a few of her dingy, old worn-out clothes still inside. Her lovely new clothes would get old someday too, but right now she knew she'd never have nice new things like this ever again. Oh well, after brushing her hand across her new soft flannel pj's, she shut the drawer.

Eilleen picked up the shopping bag she'd carried upstairs

and announced, "Everyone sit down and close your eyes. I have a surprise. You too, Grandmother. Hold out your hands everyone." She reached in and selected the scarf and a pair of gloves for each of them and said, "Don't open your eyes, even when you feel something, wait until I say the word. OK. GO!"

The girls were thrilled to see lovely scarves of spun wool in beautiful rich colors and a new pair of gloves. "I picked these out for you." Eilleen said proudly, "However, Dad paid for them, he's wonderful like that you know." The girls were tossing their scarves over their shoulders and parading around like movie stars. Grandmother stroked her scarf then brushed it to her cheek to feel the softness of fine, luxurious fibers. It had been a long time since she'd received a gift that was both new and of such fine quality.

"Now, it's time for this one," Eilleen grunted, as she dragged over and opened the bulging Wanamaker shopping bag revealing a beautiful wool plaid blanket with wide, pink silk binding stitched around the edges. It was made of soft, carnation pink and buttercup yellow plaid with traces of a deeper rose and moss green running between the squares. Jene and Marie helped Eilleen spread it on top of their covers, so they could enjoy its beauty along with the warmth it promised. They admired what a cheerful change it made to the whole room with those happy soft colors.

"Be sure to tell the Wharton's thank you. This is a wonderful day! Having you home and surprises like this, from Wanamaker's too, woo-hooo!" The sisters began jumping on the bed, bouncing on top of the new blanket.

Eilleen had a slight frown thinking, *Tell them thank you? When in the world will I be able to do that?* And it dawned on her, she might not get to speak with them until next summer and a chilling wave of emptiness washed through her, stealing her smile. It was a feeling that would become all too familiar to her in coming weeks.

That night, under the cozy pink plaid blanket, the girls snuggled together the way they used to and Jene and Marie begged to hear more about the summer. Eilleen decided to tell them about the Kent and Sussex Fair and the animal barns when suddenly, they noticed they were getting way too hot, having far more covers than they needed for a mild September night.

As Marie peeled back the top blanket she said, "Hey girls, guess what? That was just a sample of how warm we are going to be when it does get good and cold in here. Good grief, we were cookin' in here like an oven! Aren't we the lucky ones? Thank you again Eilleen." Marie said, and she kissed her little sister's cheek. Knowing they would be toasty on the coldest of winter nights was reason to celebrate.

Shortly, both her sisters fell asleep, but Eilleen lay wide awake, so aware of her surroundings, finding it strange and not feeling at all how she expected or remembered. Turning her head on the pillow to look out their dingy window, she viewed the small patch of night sky with so few stars. She couldn't see the sky blocked by so many close buildings and she felt cheated, knowing there really was a big, expansive sky and thousands more stars to see. Days ago, she'd been privileged to glimpse at the full, unobstructed sky with so many stars she couldn't begin to count them all, right from her bed. Not anymore. She wanted to track the phases of the moon and witness all that was shining in the night, see the whole thing as nature laid it out. She laid there feeling trapped and closed in.

And those stairs! Dad carried her up one flight to bed each night because he loved it and of course, she did too. They'd think she was such a fool or some big old baby to love being carried to bed. In Delaware, she was tired every night, but from swimming and jumping rope, not walking long city blocks and carrying things up six flights of stairs.

She had escaped for a few weeks, sampled a new life and it deeply worried her. *How am I supposed to be happy now?* She thought. She missed Mother and Dad, she missed her friends, and her nice bed with her expansive view overlooking the wide-open marshlands that softly glowed every evening bathed in moonlight. Eilleen closed her eyes to remember and she could see it clearly, with all the stars in the Heavens. That's when she drifted off.

School started with Eilleen enrolled into first grade, Miss Marshall's class. She walked to school each morning with her sisters and tried to make friends, but these weren't very happy girls. Oh, sometimes they were, but Lucy bit her fingernails so much sometimes you could see her fingers bleed. She reminded Eilleen of a frightened puppy, always dropping her head, shrugging her shoulders and dipping her chin, cowering down and rolling her eyes upward to sneak a peek at you like someone was going to strike her with a rolled-up newspaper or something. And Mildred was such a whiner. She got so tired and cranky in the afternoon she would sit in her seat and start to cry, right in class. Sometimes, they had to put her chair out in the hallway. At recess, Eilleen suggested games, but the girls were reluctant to join in. It was as if they'd never played games in their whole lives, for gosh sakes! Then Eilleen realized, that was probably true, so she decided to teach them how to jump rope and soon all the girls in the whole class were lining up to take turns. Miss Marshall told her she was a real leader.

Learning was fun. When Miss Marshall read out loud, that was the best. During class, the days moved along well, but Eilleen wished she was in school with Eileen, Frances, Gertrude and Elaine, always wondering what they were doing about now. "Boy, if they were here, they'd show these girls how to jump some double-dutch. But they're not, so that's never going to happen."

When October rolled around, temperatures grew colder and Eilleen got out her new blue coat and bundled up for her walk to school, feeling like a million bucks. She felt so warm and it fit just right with a little room to grow and it reminded her of Mother and Dad. She remembered how Dad smiled when he saw her try it on and how he told her it was her birthday present for turning six and that every time she wore it, he wanted her to feel a warm hug from them. Yes, she loved her coat. Her sisters wore their new scarves, and they all walked to school with a bounce in their step.

Approaching the school grounds, some kids started calling out mean things, yelling, "Look at you, would you! Aren't we all *fancy-smancy?* Who do you think you are, the *rich kids?* Hey! Who d' you steal the coat from, tootsie?"

"Keep walking Eilleen, they're being stupid," Jene said.

"And acting like real knuckleheads," Marie added.

"It's just a coat," Eilleen said as she frowned because their words made her feel awful for wearing her nice birthday gift. "Mean kids don't live in Delaware, or at least, none that I ever saw!"

"Look around Eilleen. Most of these kids don't even have coats and if they do, they're practically rags, or some patched up old hand-me-downs. They're just jealous, that's all," Marie said. "Wait for us inside the front door after school to walk home. And keep your coat in your arms until I get here before you put it on, OK?"

"Sure. See you later," Eilleen said deflated, as she walked to her classroom without the bounce.

That was the just the beginning. During the next weeks, it became clear, no one shared what made her happy. Her beautiful clothes made everyone roll their eyes or become annoyed. No one wanted to hear any more about Delaware or her past fun, or especially anything about the wonderful meals and different foods she got to try. One evening during a dinner of potato and parsley soup with a slice of day old bread and that awful powered milk, Eilleen mentioned, "Did you know that New England clam chowder is made with cream, but Manhattan clam chowder has vegetables, broth and cooked tomatoes? One is white, like this soup and the other one is red. I like Manhattan the best. Frances's father always gave us fresh clams from the bay," Eilleen said, "and other neighbors gave us the tomatoes."

"That's enough Eilleen!" Grandmother Anna barked, almost scolding. "Just sit here and eat your dinner and be grateful you have some. Folks around here don't eat clam chowder and I don't believe it does you—or any of us, any good to hear about what you ate in Delaware while we're sitting at the table."

"Yes Grandmother," Eilleen answered, realizing that what she thought was interesting sure didn't make Grandmother happy.

Marie changed the subject and began telling a funny story

about Mary, her friend at school while working on a project together. "Mary's so much fun. We do the work, but we have to whisper to each other in between and it's so hard not to laugh in class."

"I know how you feel Marie," Eilleen said, "Elaine, Eileen and Frances and I laughed all the time. Mother said if we couldn't behave ourselves we couldn't sit together in church. But we really couldn't help it!" She giggled just remembering the moment.

"Eilleen, who are your friends here in school?" Grandmother Anna asked in a stern tone.

"Lucy and Mildred, I guess, but it's not the same thing. Elaine, Eileen and Frances are my best friends," Eilleen said.

"Well, maybe you should try a little harder and be a better friend yourself. We want you to have friends here, where you live." Grandmother suggested as if this would be helpful, but it let Eilleen know again, for some reason the things that made her the happiest, didn't make anyone here happy at all.

Eilleen decided right then, her memories of Delaware, the trips, her best friends, her Aunt Mimi, cousin Dorothy, Slaughter Beach, and most of all, Mother and Dad, and all of those special memories would be just hers to keep secret from everyone. She could make herself happy anytime she wanted to, just by thinking about them, but never again was anyone going to ruin a single second of what she felt were the happiest days of her life.

Nope, no one's going to hear me say a peep about Delaware anymore. She decided. *They don't understand. But, how could they? They've never even been out of this stinking old city. They don't even know how ugly and sad it is to live here. But*

I sure do.

CHAPTER 21
GOING BACK

Sarah knew they were in for one long and quiet drive, as they began the two hundred-mile trek toward home in total silence. When they stopped for gas and to check the oil, she climbed in the back and reached for the small pillow she'd put in for Eilleen, to rest up awhile and wished she'd packed a small blanket too, but honestly, figured they'd stop for the night like they usually did. But Bayard wasn't in any mood to stay over, or even to have dinner in Philadelphia at his favorite restaurant, Bookbinders, where they would eat every time he was anywhere near Philadelphia. Exhausted from the tension of the day, she dozed off.

Bayard was hell-bent on driving all night if that's what it took, for the only thing he wanted to do was to get back home. He did decide to make a pit stop at a clean-looking road side diner, just for a quick bite, he didn't want Sarah to be hungry on account of him. They ordered open faced, hot turkey sandwiches with mashed potatoes and cranberry sauce that Bayard was surprisingly able to eat, finding he was hungry, even being as upset as he was. He asked for seconds on coffee too. It was some strong, good coffee, and he figured it might be a smart idea, facing such a long drive. As soon as he swallowed the last sip, they were back on the road.

Traveling on without any conversation for the better part of the trip, they were approaching the Delaware state line near Wilmington before Bayard finally spoke up. "Thank God it's pitch black outside tonight. I don't think I could stand looking at a field with any of those damn sweet cows standing out there right about now."

"I know, Bayard," Sarah responded softly with deep regard for his feelings, "I know just what you mean. I think we're both in for a few rough weeks, but you know what? Right after Thanksgiving it will be Christmas, then it will be 1934 and, in a jiffy, spring will be here and before you know it, Eilleen will be returning for the summer. We'll keep ourselves busy making all kinds of plans. Who knows, maybe we can drive up and get her as soon as school lets out. I bet you anything, she'll be as ready to visit us as we'll be to have her back."

There was a long pause before Bayard responded, his eyes staying fixed on the limited, lit view of the dark road that stretched out ahead. "Let me ask you something, Sarah. Did you have any idea we'd bring home some strange child for a Fresh Air visit and end up feeling like this? Did *any of this* ever cross your mind? 'Cause it sure as heck never crossed mine. To come clean, Sarah, I kind of thought at first I was just helping you out. I figured it was some fleeting whim you got in your mind and if a child came for a few weeks, it would make you happy. I didn't think I needed anything to be happy, why, quite frankly, I thought my life *was* happy and just about damn near perfect! And I believe it was too. Or at least that's how I remember it. Well, Sarah, I'm sorry to have to say this, but that's all been shot to hell now!"

"Oh Bayard, I know. I don't know what to say to you, or even what to think myself. One thing's sure, I don't regret this summer. No, I don't. Not in the least. Why, we've had nothing but more fun than I can remember, and right in the midst of such financial ruin that's all around us, and the storm damage and flooding and who knows if our own cottage is even still standing? But the time we spent with that child? Lord have mercy, no, I wouldn't trade these weeks or meeting her for all the tea in China. She's a rare, extraordinary child you know. How could we not fall in love with her?

"Let me ask you something, Bayard. If you knew everything you know, right now… right up to this very moment, would you want to go back and do any part of it differently? Would you still change her tag? Or, would you choose to bring home Grace Anne this time?" Sarah asked.

There was a pause and thoughtful sigh before Bayard replied, "My heart is breaking here Sarah, so I'd like to tell you I simply wish we were just never involved with any of this Fresh Air mess, so that none of this would have ever happened and we'd be just rolling along the way we were, before that damn train arrived! That's what I'd like to say, but it would be a big-old, bald-faced lie. When you put it like that, I have to fess up and say, no, I'm with you, I wouldn't change a single thing." As he finished, the bottom corners of his lips began curling downward.

Tears filled Bayard's eyes before he continued. "Problem is not the past Sarah, not with the summer or even now, taking her back to New York. MY problem is I don't know how to go back into our house and look at it, empty, without her in it. The problem is I don't know how to fix this overwhelming sad feeling I have. How do you go on, Sarah? I don't know if I can. They say you never miss what you never had, but Hell, guess what? *We had it!* Do you know what we had Sarah? Do you know what the *'it'* really is?" Bayard's voice was slightly raised and tense as he blurted out his feelings.

"Yes, of course I do. We love Eilleen," Sarah replied as tears spilled.

"Yes, we love her, of course we love her, but it's much more than that. Sarah… we were a family!" Tears were rolling as he opened up and his lower lip continued to quiver as he went on, "I love our family, Sarah. I love being a family. I've never loved you more than seeing you be a mother, and you know how much I've always loved you. You're such a great mother! I loved *us. All of us.*" Tears dripped off his chin as he tried to continue, speaking between breaths the way you do when you try to talk but end up barking out groups of words in short clusters as your tightening throat chokes off your sentences. "And it felt right… and complete… and damn it... I don't know if anything... will ever be... right with the world... ever again!" Then he turned to look at Sarah straight-on, "And I mean that Sarah!"

"Pull over Bayard. Come on now. Let's just stop right here for a few minutes." Sarah suggested gently in her take-charge tone.

Bayard turned the wheel, directing the car onto the tall grass along the paved road and as soon as the car stopped they reached for each other and curled together like parentheses framing their shared thoughts, embracing and crying like little children lost in a deep woods; done in and giving up, no longer knowing which way to turn but knowing full well plenty of hungry wolves were lurking nearby, ready to close in and pounce any second. The situation may be different, but the feelings so similar. They were both scared for what was next with so many dangerous situations all around them just like those imaginary wolves, lurking in every direction... and they were both desperately sad, deflated and drastically spent and bone tired.

It took a few days to recover from that exhausting road trip. Mentally, the sadness began taking over Bayard in a form of grieving. It was indeed a loss, pure and simple, however, Eilleen was still alive and well and would soon be returning. That was the counterpoint Sarah kept reminding Bayard of, that in a few months school would be out, and she'd be back with them. While he knew it was true, he couldn't bounce back, though he really wanted to.

"You know Sarah, I think I convinced myself our adoption idea would please Anna, be a real answer to her prayers, and that Eilleen was never going to leave us. I should never have assumed such an outcome or planned for it at the level I did. Just give me some time, I'll be alright."

The following Sunday brought a cool and sunny afternoon. After church and another cup of coffee, Bayard put down his cigarette and the Sunday paper and suggested, "What do you think? Let's take a ride, a short one I assure you, but I think it's high time we go down and assess the damages and have a first-hand look at the cottage. I've heard reports the old homestead's still standing, but I think we need to see for ourselves."

Driving into Slaughter Beach, they noticed sand drifts across the road and tons of sand piled where it had never been seen before, but overall, things seemed to be in place with extra drifts of sand in their yard that were not there before. Opening the back door to the kitchen revealed how much dust and dirt had blown in covering over almost everything, but it wasn't the first time they'd seen a mess like this. The floors were covered and gritty, but they might as well wait to clean because they knew they would just have to do it all again in the spring, anyway.

Sarah brought in some cardboard boxes to take home the rest of the summer jelly and anything they might want back in Milford for the winter, while Bayard went to inspect the front porch screens and the rest of the cottage, when suddenly, Sarah heard a loud, painful cry that sent her running.

"Bayard! What is it?"

Bayard was down on his knees, bent over and curled up, on the living room floor, crying out. Sarah rushed to his side to see if he was having an attack when she saw it.

"Oh my God," she said, covering her mouth with both hands. She froze in place, her mind racing, wondering what to do. No answers were coming.

It was CC. He was clutching CC to his chest, the Cupie Doll Eilleen left behind on the sofa. Bayard looked straight up at Sarah with such sorrow in his eyes it broke her heart, then desperately he screamed out, "I can't bear this! CC is right here... but our Eilleen isn't!" He sobbed, feeling the depths of intense grieving overcome his thinking. Seeing CC on the sofa triggered a flood of beautiful memories that overwhelmed him.

He stood up frantic and wild eyed, searching for other things. "Sarah, I cannot and will not look at these things! I can't bare it!" Bayard hollered as he stomped up the stairs to Eilleen's room where he flung open the door to see what remnants of hers remained there to torture him. There were her beach shells, all lined up where she left them. He froze thinking for a second what to do and turned around and headed to the garage like a man on a mission where time was critical, the way a fireman would rush for a water hose to combat a fiery blaze, acting quickly before more damage is done.

In the garage, he grabbed her tin pail and shovel, the jump rope and then eyed the inner tubes, for some reason, he was OK leaving the inner tubes behind. He jerked his garden shovel off the hooks and propped it outside the garage, then went straight into the house toting the little pail and charged up the stairs and started filling the small bucket with all the treasured sea shells he scooped up by fistfuls. At the bottom of the steps, he lunged for CC, snatching her up with plans to destroy her as if she were a poisonous snake responsible for all of his pain, knowing she could strike again anytime if he as much as looked her way, inflicting these wounds all over again. He stomped straight outside with the pail of shells and CC stuffed under his arm. Back in the garage, he found his wading boots and began urgently pulling them on then snatched up the jump rope.

"What on earth do you think you're doing Bayard? Stop this!" Sarah cried when she saw him reaching for his shovel. "You know she's coming back! Those are her precious things! She'll be looking for them when she comes back here. Don't do this! You can't do this!"

"Oh... I most certainly can! And, I most certainly am! What I CAN'T DO, my dear is LOOK at any of this! I JUST CAN'T! Sarah, you just have to let me go." He was crying in a way Sarah had never seen him, or any man, ever cry before.

It was heart breaking and scary. She desperately wanted Eilleen's special things to remain with them, waiting. "Bayard, what happens when she comes back? What will you say to her when she finds all of her favorite things are gone?"

"Well, Sarah, I shall buy her new things. But I'm telling you this, I won't live to see her return if I have to look at any of this a moment longer!" And with that, Bayard picked up his shovel and the toys, turned and walked off, still crying uncontrollably as he left the yard. He continued walking down the road, a grown man, pitifully crying and blubbering, carrying a jump rope, a sand bucket full of shells and CC. It was an unimaginable sight. After a short distance, he turned and headed walking straight out into the back marsh. It seemed he walked on forever, sinking in the mud going slower and sinking deeper, pushing on and fighting harder to walk the farther he went, sinking down with each step.

Sarah sat on the sand-covered kitchen steps and quietly cried, but not for herself or even the sadness of it all. This time, all her tears were for poor Bayard. As much as she was painfully sad, she knew it had to be far worse than anything she could imagine for this dear, tender man.

From the distance of the back steps, she heard the horrible sounds of agony travel across the flat back marsh. His loud cry was pouring out from the depths of his soul with not a thing out there to stop or buffer it. There weren't very many people around Slaughter Beach that late autumn afternoon, but the few that were, heard it too. A couple of folks walking near the little store, stopped in their tracks when they heard the pathetic cries. Why, even a store clerk who happened to be there on Sunday doing paperwork, walked outside to see what on earth was going on. The sound was that of a wailing so sorrowful, it would make a grown man's blood turn cold. No one who witnessed the sight of Bayard Wharton, standing all alone, way off, out there in the middle of the vast muddy marsh bent over his shovel, burying Eilleen's precious things, would ever forget it.

CHAPTER 22
WINTER IN NEW YORK

"Would you girls please wash up the breakfast dishes? Marie's coming with me to help carry the rations home." Grandmother was feeling far too tired and weary for the task this morning. "That line gets longer every week." She took a deep breath, shook her head and exhaled a deep sigh, unable to imagine how things could get much worse.

"We'll be gone until mid-afternoon I'm sure. I wish they'd allow the eldest child of the family to do this, but they won't even distribute a slice of stale bread to a child. Tonight, at supper remind me girls, we must pray for jobs. Lots and lots of jobs. Our men need to get back to work to put an end to this awful Depression." Grandmother said, knowing if it weren't for rations and soup kitchens, the people around here would be starving, and truth be told, she knew some already were.

The market had all but closed for winter since no one had any money these days, heck, three out of four men were out of a job and times had become so bleak, if you had something to eat and were under any kind of shelter that kept you out of the elements, you were doing well. Anna had started taking in ironing for pay while the girls were at school, it's no wonder she was exhausted. Her swollen legs were aching, making standing in a long line today practically torture.

After they left, and the door closed, Eilleen stomped her foot and stated, "That darned Depression. That's all we ever hear about! New York must have more Depression going on here than anywhere else in the whole United States. I don't know if you know this or not, but there are other places in the world where things are not this bad."

"Really? Gee-whiz, let me guess. Could it be *Delaware?*" Jene was mocking, "Of course, it is, it's paradise there. Delaware is where they have a big sky, and everyone eats fresh seafood right from the bay and pick ripe vegetables straight from their own gardens! Yep, I do believe I've heard *all about it,*" Jene said sarcastically, tilting her head from side to side, emphasizing each statement and fluttering her eyelashes for added drama.

"You can make fun of me if you want," Eilleen screamed back, clenching her fists, "but it's every bit true! We should be running away from this place instead of walking blocks across the city to stand in line all day for food." She yelled back, stomped her foot again out of frustration and instantly felt overwhelmed and deeply homesick, so she retreated to her room to curl up and cocoon with Tony on top of her beautiful blanket in their ugly old room where this time, she couldn't stop herself from crying. She wanted Mother and Dad to come here and beat down the front door and storm inside to swoop her up and take her home with them! They would rescue her too, she felt sure of it, if they had any idea what was going on. Missing them was far more painful than being hungry.

This must be how a caged bird feels, she thought, *one that was allowed to fly free and wild across the beach but now is trapped and can't live its natural way. That's how I feel. I got to live just like a free bird all summer. A beautiful songbird. No wonder I don't want to sing anymore.* She calmed down as soon as she began to remember those happy days of frolicking on the beach while staring out her dingy, soot-streaked window to a view of nothing but other drab old buildings and a narrow peek of a gray, overcast sky, for everything bright and colorful only could be found inside her head.

November continued with each day growing a bit shorter and becoming darker earlier as the temperatures dropped. One evening while Grandmother Anna was at the stove, sizzling chopped onions in the frying pan to be mixed with rice and beans, she heard something unusual. Looking over, she watched Eilleen remove the lid off the sugar bowl, stick in her fingers, then quickly lick off the sugar and dip in for more.

"Stop that! What in the Dickens do you think you are doing?" Grandmother demanded using her strongest, booming German tone while slamming down her wooden spoon on the counter with some surprising force. "Merciful heavens child!"

Eilleen froze, sticky fingers midair, looking stunned as she realized Grandmother was very angry.

"That bowl of sugar is all we have! It's not a candy or treat for you to just dig in and help yourself. Who do you think you are, anyway? Well, I'll tell you. You're spoiled! You just spent the whole summer living like some rich kid that you're not! And to be honest, I'm sick to death of hearing about it. I'm sorry I let you stay the summer, which was my mistake, because it's ruined you!" Grandmother Anna shouted as she waved her hands. Suddenly she grabbed Eilleen's arm, snatching her almost off her feet and began dragging her down the hall, shaking her the whole time as she continued yelling. "You should have more respect than to help yourself to whatever sugar *you want,* but that is exactly what happens once a child has had too much given to them. Well, young lady, it's not like that here! Do you think I stick my fingers in the sugar bowl after you've gone to bed? No! Not even a little bit extra do I ever put in my tea. Why? Because I want to be sure we all have some...unlike YOU!"

In one swift swoop, she spun Eilleen around and shoved her in the hall closet and slammed the door and continued her rant practically screaming, "I want you to stay in there and think about what you've done. And while you're in there, think about this too...there are other people living in this home besides just YOU!" Grandmother Anna powerfully enunciated each word, she was so worked up, feeling almost ready to explode. Raising these children was taxing enough, but, Lord have mercy, she refused to tolerate any one of them to feel more entitled to the little they did have. No, there would be no special ones... not in this house. Not while she was still living.

Eilleen sat in the dark on the closet floor, stunned by Grandmother's outburst. She tried to remain quiet, so as not to anger her any more than she already had, but she couldn't help crying. Her heart beat had doubled and was pounding in her ears. Scared and afraid to make any more noise than necessary, she sat trembling on the floor, seeing nothing in the dark but the crack of light from under the door while she tried her best to stifle her desire to really bawl. She held her breath, fighting as hard as she could to hold it all in, but the tears and sobs came. Never in her whole life could she ever remember upsetting anyone so much.

During the duration of her cry, the reason for her tears changed from being scared and punished, to purely and thoroughly missing Mother and Dad. This moment crushed the last spark of light inside her for she simply couldn't think of a single reason how or when she would ever be happy again. She was so desperately homesick.

Twenty minutes later, she stopped crying and by then had decided no matter how bad things got, she would always have her summer memories. After all, a girl who was part bird and allowed to fly free on the beach still had enough sunshine inside her to warm her own heart anytime she wanted. That would be her secret plan. Seems it was all she had and by God, she was going to cling to and cherish every memory she possessed forever. Stifling making any sounds while continuing to have such an enormous, upsetting cry left her with swollen eyes and a pounding headache.

Late one November afternoon, there was a knock on the door and there stood Butchie Holloway in the hall with a delivery. Thanksgiving was in a few days and the church had sent over a box of food, enough to make a Thanksgiving meal complete with flour, eggs, potatoes, fresh kale, an onion, six apples and a fresh chicken. Anna was very grateful to see the food but in the same split second, felt guilty since food was desperately needed by so many families this year. She hated being on the receiving end, but the church had made the list of the neediest, and while it was not a list you want to be on, you had to feel grateful if you were. Mrs. Geneille probably had a hand in making sure they were included.

"Thank you, God, for good friends and our caring church," Anna announced "And, thank you Butchie, Happy Thanksgiving." Unpacking the box, they discovered a round tin filled with oatmeal raisin cookies and some tea. Anna felt sure that surprise came straight from her dear friend, Mrs. G. herself.

Thanksgiving dinner was served with Jene, Marie, Eilleen and Anna all gathered around the first hot meal they had to eat in weeks. The kitchen smelled delicious with the aroma of baking bread and roasting chicken, making the entire day wonderful long before it was time for the first bite.

Grandmother gave the blessing as they held hands. Eilleen felt troubled though. She wanted to be as grateful as the rest of them, but somehow, her heart wasn't in. She had begun to feel a strange bitterness and a lot of anger lately too, feelings she wasn't at all familiar with. Maybe Grandmother Anna was right, calling her spoiled.

I don't want to be bad, she thought to herself, *I just want to run away from this place more than I want to sit here and be grateful for one old stinking hot meal. I want to feel grateful for everything, all the time... the way I did this summer. It was easy to feel grateful in...* she stopped herself. Oh no, there was the proof... she was spoiled. In that split-second she decided, *Maybe I better be grateful for whatever good does come my way, even when things aren't easy. And I guess I better start right now, because I don't think life will be easy for me ever again. Today we do have a perfect dinner on our table, and I am truly grateful for that, I really am.* She sincerely smiled for the first time in a while and she felt much better.

"Hustle along now girls, don't dawdle. This is the first Sunday in December and you know we begin lighting the Advent Candles. The church will fill up faster than normal today. Oatmeal's almost ready, hurry up, we don't want to be late," Grandmother Anna informed the girls as she got out bowls and spoons for hot cereal.

Coming to the table one by one, each looked worse than the other. “I don’t feel well at all,” Marie said, with glassy eyes that were shadowed by dark circles and she began to cough.

Eilleen pulled up her chair only to plop her head down on top of crossed arms on top of the table just as Jene walked out sneezing and blowing her red nose.

“Would you look at the three of you? Runny noses, stuffed up heads and those tired eyes, it’s certain you’ve all come down with something.” Grandmother felt their foreheads to see if anyone was running a fever.

“Looks like we’ve become the sick room overnight. Just what we need around here, everyone ill,” Grandmother Anna said, wearily shaking her head. Sighing, she took the hot kettle off the stove to make each girl a piping hot cup of tea. “Try to drink your tea girls, but there will be no church for you today. Stay wrapped up and keep warm.” She got down a bottle of Bayer aspirin and laid a tablet beside each tea cup. “Take this when your tea cools down, it will help. Mostly, you just have to let a winter cold run its course.” She mashed Eilleen’s tablet between two teaspoons and mixed it with a little tea to make it easier for her to swallow.

Since the girls didn’t seem to have a fever, Anna decided it would be alright for her to walk on over for church. She needed this week’s uplifting message to give her proper things to think about for the upcoming week, and she loved how the organ music made her feel as it filled the church, and when the melody washed over her, it provided her a few wonderful moments of comfort and peace. Plus, after the service, she always enjoyed chatting with her friends who after all these years had become her family.

Once she'd explained it this way, "Girls, I'm just like an old German wind-up music box, by the end of the week the music is almost over. Each note begins to play slower than the last, and just when it's about to stop, I go to church and get cranked up, so my music can play for another week. I do get strength from church, girls, I can't explain it any other way. You need to know I sure couldn't do all this without His help and that my dears, is the absolute truth."

Inside the church, Anna took her seat beside Mrs. G. and Maggie. Fresh cut pine decorated the alter and was placed all around the Advent wreath. The cuttings filled the church with a woodsy, fresh pine fragrance. Anna loved the Christmas season celebrating the birth of the Christ child and never grew tired of listening to the story.

The pre-service organ music ended as Pastor O'Riley stepped forward, shuffled a few notes and began. "Welcome one and all. Today's sermon is all about pure love. The greatest love the world has known, brothers and sisters." The minister deliberately paused to scan the interior of the church as he looked out across the congregation with a sweet smile for each one who had gathered this morning before continuing.

"God so loved the world, he sent us his only son." He paused even longer this time before saying softly, "Please bow your heads. Let us take a moment to reflect on these powerful words… He gave us his only Son. Can any of us even imagine? Let us pray in silence as we take a moment to really think about such a wondrous gift."

Truly it was the greatest gift the world has known, Anna thought, as she bowed her head, *there couldn't be a bigger one.* Staying focused on that thought, Anna wondered, *how did*

God feel, giving us his son? How hard that must have been? Now, that's some real love. And precisely at that moment, a realization dawned in her spirit. *Pure love is unselfish.* Oh, it suddenly became crystal clear in her mind, intensely vivid with one word jumping out... Unselfish, defined as not thinking of self... loving others more than yourself. She knew it to be true. That could be the only way to ever love... like God does.

It's *how* we love that distinguishes the difference between selfish love and unselfish love. Anna's body suddenly grew warm from within, and she felt goosebumps rise on her arms as this powerful shift of clarity occurred. Tears welled in her eyes.

Thank you, God! Anna thought, *I've got it, loud and clear. Oh, what a fool I've been. Why, look at me, I've prayed so often and yet when the answer came, I refused to see it. Eilleen's just a little girl and I've been so angry with her because she found a happiness that I can't give her? But indeed, I can! Why, it's the very happiness God himself intends for her and here I, the child's own grandmother, didn't love her enough to allow her to have it? I've kept her here, selfishly, with me. Why, that dear child has been so homesick for those folks and look, she's home with me right now getting sick, condemned to this pitiful poor life. But, the chance for a beautiful life? The very one God arranged? Was denied because of me? Yes, because of me.* Tears gently began flowing down Anna's cheeks, *Because I think I love her so much.* Anna reached for her cotton hankie to dab the tears.

No. Thoughts in her mind began to race, *I do love her enough. Why, for me to keep her here is nothing but cruel and certainly not Gods plan, I know that now. Well, what do you know? The answer to my prayers did come. Even Bayard mentioned it to me himself. How could I have been so blind? They do say Love is blind. Please forgive me Lord for being such a selfish, foolish old woman.* She had a life history of discovering that answers did sometimes come in surprising and unexpected ways and look, here was even more proof.

The sermon had been in progress quite a while and was about to end, yet Anna never heard a word of it. She looked around and felt as if she had left the building and circled the earth a few times before being plopped back to the same spot while not a soul around noticed her absence. She felt so light, like a burden was lifted, and she was delighted and completely sure, knowing exactly what she must do, and it filled her with joy, just pure joy. Her eyes were bright and sparkling there was a blush of color to her cheeks and she was smiling a sweet contented smile that shone straight up from her soul right out through her eyes.

Mrs. G. noticed and leaned over, poked Anna's arm, and whispered, "Did you happen to hear something in the sermon that I missed? Cause it sure looks like you got something out of it I didn't. Why, Anna... you look like you've been touched by the spirit!"

"You've got that right. I just got a message straight from God. Oh, I've been such a stupid old woman." Anna announced in a bold, uplifted tone, while looking nothing short of radiant wearing a bright smile.

Being a stupid old woman certainly didn't seem to be any kind of reason to look so pleased and delighted, but about then, Anna reached over, latched on to Mrs. G. and gave her a great big hug and was obviously so happy, it left Mrs. G. leaning back in the pew stunned, bewildered and totally puzzled.

Anna grabbed up her purse and tucked away her hankie. She

swung her new woven scarf about her shoulders and proceeded to head out of church without the foggiest intent to linger but found herself hugging everyone she knew patting arms and greeting faces with the brightest smile they'd ever seen on her as she made her way outside. She had to think. Her role was to carry out God's plan. And this time, by gosh, she was going to get it right.

Once outside when she reached the bottom of the church steps, she paused and couldn't help but notice how quiet and peaceful everything around her was. A soft snow had begun to fall, and the state of the world around her seemed to be so still and at peace, and it seemed to match her mind that also seemed calm and void of bouncing thoughts. Then suddenly, a plan surfaced, formulated and came into focus, perfectly clear in her mind. Yes, tomorrow morning. She'd return to the church, have them place a telephone call for her to the business establishment of Wharton and Barnard in Delaware, where she'd ask to speak to Mr. Wharton himself. Won't he be surprised! Anna smiled, the way you do when you're the only one in the whole world who knows the delicious secret.

A few doubts began to seep in to cloud her thoughts. *What if they've changed their mind? Or decided it all worked out for the best, realizing what a huge obligation raising a child could be? Wait... never mind any of that. I have absolutely nothing to worry about. That's not my part. God got me this far and I know what I'm to do, so who am I to worry about any of the particulars?* And just like that, total joy returned to her as completely as before.

The air outside was as still as could be. The grounds and trees had recently turned white, lightly covered in a soft dusting of the most beautiful snow, the kind that covers things quickly when pure white, large flakes float loose, sashaying down one by one without sticking together. As the snow fell, slow and straight, flakes landed on Anna's black wool coat sleeves where she could clearly detect individual frozen patterns and she noticed the random and various designs sparkling in the noontime light that was softly filtered through the thick, gray snow clouds. Anna sat down on a wood bench, fascinated by this unexpected beauty, and watched as snowflakes landed in her lap. Each one was crystallized and dazzling. Sparks of rainbow colors became visible when she lifted her sleeve to look closely.

She hadn't done this in years, not since Caroline was a little girl. She remembered how they used to sit outside and observe the falling snowflakes, inspecting each one, impressed by the wonder of Mother Nature and how she could create millions of patterns where no two were ever the same.

Natural beauty had her so completely engrossed in the moment that it silenced her thoughts and prompted vivid memories of those old days to come rushing back to her so perfectly clear they felt surreal. *Why, it's a sign. I believe it truly is. I believe my Caroline must approve too!* Anna thought. Everything felt pure and somehow guided and perfectly right. It was exhilarating.

Anna tilted her head as far back as she could and gazed straight up to the heavens as if she might just be able to catch a glimpse of her daughter peeking down from behind the grey clouds and watched as snow fell from as high up as she could possibly see, falling directly toward her eyes. She blinked when snowflakes tickled her eyelashes and deeply breathed in the crisp, fresh air. Unexpectedly, she laughed right out loud with a free spirited, little girl giggle she didn't even remember she still possessed.

CHAPTER 23
THE UNEXPECTED CALL

This was going to be a Monday the likes of which any businessman worth his salt would surely dread. Bayard left home early, knowing they were going to be in for a rough one. One of their supplier's delivery trucks got a flat tire in route so it didn't arrive last Thursday or on Friday either, and if that wasn't bad enough, their last train shipment that arrived was short of one of the most important parts they'd been waiting days for. Their phone would be ringing off the hook with complaints and they'd have plenty of difficult explaining to do.

Joseph Motor Co., C. M. Hammond & Son and the Atkins Motor Company all needed important parts *last week* and who knows when in the world those blasted Studebaker pistons would ever arrive? One thing was sure, if Wharton and Barnard couldn't deliver parts because they didn't have them or couldn't get them, that was a formula for some bad business when your only job is selling automobile parts. Nobody buys parts until they're desperately needed anyway.

"Yes sir, I certainly hear what you're saying, Jim. I know. Now, you know your company has always a top priority with us. As soon as it comes in, we'll be out the door and headed your way. We DO appreciate your business, Jim. Some things can't be helped, but please know, we're going to do our best over here, I promise. Thanks again Jim," Bayard said and as he hung up the receiver he leaned back in his chair, released a big sigh and rubbed his forehead.

Rem popped his head in the door and said, "What a tough morning. Ooh-Wee! You know, it's the craziest thing, we do our damnedest all year yet when others hold us up, somehow, *we* end up looking like the bad guys. Ahh, don't worry, soon we'll have everyone happy again," he said, understanding how tense the frustration could be, helplessly waiting on orders from outside sources.

"Mr. Wharton, you have a call," Delores said as she knocked on the edge of the open door to Bayard's office.

"No Delores!" Rem jumped in and spoke up as he raised his hand with an open palm toward her like a traffic cop, "You tell that son-of-a-gun, whoever it is, that Mr. Wharton is in an important meeting... about those damn missing parts! Taking more of these calls right now won't do a single thing to speed it up."

"Yes sir," she replied as she turned to return to her desk.

Rem hollered a few more instructions after her as she walked down the hall, "And tell each one of them we've put them on our top priority list too! That should shut them up a few hours. Good Grief, it's not like we don't know they're waiting."

"Thanks Rem," Bayard said and they both shook their heads and laughed a little. Buying a little time was a great idea.

"Mr. Wharton, excuse me again sir, but you have a call," Delores said as she stood in the doorway looking a little nervous.

"Now, Delores, I just told you," Rem said, "we're not taking calls, just take down their names. These guys can be ruthless. Tell them he's in a meeting across town if you need to!" Rem added.

"Well sir, yes I will, or I would...but this is..."

"I don't care who it is!" Rem blasted in a raised, agitated voice. "Why, they all think they're big shots. Until the parts arrive, we've got nothing to tell them!"

"But, this isn't a dealer, sir. Mr. Wharton, it's a telephone call for you from New York City. I thought you would want to know."

Bayard jumped up so fast he knocked over his pencil holder and things went scattering. "Why, of course, yes, I'll take the call. Thank you."

Then he froze as he looked over at Rem and they locked eyes. They both stood dazed as they processed several imagined possibilities for the call, something could be wrong or someone's sick... but nothing that came to mind was anything good. Bayard sat down hard and took a deep breath before answering.

"Hello, this is Bayard Wharton," he said in his automatic, professional tone.

"Good morning Mr. Wharton. This is Anna Mawlback, Eilleen's grandmother." Anna said, but before she could breathe and continue, Bayard interrupted.

"Anna is everything alright?" He asked in an anxious tone.

"There's no need to worry, we're fine. There's nothing wrong." Anna said in a gentle and kind tone that put Bayard's fears to rest.

"The reason I'm calling is... I've had some time to think. You know, it's very different when you think about yourself than it is when you take time to put someone else first. What I'm trying to say Bayard is this, I believe I made a big mistake when you asked me if Eilleen could come and live with you. But please understand, I wasn't prepared to make that kind of a decision right there, on the spot. While I still don't want to give her away, I decided I do wish to give her the best life possible, and I discovered I love her enough to make this call. It seems, my choosing to keep her here with me would also make me responsible for preventing what I believe is God's plan for her life, and I have come to believe that's for her to live in Delaware with you and your wife, Sarah."

Bayard was speechless. He sat unable to move as Anna continued.

"Before I can go on, I need to have the answer to a pressing question I have Bayard. Do you and your wife still wish to have Eilleen come and live with you? Or, have you had time to have second thoughts?"

"Oh Anna. You're asking me? *Do we want her?* YES! Of course, we do! She's all we ever think about! Why, all we ever talk about, all the time are plans for next summer. Heck, I'm only still living because of next summer! Anna, you need to know that Sarah and I truly love Eilleen. We didn't just enjoy her, we fell in love. All of us, it's something the three of us share, I can't explain it. But it happened, and it's for real, Anna. No, heavens no, there are no second thoughts here."

"OK, then it's settled. Life is hard here, Bayard. I don't need to say any more about that. I'm getting older every day and there isn't much I can do for these girls, but by GOD, *I can do this!* I can give my permission to have her grow up with you, so here it goes. I, Anna Mawlback, after much prayer, declare it's my heart's desire to give my granddaughter a better life where she will be loved, safe, happy and cared for. I'm going to give her to you and by doing this I'm giving her the greatest gift a poor old woman can, two loving parents.

"Bayard, you need to know that this dear little girl has missed you both something terrible." Anna said as her eyes filled with emotional tears. She couldn't help but begin to cry a little, adding, "This is hard for me Bayard, but it's the right thing to do. God's hand has been in this since the very beginning, I know that. What were the chances of her ending up with you? Why, she wasn't even registered to be in the program in the first place, did you ever know that?" Anna couldn't prevent openly crying as she continued, "Just that alone tells me it's God's plan. And I know that I'm crying, but I'm happy and very relieved too. This whole thing is an answer to prayer. Just like you said."

"Thank you, Anna, from the bottom of my heart, thank you. You've done a brave and very loving thing today. I know you understand this will change everything for Eilleen's future. You'll never have to worry about her wellbeing, I can promise you that." Bayard said, "So what do you think we should do next? Does Eilleen know about this?"

"Oh, no. I needed to find out how you felt first. She knows nothing, in fact, no one does, not even my closest friends," Anna said. "The girls still have another two weeks of school before they are out for the Christmas Holiday on the 15th. I'm thinking I should talk to Eilleen tonight and that would give her time to prepare and get ready for such a big move, but to be honest, I don't think it will be the least bit hard for her. She's belonged to you long before she ever came back to NY. The hardest part for her will be waiting for you to come get her."

"My only concern with that Anna is that I don't want Eilleen to feel like she has to choose us over you. Or for her to hear any comments while she is waiting that might upset her," Bayard said while he was thinking. "How about this, we tell her we're sending her here for a Christmas visit and then I'll ask her what she thinks about making this a permanent arrangement after she settles in. Maybe on Christmas day. Here's an idea. I could tell her that you've given this idea your blessing Christmas day, as long as that's what she'd like to do. I don't want her to have any more stress than she has already had in her short life."

"That's a great plan, Bayard," Anna agreed, "after all, we are the adults here. I really like that idea."

"Bless her little heart. Alright then, it's settled," Bayard said looking at his calendar, "The last day of school is the 15th so how about we plan to drive and pick her up on Saturday morning, December 16th. We can be there about 10:00 to 10:30? How does that work for you?"

"Saturday will be just fine. Thank you, Bayard, for everything. We'll be waiting for you on the 16th. Eilleen's about to get the greatest Christmas gift of her life. She might think it has something to do with some old wish she made on the stars, but we both know better, don't we? Good-by Bayard and God Bless," Anna said.

"Goodbye and God Bless you too, Anna." Bayard hung up the phone and just sat there, still as a statue, his hand remaining gripped to the receiver of the telephone, stunned.

What just happened? Right in the midst of the worst day, everything turned on a dime and became the best day of my life in what, the stretch of a three-minute phone call? Bayard Wharton knew, everything in his life was about to dramatically change, again. This was it! All he and Sarah had ever wanted, wished and hoped for and even dreamed about would be coming true in a few short weeks.

His mind was racing, he could hardly wait! *I have to go home and tell Sarah. Wait till she hears this news. Boy-oh-boy, do we have to get it in high gear. It's hard to believe, but she'll be here before Christmas.*

As Bayard sat there, letting it all sink in, wearing a big grin when Rem walked in, took one look and asked, "Is everything OK, Bayard? You sure don't look very upset."

"Am I OK? No, Rem I'm not. I'm way better than OK, I'm swell... and everything in the world is peachy keen! Isn't that what the kids say these days?" Bayard announced as he jumped up and grabbed Rem's upper arms, "You're not going to believe this Rem, but we've got to get everything ready." Then he started shaking him. "Rem, we're going to go back to New York and bring our little girl home! Delores, tell everybody that calls for me, I'll talk to them tomorrow, 'cause, right now, I'm going home!"

Rem gave Bayard the biggest old bear hug then Bayard grabbed his jacket, and in a flash, he left the office practically in a run. As far as he was concerned there were no more missing parts in his life! And very soon, none to be in Sarah's either.

Those auto parts finally did arrive that very afternoon, every last box of them, making all the W&B customers happy, too. It was one day that certainly ended far better that it began.

CHAPTER 24
ALMOST CHRISTMAS

Isn't it funny how the world can seem so different as soon as one little thought in your head changes? Anna pondered and considered that new awareness of hers while walking to the butchers house a few blocks over to deliver their fresh ironing.

To think I was so set against Eilleen moving to Delaware, but now, not only does it feel right, but do I believe there's a lot of good to come from it. First, there are the obvious advantages for Eilleen, of course, but look how this will free up Jene and Marie too. They've cared for Eilleen most of their lives. I know they were happy to do it, but it's a lot of responsibility for girls their age.

Why, Marie recently turned down a job Sophia offered her at the coffee and cocoa stand and now, there's no reason she can't take it since I won't need her to help me as much. It will be good for her to wait on customers and have the chance to do some real work. More importantly, the market vendors look out for one another and once Marie becomes a worker there, she'll have her foot in the door and while she might still be poor, she'll no longer be thought of as a street beggar. They'll look out for her too; plus, think of all the grand business skills she'll learn.

Jene's old enough to deliver the ironing for me, once she won't be busy helping with Eilleen's homework after school, too. Anna thought.

Thinking about the girls helping, doing odd jobs, and

how wonderfully quiet it would be in the house with just the two older girls around, Anna realized the quality of her life was about to improve and for the first time, she felt just fine admitting it without feeling any guilt.

Jene and Marie will be able to make their way much better in the world together, should something happen to me, especially if they don't have the worries of caring for a young child. Yes, this is a blessing for all of us, I truly do believe it is.

At the butcher's house, Anna collected five cents a garment for the ironing which totaled forty-five cents. Mildred invited her to come in, but Anna said, "Thank you, but I need to get back for the girls."

"Would you care to have a nice ham bone with quite a bit of meat still on it? Being a butcher's wife, we're never at a loss for fresh meat, but at the moment, we're a bit 'hammed-out' if you know what I mean. I've already wrapped it up for you," she said laughing. Anna laughed with her, but wondered how one could be "hammed-out" and what did she mean by that? Was she tired of having plenty to eat? No, Anna sure couldn't remember feeling anything like that.

Mildred returned with the ham nicely wrapped in brown butcher's paper. "Here's a small sack with a few potatoes, carrots and onions too. Thank you for delivering our ironing and Merry Christmas to you Anna!" She said, waving as she closed the door.

"Thank you so much Mildred, and Merry Christmas to you too!" Anna said, knowing that it would have cost her far more than the forty-five cents she'd just earned to purchase the food Mildred gave her. Oh boy, they were going to have a fine dinner tonight and tomorrow night as well. Think of the soup she would cook up later with that wonderful bone. What a day this one turned out to be with just one big old surprising blessing right on top of another.

Their delicious supper was about over with the girls practically licking their plates clean when Grandmother Anna, smugly smiling with a gleam in her eye, announced, "Girls, when you're finished, clear the dishes for me then come back to the table and have a seat, we need to have a little family talk about some news I have." Grandmother said in a way that planted a seed of mystery.

They proceeded to clean up in a jiffy and sat back down. Grandmother folded her hands in front of her on the table and looked at the girls faces knowing for once, what she had to say was really good and she was excited to watch their reactions.

"Let me get right to it, I had a nice phone conversation today with Mr. Wharton in Delaware. It seems he's invited Eilleen to spend Christmas with them. So Eilleen, would you like to pay a visit to Mother and Dad, cousin Dorothy and Aunt Mimi? I know how much you miss them and it seems like they sure have missed you too, honey. I personally think it's a wonderful idea," Grandmother said with a kind tone in her voice.

Eilleen sat very still in her chair and her bottom jaw dropped open a little, she was lost in her thoughts, not saying a word, for she couldn't believe what she just heard.

"But, before we put any plans in motion," Grandmother added, "I need to know how you feel about this idea? After all, it's your choice."

"Gee whiz," Eilleen said in a voice so soft it was almost a whisper, sitting there, not moving while her bright blue eyes darted around matching thoughts that were wildly bouncing inside her head. "They really miss me? And they want me there for Christmas? Oh, my stars."

There was a brief silence that was abruptly broken with a shout of "Holy Cow... YES!" She continued in a spirited voice, "I'll have to pack up my things and Tony, too. I'm *really* going to go see Mother and Dad? I love you so much Grandmother Anna!" Then her voice grew very soft again as she added, "And I do really love Mother and Dad, too." She looked across the room as though she was watching a screen play out her memories and said, "It felt like we were a real family when I was there. I was their only little girl and Dad carried me upstairs to bed every night to tuck me in and read me stories." Then she looked back at her family and tears filled her eyes, "but I love all of you too! It's really OK that I go?"

"Of course, Eilleen. You have to go! I'd sure want to go if I were you." Marie said.

"You're going to have so much fun," Jene added. But the older sisters were a little bit surprised, so mostly they sat quietly and listened.

"I have to agree with your sisters," Grandmother Anna said. "You should go visit them and see the friends you made last summer and have a wonderful time. Your poor old Grandmother can't think of a thing I could give you for Christmas that could make you any happier. You have my permission. I think you deserve a little spoiling right about now, don't you?"

"Whoo-hoo! Hot Diggity! Tony, old boy you better get ready! We're going back to Delaware for Christmas!" Eilleen jumped out of her chair and began dancing and twirling.

"Just a minute, we're not done, I've got some more business to discuss while you girls are here," Grandmother said. She sincerely wanted to give all the girls a piece of good news.

"Jene, I'm putting you in charge of helping me deliver the ironing from now on. You can pick up and deliver in the neighborhood and of course that means I am going to pay you for your work my dear."

"Holy smoke... really? See, I told you I was old enough to help. I know everyone in the neighborhood for blocks around here. I promise I'll do a really good job for you, Grandmother. Whoo-hoo! Hot-Diggity-Dogs!" Jene sang out, clapping she was so happy with the news that made her feel that she was finally growing up.

"There's just one more thing. Marie, I think you should tell Sophia you'll be happy to take the work she offered you at the coffee stand." Grandmother said leaning forward so not to miss the expression on Marie's face knowing her eyes would pop with surprise hearing this.

"Really? You think it's OK? OH, MY GOODNESS! May I start right away? At the next market? This is great! They get so busy before Christmas and you should see all the customers she's been getting. They're roasting their own beans and selling them by the bag and it's been a big success." Marie was so excited she was about to burst, and yes, her eyes were lit up just as Grandmother expected. It was a wonderful sight to see.

"Yes, my dear, you can start whenever you want, just remember you must keep up with your school work," Grandmother said. "You girls have all earned this!"

Marie jumped up from the table as giddy as her sisters. They were clapping and jumping and giggling all at once. It was marvelous to know at that moment, everyone was full, happy and excited about something in their future. That sure didn't happen often, not around this old place.

"We're going to be just fine girls!" Grandmother said as she wrapped an arm around both older girls and gave them a double squeeze. "It's high time for a few things to change around here and I think with the Lord's help, that's just what's going to happen. We have to simply trust that life unfolds exactly the way it should... eventually. Sometimes it sure does come along and unfold in some unusual and unexpected ways, just be sure you don't become too old and stubborn you miss it.

CHAPTER 25
CHRISTMAS IN THE AIR

Bayard arranged to take off from work Friday, December 15th. You best believe he wasn't planning to drive straight through to New York ever again. In fact, he knew he wouldn't even be able to coax Sarah to climb in the car, if that was his intent.

After placing a few necessary long distant telephone calls, he'd made reservations to stay over again in Philadelphia at the Bellevue-Stratford for both Friday and Saturday evenings. After all, it was the ideal driving distance from New York, perfect for staying over and resting up, both coming and going. Plus, this time of year, the sights of the city at Christmas would add a special touch, like a bright sparkling cherry right on top of his happiness sundae.

Next, he telephoned Bookbinders and made reservations for Friday evening, 6:45 for a memorable dinner for two. Might be a long time before it would be just the two of them having dinner alone, a thought that absolutely delighted them both. They'd already had a darn lifetime of blasted dinners for two.

His final call made reservations for lunch on Saturday afternoon for them at The Crystal Tea Room in Wanamaker's. They'd go see Santa and do some shopping. Eilleen would need a holiday dress and a new pair of patent leather shoes to go with it. This was going to be one Christmas season they were going to celebrate like never before. He couldn't be happier.

"Let's get on the road, Sarah," Bayard said as he tugged

on his beret before tucking a basket of lunch in the back and lighting up a fresh cigarette. "It's almost full light and I want to get going so that we can be on the lookout for every field of black and white cows we can spot from here to Philadelphia and enjoy seeing them for a change. Why, I'm going to laugh right out loud every time we do. Won't that be some grand fun?"

"Almost ready. You and those darn cows. I can't wait to see our little girl again," Sarah said. "I called Mimi and Dorothy and gave them the telephone number to the hotel. They're as excited as we are. Mimi's been knitting Eilleen a cardigan in a cream-colored yarn and plans to add those crystal buttons she loves, to give it to her for Christmas. Isn't that sweet? She's the best sister. She started knitting even before Eilleen left, I hope she hasn't grown so much it doesn't fit."

"Grown? Well I personally don't care if she's five foot nine and weighs a hundred and fifty pounds, she's going to be our little girl!" Bayard belly laughed at his silly notion, teasing Sarah.

The Wharton's loved Philadelphia, far better than New York. Probably because they knew their way around since they were privileged to visit every now and again.

The drive up was easy. Parking and check-in went smooth. The hotel was absolutely stunning the way it was decked out, dressed up for the holidays. Every place you looked was decorated with garlands of fresh evergreens and trimmings of gold and silver. Near the staircase stood a gorgeous, giant evergreen, lighted with strings of Christmas lights, glittering with gold and silver glass balls and dripping in perfectly placed tinsel that shimmered when drafts swirled in from the revolving door out front. Gilded pots full of crimson blooming poinsettias were everywhere you looked. A pot had been placed on every step near the brass railing, to frame the staircase in holiday colors of red and green. The hotel's interior looked like one of those fancy, glittery Christmas cards had come to life, right there in the main lobby.

After a short rest, the couple left for dinner where they enjoyed some perfectly seasoned seafood platters that were as delicious as any they had ever eaten. Live music played while they dined, and it seemed the entire city was hosting a festive celebration, prepared just for them.

After strolling through city streets and spending time window shopping, or peeking as Sarah would say, the couple headed back toward the hotel. Strings of holiday lights were everywhere you looked, and the department store window displays were beautifully done up, surpassing anything they ever saw back home. Why, even the automobile tail lights that zoomed by streaked with more red lights than you'd ever see hung in the entire downtown back home. Even as the hour grew late, they just kept wandering; for these two weren't the least bit tired, they were far too excited, just like all children at Christmas time.

Sarah woke up the next morning and looked at the alarm clock. It was a little after 6:00 a.m. Bayard had already dressed and left the room. She could just imagine him pacing in the lobby, she was sure he'd gone down for coffee and to read the paper. *Good luck staying focused on the news of the world this morning, Mr. Wharton!* She thought smiling as she pictured his every move, she knew him so well. He might be going through his regular routine, but he was about ready to jump out of his skin and would never be able to focus on news or remember a word he read, not today.

Sarah found him downstairs doing exactly as she imagined. Together, they shared a hearty breakfast of bacon and eggs with chilled glasses of fresh squeezed orange juice in the hotel. After Bayard's second cup of rich, imported Brazilian coffee that he loved so much, it was time to get on the road toward their long-awaited destination.

Pulling up in front of the old brownstone building, Bayard checked his watch. They arrived in New York at precisely 10:02 a.m. As soon as he took the car out of gear and pulled up the brake lever, Eilleen came bolting out from behind the massive front door wearing her new coat, and looked like a blurred streak of blue, she was running so fast, straight toward them; with a smile as bright as Broadway. The rest of the family came out to greet them too and gathered around the car.

There was plenty of embracing and hugs for everyone. Several special winks and coded glances were shared between Grandmother Anna and Bayard, for they knew the big secret. A small suitcase and several bags were packed in the trunk box Bayard had installed on the back of the car. Smaller parcels got tucked behind the back seat. Eilleen bounced in with Tony bear, taking her spot right behind Mother and in less than two shakes of a "cow's tail", Eilleen was off—for the second time in her life—to Delaware.

The wheels of the Model A Ford cut a hard left and began rolling as Dad tapped the wheel. It was done, the whole family was back together again. What a feeling!

Eilleen began rapidly firing questions, "How is Aunt Mimi doing? How 'bout Cousin Dorothy? Have you seen Frances and the 'other Eileen'? What about Elaine & Gertrude, how've they been? Do you see them in church? How did the cottage hold up after that bad storm?" and so it went for the entire ride, with Mother and Dad taking turns supplying the answers, smiling the entire time. Her little voice sounded as sweet and refreshing as a summer rain pinging on a tin roof after a scorching hot day, so welcomed, refreshing and pleasant, you just can't get enough of it.

They arrived back at the Bellevue, parked the car and hustled inside just long enough to drop off the bags in their room. Then in short order they walked down the staircase, straight through the lobby and out the glass revolving doors to the sidewalk, holding hands, heading straight for Wanamaker's. They played an old game like they used to. When it was time to cross into the street, they'd lift her up off the sidewalk and swing her over the curb. She loved that game.

The entire day was magical, a huge dose of Christmas splendor. There was delicious food and merriment mixed with Eilleen's pure delight of it all, blended with colorful holiday lights and music and plenty of seasonal hustle and bustle, topped off with church bells chiming off in the distance.

Just entering and walking through Wanamaker's to the elevator was breathtaking for Eilleen. Christmas carols filled the store and when the Organ Concert began playing the holiday songs, music rang out to the rafters. Colorful decorations and sparkling lights turned the store into a fantasy world, so glittery, fancy and beautiful, she'd never forget it. Mother and Dad surprised her by taking the elevator straight up to the ninth floor in time for their reservation at The Crystal Tea Room.

Lunch was served on fine china plates by men dressed in formal suits. Fine cloth napkins were folded in a fancy way at each place setting next to so much shiny silverware. A fresh cut floral centerpiece of red carnations and holly graced the center of the table. Then there was the meal itself, so grand and yummy you might think you were dining at a real palace.

After lunch, they took the elevator down to the eighth floor to Toyland where they allowed Eilleen to take her time and wander at her pace through the many displays of dolls, games, puzzles, stuffed animals and trains before they got in line to see old Santa Claus himself. Eilleen covered her mouth with both hands in disbelief when she saw the bearded fellow, wearing his rich, red velvet suit trimmed with soft white fur that matched his beard. He sported black shiny boots too and was perched up on a huge golden chair so ornate it looked like a throne fit for a king. She had seen Santa before, but only as a bell ringer or at the church as he was handing out gifts; but they sure didn't look anything like this! Their suits were so tired and old they had to have been Santa's helpers. Never once had she ever had the chance to spy the real fellow himself, the very one who was famous with children all over the world. But there he was, she was sure of it.

When it was her turn, Eilleen approached Mr. Claus focusing on his every detail. Hopping up in Santa's lap she rubbed his velvet sleeve and felt the fur on the cuff of his jacket… it was *real fur!*

Santa smiled beneath his beard, he asked, "Young lady, what would you like for Christmas? Have you been a good little girl this year?"

"Oh yes, I've been good, most of the time, anyway. I do always try to be. What do I want?" She thought about Santa's question. Tilting her head and looking right at him, she replied,

"I'm here right now with my Mother and Dad. That's them, right over there," she said, pointing them out. "What I've wanted for the longest time, was just to be with them. We're going home to Milford tomorrow. I'm going to get to see everybody I've missed for months now. So, I really can't think of anything else I want, but thank you for asking."

Santa gave her a hug. His eyes were glassy when he said, "Merry Christmas dear child, here's a candy cane for you. Your parents must know they are lucky to have a marvelous little girl like you." Here was a child that didn't ask for a single thing, bless her heart. What a far cry she was from some of the spoiled rotten brats he'd seen lately.

They rode the elevator down to the fourth floor, to "Little Girlswear" to shop for winter things. Mother and Eilleen "oood and ahhh'd" over the dresses, having the most fun and tried several on before picking the "just right" one, a classic, made of slippery taffeta in rich red and green plaid with a full skirt and a black velvet sash. They selected a new petticoat and a pair of ruffled socks, then it was off to the shoe department to complete the outfit. After trying on a few, they settled on a pair of black patent leather Mary Jane's that fit perfectly. Eilleen loved them and of course, she didn't want to take them off.

Bayard stooped beside her and said, "These are Christmas shoes, Eilleen, to wear for Christmas. *And...I'll tell you what...* it sure feels like Christmas to me! So, you better not take them off, young lady, today's mighty special and besides, they're far too pretty to keep inside of that old shoe box!"

Eilleen giggled, giving Dad a look, knowing she was being more than a little bit spoiled right now, and she loved it.

The day flew by as they shopped and explored the city,

looking in the department store windows and taking in the holiday sights. It was cold by the time they walked outside after leaving an Italian restaurant where they'd stopped for some authentic Italian spaghetti and meatballs. The Christmas lights strung across the city stood out bright and crisp against the dark night sky and various church bells chimed holiday carols in the distance as the three quietly walked back to the hotel.

In the hotel lobby, a pianist was performing Christmas carols for hotel guests on an ebony baby grand piano stationed beneath that enormous, elaborately decorated Christmas tree. The Whartons wandered nearby and decided to sink into a couple of those beckoning, plush lobby chairs to relax and listen a few minutes before going upstairs. What an unexpected treat at the end of a wonderful day and boy, were they bushed.

Both Whartons got lost in music before they noticed Eilleen was standing right beside the pianist. She watched his professional fingers dance across the keys until the very last note. When the next song began, "Silent Night", Eilleen began singing. Her clear voice had perfect pitch and demonstrated the quality of someone who was trained, but she was only six. Where was all this coming from? Sarah and Bayard sat straight up in their chairs, amazed but they sat still and allowed her to entertain those who were in the lobby, also struck by the power of the music and simple words she sang so beautifully.

Bayard leaned over and asked Sarah, "Do you think the day will ever come when she doesn't surprise the soup out of us?"

"Probably not. I think you better get used to it, Dad." She could see he was beaming.

A few songs later they ended the evening and went up to their room and plopped Eilleen into a luxurious hot bubble bath.

Sarah noticed she had placed her shiny patent leather shoes carefully right beside her bed. Soon she was squeaky clean, smelling as sweet as a sugar plum wearing her soft, new pj's and Mother tucked her into bed with Tony. She looked so small in the big bed, her little head cradled by the puffy, overstuffed feather pillow. They said prayers and turned off the light. Tomorrow was another big day—they were going home.

Bright and early the next morning they packed up, then went down stairs to enjoy a wonderful breakfast of pancakes, fresh juice and a few more cups of that fabulous coffee that Bayard loved. Afterward, they turned in their room key, loaded the car and stuffed in those extra shopping bags that just about filled the entire car, and it was time to go.

Bayard started the engine, but Eilleen started to panic, frantically looking all around in the back seat and she began to cry.

"What on earth is wrong, Eilleen?" Sarah asked as she looked over her shoulder.

"Tony's not here. I can't find him. *Where is he?*" Eilleen was becoming more upset the harder she searched.

"He was in our room. I remember seeing him there," Dad said, "so he can't be far. Don't worry. Wait right here and let me go check." Dad jumped out of the car and into the role that Dad's sometimes have, off on a mission to rescue a treasured toy before they are lost forever. Sure enough, he returned the super hero, displaying Tony in his hands just a few minutes later.

"He was right in the floor, near the bed. Glad we're still here at the hotel. This could have been a much worse situation if we were about a hundred miles away from here, I'll tell you that!"

South of Wilmington, they passed multiple fields of beautiful black and white cows and enjoyed seeing every one of them, and in a few more hours the Wharton's reached the outskirts of Milford. The evening sunset painted the sky with some of those glorious, vivid orange-pink mixes, perfect to represent their inner joy. Why, the old homestead looked practically like it was glowing surrounded by the stunning golden sunset when they turned into their driveway. How fitting.

It was the best part of the trip for Bayard, the moment he had been waiting for. Turning the key and shutting off the engine, he had to sit there in the quiet, take a deep breath and savor the victory. They were home. By God, the whole bunch of them, even Tony. This was one of the greatest days of his life, one that he would never forget, not for as long as he lived.

From that moment on the days simply flew by. First on the list, they went straight to Aunt Mimi's house and as soon as she hustled across the room to give Eilleen a big hug, she started to bawl. "Do you have any idea how much I love you, you sweet little girl, you? To the very moon and back that's how much. Why, you won't live long enough to ever really know. I'm so glad you're here!" Aunt Mimi told her, squeezing her so hard she could hardly breathe. Cousin Dorothy was beaming waiting her turn for hugs.

As soon as the word was out that Eilleen was back, old summer friends came over to the house. Other days, Mother walked her to pay a visit at their homes. It was the best fun seeing everyone. They had missed each other terribly and all of them were excited for Christmas.

Before long, it was the night of the Christmas Eve Concert at Avenue Church and everything was beautifully decorated in evergreens, red bows and candles. The advent wreath had four lit candles and during the sermon, they would light the center candle announcing the birth of baby Jesus. Near the end of the service was the best part. All the lights would be turned off leaving the entire church totally dark at first except for the lit wreath. Then, one by one, everyone lit their candle from one that was shared from row to row and soon the entire church gleamed; bathed only in candlelight. "Silent Night" began, and everyone sang without the organ. In the soft, natural light, one couldn't help but feel the true meaning of Christmas wash over them as the music, the message and candlelight worked its magic.

There were plenty of pats and hugs to go around that night after the service. Everyone was delighted to see Eilleen home again even if it was just for the holiday. It was a night of sweet Christmas joy.

Later at home, after Eilleen hung her stocking, Dad carried her up the stairs the way he always did, read her a story and tucked her into bed. He checked back in about fifteen minutes and once convinced she was sleeping; he slipped out back behind the garage and came inside toting a live pine tree. Sarah had been getting out the decorations in preparation for them to do some trimming.

They could hardly stand it, trying to imagine Eilleen's reaction to seeing a decorated tree at the bottom of the steps, and gifts waiting for her Christmas morning. Bayard strung the lights and Sarah hung the balls. It looked spectacular,

After the tree was decorated, they scurried around to find all the hiding places they stashed Eilleen's wrapped gifts of paper dolls, a slinky, new crayons and coloring book and a baby doll with little doll clothes. Then Bayard went out in the garage and came in with the big one, a tall three wheeled bike with chrome handle bars that would be just her size. It was too big to wrap, so they rolled it under the tree and tied a big red bow on the handle. These two were having more fun than they could imagine, and soon they became punchy and got down-right giddy. It seemed the harder they tried to stay quiet, the more they laughed, until they finally lost their breath and their ribs hurt, just like a couple of ornery little kids.

Early Christmas morning, Mother and Dad Wharton were up and raring to go at dawn, but the problem was, Eilleen slept in. How could she? This dear child didn't have a clue what was waiting for her since she never experienced a Christmas morning like this before. Sarah and Bayard ate some cereal. He had a second cup of coffee and she made a cup of tea and they waited some more. The lights were shining, packages were wrapped and ready. The only thing missing was a little girl to rip into all of it and make Christmas come alive.

Before long, they heard footsteps upstairs. Both Dad and Mother took seats in the living room and positioned themselves just right to watch her big reaction when she came downstairs to discover what was waiting. They could hardly wait.

"Here she comes." Mother said in a hushed voice, poking Dad with her elbow.

Eilleen got about half way down the stairs and sat down on a step, folded her hands and placed them in her lap. "Good morning!" She said.

"Good morning. Merry Christmas, Eilleen. Aren't you going

to come down and open your presents?" Dad asked, wondering what was up.

"No, I'll wait for the other kids. Isn't the tree beautiful?" She remarked.

"What other kids?" Dad asked, feeling really puzzled about now.

"The other kids from needy families. We all sit under the tree and wait until somebody passes everything out. We'll each get a present. I wonder which one mine is. When do you think they'll be here?"

"Sweetie, there are no other children coming. This is your Christmas. Come on down and see. It looks to me like Santa's been here. You did speak to him in Philadelphia you know," Mother said.

"Really?" Eilleen replied, still sitting frozen on the step. At first her eyes started looking all around, then she popped up and hollered, "Holy Cow! MERRY CHRISTMAS! Santa came here and brought this for me? This is all for me? Oh boy. Look at that swell new bike! Is that really mine? It's so beautiful.... and shiny!" Her voice was so high she was practically squealing. She eagerly began unwrapping her gifts, but very carefully, savoring each one and remained in squealing mode and totally delighted the entire time. Her cheeks turned bright pink from all the excitement.

After the gifts were unwrapped, Mother and Eilleen sorted and displayed them under the tree so when Aunt Mimi and cousin Dorothy came over she could show them what Santa brought. They would be over soon. Then they'd go to church, then back to Aunt Mimi's and cousin Dorothy's for a big Christmas dinner.

The day played out with every detail you'd find in a Norman Rockwell painting captured and coming to life. It was picture perfect, filled with fresh cut pine, loved ones, holiday lights, glowing candles, wrapped presents being happily exchanged, a child's joy filling the room, church choir voices singing to the rafters the message that baby Jesus was born. Life right now was delightful and a true wonder, even with all this year's hardships stirred in.

The Wharton's life had been suddenly filled with a love and joy they had never experienced or expected just weeks ago. In church that Christmas morning, Bayard Wharton bowed his head to say a prayer.

"Dear Lord, I've thanked you many times for my blessings, but this new plan of yours, the one that brought Eilleen into our lives, well, I want you to know I've never been more thankful for anything my whole life. I promise I'll do my very best to raise her and try not to let you down. Thank you, God, and please, help us to be the best family we can. Please bless Grandmother Anna, too. And God, I am sorry I got a little bit out of character back a few weeks ago, but thanks for listening. I really don't believe any of us would be here right now without you looking out for us. Amen."

The Christmas dinner Aunt Mimi and Dorothy prepared was so fabulous, it's fair to say, they out-did themselves. They served roasted turkey with sage dressing, mashed potatoes and gravy, jelled cranberries, mashed turnips & turnip greens with vinegar, bread and butter pickles and hot buttered yeast rolls. And it goes without saying, there was a fresh jar of beach plum jelly sitting on the table too.

For the grand finale, you had your choice of warmed minced meat or apple pie if you had saved enough room. Dorothy always turned off the oven as soon as the turkey came out and would slide in the pies, so they'd warm up during dinner. It worked perfectly every time. Of course, there was a plate of sugar cookies with some red and green sprinkles, for how could it be Christmas without a tin of cut out sugar cookies?

Eilleen filled her plate with Christmas dinner, but she could hardly wait to spread some of that homemade beach plum jelly on her roll and take a big bite. "You are right Mother, this does taste even better in the winter. It surely does. Mm-mm, do we know how to make some good jelly, or what?"

While slicing the pies, Mimi began reminiscing and sharing old stories from way-back-when she and Sarah were both little girls growing up at Christmas. Eilleen tried hard to imagine these grown women being sisters and little girls her age while she helped pass around plates of the warm, sweet smelling desserts.

After the last bite, Bayard scooted his chair back and said, "That certainly was a wonderful dinner, Mimi and Miss Dorothy, I do thank you ladies." He leaned back in his chair and added, "Been pretty much a wonderful year too, except... for the time when we had some important parts missing. Now, there's nothing wonderful when you have a crucial part missing, because the whole thing just doesn't work. Isn't that right, Eilleen?"

Eilleen looked at Dad, nodding her head to agree with him, since her mouth was full of pie.

"Whoops, now hold on. I bet you think I'm talking about work and some old automobile parts?" Dad asked with a gleam in his eye, "Am I right?"

"Yes. You need parts, or the cars won't run." Eilleen answered still eating apple pie.

"Na-ah...that old stuff's just business. I wouldn't let that ruin my day. The missing part I was talking about... was you. Why, you need to know, it was just plain awful for all of us around here after we took you back. Life wasn't right at all. You were gone, and we weren't a family anymore without our little girl. So, let me ask, how was it for you after we took you back to New York?" Bayard turned in his seat and leaned toward her for a close-up look at her response.

"It was plain awful! I missed you both so much. I wanted you to come and get me and bring me home with you. I wished it on the stars out my window every night." Then turning both hands palms up she added, "How can I have a family like all of you, and my best girlfriends too and not miss them? Most of the time, I was really sad, and sometimes I cried in my room, because I never thought I'd get to eat beach plum jelly in the winter. Not ever."

"Now, by gosh that's awful. See what I'm talking about, it's just plain awful. I think this is a situation that we have to do something about. Don't you Mother?" Dad asked in a booming voice as he winked at her. He continued using a softer tone as he leaned close to Eilleen.

"Eilleen, Mother and I have talked a great deal about this and we both want you to stay right here and live with us from now on. What do you think? It's up to you of course, but first, you must know your Grandmother Anna thinks it's a pretty good idea too. We all feel that God's been looking out for you and who are we to mess up His great plan? I think the whole thing started the minute you got off the train and were plopped down, right in front of me. I don't know, but something came over me and you were the one I wanted to bring home, so I switched those name tags and look at us, here we are.

"What do you say Eilleen, would you like to make us your official Mother and Dad for Christmas and for the rest of your life? We'll throw in a sweet Aunt Mimi and a pretty nice, old cousin Dorothy too, for good measure, so we can all love you to pieces and try our best to spoil you rotten? But you can't become too rotten, you gotta promise me that though."

Eilleen's hands were pressed over her mouth in disbelief as her blue eyes grew large and darted to every face at the table before she spoke. "You mean it? For good? This will be my real home... starting right now?"

"That's exactly what we all want," Mother said with a big smile.

"Oh, my stars! My wish came true! Yes. Holy Cow...yes! Of course, I want to live here, with all of you. I always wanted to, but I never knew you wanted me too. You're right, Dad, we need to keep our parts together!" Eilleen jumped right up in Dad's lap and gave him a big hug.

"I love you all so much!" Eilleen cried out with all the enthusiasm she could. Then she jumped down and started hopping, clapping and twirling in her new taffeta plaid Christmas dress, her cheeks blushing from the excitement, and her blue eyes sparkled.

Aunt Mimi and Cousin Dorothy were both crying and hugging Sarah. Poor old Bayard was done in from it all. He buried his face in his dinner napkin and dove face down on the dining room table, bawling like a baby. He had to use his dinner napkin to absorb the tears, he blubbered and sobbed but he couldn't help it. It was just that kind of moment.

It was official, they were a family. Not one of them could have imagined this kind of joy a few weeks ago. It took chance, circumstances, luck and many prayers but in the end, it was unselfish love that made it happen. Sometimes answers certainly do come in strange and mysterious ways.

EPILOGUE

The love that filled Aunt Mimi's dining room that evening stayed in Delaware from that day on. Eilleen continued to love, delight and surprise the ever-loving soup out of the Whartons as they enjoyed every second watching her grow up in their home in Milford and at their cottage in Slaughter Beach, right where it all began.

Eilleen became a member of Avenue United Methodist Church where she sang in the choir as lead soprano and graduated from Milford High School in 1945. She attended her first year at Sullins College in Bristol, VA, only to complete her education back in Delaware at Wesley College, graduating with an associate degree in business in 1948. On June 25, 1949, she married Dr. William E. Spence, a Dover Veterinarian, and they had three children, Debbie, Bayard and Tommy. The family became members of Wesley United Methodist Church in Dover.

Collecting lifelong friends began early during her younger years and never stopped. She added many more lifelong friends while her family grew. Eilleen delivered a breath of fresh air and plenty to laugh about, plus she was more than happy to share all she had and always included everyone she could. If you were one of the lucky ones who knew her, then you know exactly what I mean. Her natural spirit remained fun, pure and childlike her entire life. Her mission was simple... to give love to everyone, everywhere. After all, that's what had happened to her.

Reflecting on her true story, the sheer number of strange and chance circumstances that came into play were staggering. What if one of the Fresh Air Program's children hadn't gotten sick? What if Sarah didn't have a headache the day the train arrived, or if Bayard never changed the tag? Or, if Grandmother Anna had all three girls with her that day in church? Would it have become clear to her what to do?

My daughter knew this of Eilleen's story as a child and told me how she was going to host a Fresh Air child someday and meant it. Jaime and Ed now have a lovely family with four boys and this year will be their tenth summer hosting Andre—an adorable, bright boy we all adore. Other local families now also host children after meeting Andre. The stories are amazing and fun.

I know Eilleen would love nothing more than for her story to be responsible for even a few more families to join with the Fresh Air Foundation and host more children for these important summer visits.

There was that split-second when Bayard Wharton felt compelled. He took action and made it happen. Such a little thing; at the time, something he believed no one would ever notice, but, many did, in fact, because of that one moment entire families and lives were changed forever. My wish for you is that you keep on the look-out and when such a moment comes your way, be ready. Trust your heart, take a chance and when something "just feels right", take action, do the right thing and make it happen. I will forever be grateful Bayard Wharton did.

Diane Lane

ACKNOWLEDGMENTS

Many thanks go out to my dear friend and Eilleen's daughter, Debbie Spence Cromer, for her help, encouraging words, and support through this project. Debbie supplied insight for the story as well as editing help. She also shared her mother's fabulous photos taken in Slaughter Beach the summer of 1933. What a treasure.

I want to thank the friendly staff at Delaware Archives in Dover who taught me to use the micro-film system to scroll through documents and articles so I could research the events that happened during 1933. Even the newspaper ads of the day were a rich source of information and I found them to be very interesting.

Thank you to Dave Kenton, one of Milford's most knowledgeable historians who shared lots of information on various commerce, downtown stores and their locations during this time. His mother-in-law, Elaine Townsend Dickerson, one of Eilleen's first friends as they bonded making up jump rope rhymes on the Beach. The Townsend family owned the Milford Chronicle newspaper. A great deal of information came from pages of those archived newspapers.

Heartfelt thanks go to my daughter, Jaime Carter-Houck and her husband Ed. They have hosted Andre, a wonderful boy from New York through Fresh Air, since he was 6 years old. Seeing him return each summer kept the feeling alive for me, just how important their program is and, in some ways, helped me stay focused and motivated to complete the book. I am not sure we would have met Andre without the history of Eilleen's story in our lives.

Thanks go to my daughter Rachelle Lane, for helping bring all the separate chapters into one seamless document for the first time and for all her ideas and worthy suggestions. A huge thank you goes to Mrs. Frances Mason and the lovely ladies at Cadbury, who gathered for many weeks, listening to the story during the early stages. They shared valuable thoughts and insights, that were both appreciated and used.

A final thanks to my designer, Crystal Heidel, for her vision that created the look and feel of this book. Her talented eye and attention to detail surpassed my wildest expectations.

With such an enormous amount of help, love and support from so many, we did it!

Made in the USA
Middletown, DE
02 June 2019